PENGUIN MODERN CLASSICS

Search for a New Land

ABDUS SAMAD is an award-winning Urdu writer and poet. He started writing at the age of fifteen and received numerous awards for his works, which include eleven novels as well as five collections of short stories. He has won the Sahitya Akademi award, the Bharatiya Bhasha Parishad Puraskar, the Ghalib Award and the Life Achievement Award from the Urdu Academy in Bihar. He has also served on the board of the prestigious Jnanpith award.

SYED SARWAR HUSSAIN is Associate Professor at the Department of English Language & Translation, College of Languages and Translation, King Saud University, Riyadh. He has been teaching English for the past forty-two years and has published several research papers in various international journals. He has authored eight books, which include a book on literary criticism and English translations of several Urdu short stories and novels.

ABDUS SAMAD

Search for a New Land

Translated by
Syed Sarwar Hussain

PENGUIN BOOKS
An imprint of Penguin Random House

PENGUIN BOOKS

USA | Canada | UK | Ireland | Australia
New Zealand | India | South Africa | China

Penguin Books is part of the Penguin Random House group of companies
whose addresses can be found at global.penguinrandomhouse.com

Published by Penguin Random House India Pvt. Ltd
4th Floor, Capital Tower 1, MG Road,
Gurugram 122 002, Haryana, India

 Penguin
Random House
India

First published in Urdu as *Do Gaz Zameen*, 1988
This English translation published in Penguin Books by
Penguin Random House India 2022

Copyright © Abdus Samad 2022
Translation copyright © Syed Sarwar Hussain 2022

ISBN 9780143446088

Typeset in Adobe Caslon Pro by Manipal Technologies Limited, Manipal
Printed at Replika Press Pvt. Ltd, India

www.penguin.co.in

Translator's Note

Translation of literary works has always been a challenge. As it requires forging a strong bond between two texts in two different languages, the building up of this relationship involves several daunting tasks. It is not only the matter of two languages but, in fact, two different styles of writing, each intensely personal and unique. The works take their own toll on the translators as well—on the one hand, translators have to be faithful to the demands of the language of the original author and on the other, invent their own devices in the language they are translating with a view to accommodate those demands. To translate is to stretch the limits of your own language to display the voice of the other.

The real inspiration to translate the present novel was the novel itself, which occurred to me as I read it in its original language. A story about exile, the compelling search for a new land and the terrible experience that unfolds, *Do Gaz Zameen* reveals the widespread trauma of partition and the unmendable alienation that was forced upon a human being from his native place. Hamid's letter to his father, towards the end of the novel, contains the crippling sorrow of estrangement that he was never able to overcome after his flight from his native Biharsharif. The emphatic story of exile, the emotions it unleashes, and the betrayal, loss, revenge, and filial dissonance that it evokes cut to the core of the human heart. The novel presents an acute insight into the debilitating impact of external circumstances on the deepest levels of the characters' psyche. These were the reasons that pushed me to explore and translate the novel for readers of English.

This highly admired novel by Abdus Samad spans three generations and encapsulates all the aspirations and despairs of the characters who have suffered the pangs of partition. It revolves around young men who left their families and migrated from the state of Bihar to Bangladesh at the time of the partition and found themselves out of place in a new land where the language, social norms and eating habits were different. For instance, Azimuddin, who migrates to East Pakistan but can never overcome his prejudices against the Bengalis, has a daughter who falls in love with a Bengali young man by an irony of fate. In his character, the novelist shows the hatred of the migrant families towards everything Bengali. When Hamid, another young refugee, marries a Bengali girl, he is arrested on the charge of abducting her. The message that the novel conveys here is that racial and cultural differences generate animosity and produce a blinkered vision that is out of all proportion.

The novel portrays how differently characters behave when they migrate to another country after making a difficult decision. In moments of crisis, the characters make complicated choices which confound their lives even more as they move from Bihar to East Bengal to Pakistan, and the story grows gradually outward, becoming more emotionally complex and powerful with each turning page. These were apocalyptic times which demonstrated how often people were surprised by the actions of those closest to them, in times that mattered most.

Like Abdullah Husain's *Udas Naslein* (The Weary Generations) and Qurratul Ain Hyder's *Aag ka Darya* (The Sea of Fire), Abdus Samad's *Do Gaz Zameen* (Search for a New Land) also portrays the ramifications of power politics in Bihar during the pre-Independence period and sheds light on the fact that the Muslims of Bihar were among the worst victims of partition and the social, political and historical upheavals that were unleashed as a result. Beginning with the story of the respectable Bihari family of Shaikh Altaf Husain and his wife Bibi Sahiba, the novel goes on to present how the pre-partition politics of the Congress and the Muslim League wrecks and ruins the lives of their children, which forces some of them to flee to East Pakistan and some to West Pakistan while the abolition of zamindari deprives those who stay back of their inherited property. This not only leaves the family truncated but also makes it alienated from its own homeland. The growing carnage of communal riots in Bihar and Bengal, and later in East Pakistan further reduces the chances of any relief for the broken family.

Fired with a bold initiative of painting a tremendously complicated canvas with a significant array of characters and situations, Abdus Samad carried his novel to a level where it shows up as a robust and accurate statement of the catastrophic experience of the partition and its aftermath. Recounting the bloody legacy of that time, Samad builds his story by spinning a fictional atmosphere in his narrative, making the work a wonderful example of objectivity and subtlety. Throughout the novel, he is constantly mindful of the message he intends to give out: it is a book about an array of men and women caught unaware in the tumultuous whirlpool of partition with all its complexities, trying to salvage their lives and identities in the worsening socio-political situation while being hounded by the politics of hatred. And it is here—through his stark narrative and subtle nuances of dialogues—that Samad builds a powerful picture of the pain inflicted by the partition.

While Samad never gets involved in the emotional upheavals that run through the story, his narrative quietly and coolly illustrates the collective destiny of Indian Muslims without ever indulging in self-pity or sensationalism.

What is most touchingly spotlighted in the story is the annihilation of hope and the moral blankness of power politics that tore well-knit families apart and compelled hapless people to leave their land and their country to find meaning and life in a world quite different from what they had known till then. The two letters—one by Akhtar Husain, and the other by Hamid, his son—describe most potently and poignantly the horrifying experiences that people on both sides of the Indian border went through. These letters recount the greatest human tragedy of partition, the traumatic memories of which cannot be wiped off anytime soon.

Syed Sarwar Hussain
New Delhi
August 2022

PART ONE

1

There is a crossroads fifteen miles west of Biharsharif. A four-mile walk on the dirt road north of the crossroads leads to a quaint, neighbouring village called Ben. Although not known for its legacy of famed inhabitants, the village prides itself on having produced one man, namely, Sheikh Altaf Husain, who has provided Ben its place in posterity. Sheikh Altaf started taking interest in national politics in his youth, when the Khilafat Movement was at its peak. While the movement appealed to the Muslim religious beliefs to a great extent, the support of many Hindu leaders had made it a national movement. Gandhiji realized the usefulness and importance of the Khilafat Movement when he left South Africa and returned to India with a passion to do something notable and unusual. For the first time, glimpses of rejuvenation and vitality started appearing in a nation that had been bowing in servitude to British rule for years. Its bent back was now straightening slowly, leading to visible anxiety on the face of its powerful colonial rulers.

Prominent Indian leaders like Maulana Shaukat Ali, Maulana Muhammad Ali, Gandhiji, and Bi Amma came to

Ben in connection with the Khilafat Movement. Every house in Ben and its adjoining villages was echoing with the song,

So spoke the mother of Muhammad Ali.
My son, lay down your life for the sake of Khilafat.

Those who had witnessed the huge public meeting organized on the arrival of those leaders to the village say that not even the Congress party and the Muslim League could, ever after, hold as large a rally as that. It is commonly recounted that when Gandhiji's chappal broke, it was sent especially to the town for repair. At that time, the gossip that Nehru's clothes were washed in Paris and that they were scented with ittar (attar or fragrant essential oil made typically made from rose petals) and other fragrances was doing the rounds among the elite as well as the common people.

Sheikh Altaf was not a big landlord. He held not more than 40 per cent share in the village land. But he had built an enviable reputation. On the edge of the village stood his grand haveli, with clay tiled roofs, large courtyards, and big rooms. Adorning the front of the house was a sizeable grassy lawn, where meetings were held. A short little trail past the field led to a pond in which the best fish food was sprinkled allowing the fish to grow better and faster to entertain the guests with tasty fish recipes. When villagers walked past the haveli, they whispered about the famed courtyard where Gandhiji roamed, or the rooms inhabited by the Ali brothers. Walking by the haveli, the villagers often found Sheikh Altaf sitting in the front yard, but it was not required of them to salute him. Whereas it was considered an offence to walk past the front of the pucca (made of solid, substantial material) two-storey houses of the 60 per cent stakeholders of the village land and not greet them. The people of the locality envied the dignity and respect Sheikh Altaf commanded.

It was generally believed that the arrival of a Sayyidani, a female descendant of the Prophet Muhammad, had changed the fortunes of the haveli. Otherwise, Sheikh Altaf's ancestors were also landlords and 40 per cent stakeholders in the village land, but they had never enjoyed such stellar reputation. His grandfather, Sheikh Imdad Husain, was a sub-inspector and was famous for having exterminated a gang of dacoits in an operation. The leader of the gang had fled away vowing that he would not rest until he took revenge. So, one dark night when the dacoit chief found Imdad Husain travelling in a palanquin, he surrounded it with his henchmen. The palanquin bearers got frightened and bolted, leaving Sheikh Imdad behind, helpless, alone and unarmed, confronted by bandits armed with deadly weapons. Though he fought bravely, wounding some of them, they finally chopped him into pieces. Only one of his hands was left to be discovered, and this hand was later laid to rest with full state honours. People in the surrounding areas remembered the stories of Sheikh Imdad Husain's courage and bravery.

When his grandson Sheikh Altaf Husain reached adulthood, the boy's mother laid down only one condition: that his bride-to-be must be a pure Sayyidani. In those days being a pure-blood was a matter of pride. And the Sayyids were held in great awe and reverence by people. They were respectfully referred to as Mir sahibs and were requested to pray for others. People feared to earn their displeasure. Eventually, after a long search, Altaf Husain was engaged to a girl from a famous Sayyid family of Sheikhpura. Hakim Syed

Nazir Husain, the girl's father, was the son of Hakim Arshad, a well-known physician. He had studied Unani medicine according to the cherished tradition of the time but was never found in his clinic. He was, nevertheless, a family hakim, especially to those with whom he had personal relations. They often requested him to prepare medications for such old diseases that had passed untreated through the hands of many hakims and doctors. Hakim Syed Nazir had a druggist who sat in the courtyard all day long, powdering and preparing drugs, leaving them to dry in large copper trays.

Only twenty people went with Sheikh Altaf's baraat (the groom's wedding procession), but thousands joined the walima (marriage banquet). Large salvers containing delicacies were also transported to Sheikh Altaf's relatives who lived within a ten-mile radius but had been unable to attend the feast.

When the Sayyidani from Sheikhpura entered the house of the noblemen of Ben as a daughter-in-law, she made her mark there in such a way that the pomp and glory of the daughters'-in-law of even the more affluent households in the village dimmed considerably. Back in her house at Sheikhpura, she could afford to have only two meals a day. Though she had little earthly possessions to boast of in her house, her family was blessed with enormous respect and dignity. At her in-law's house, she was respectfully called Bibi Sahiba, and she preserved the dignity of that honorific all her life, giving a new, deeper meaning to it. It was not easy for a girl from a poor family to adapt to the lifestyle of nobility, all the more so because everybody's mealtimes and tastes were different in the house. But things fell into place once the Sayyidani came in. Meals were prepared and served on time, and the messy affairs of the house were sorted into organized housekeeping. There was no established practice of providing children with any formal, modern education in the house. A ceremony was held with great fanfare marking the start of the Maktab education at home when the children were usually five or six years old. Well-known clerics or sheikhs were invited on that occasion. After that, a maulvi, a qualified Islamic scholar, was assigned to homeschool the children in the Quran, the books of Milad-un-Nabi, the biography and sayings of Prophet Muhammad, Arabic, Persian and Urdu. They also taught children to memorize multiplication tables. After completing the Qaida, a series of four books to learn Quranic Arabic, and the thirty parts of the Quran, their studies were discontinued. But by that time, they could read the Quran fluently, they developed good handwriting by practising on slates and could explain the meanings of Persian poems. They did not need to study more. Sir Sayyid Ahmed Khan was discredited, and children were even prohibited to utter his name. Programmes were outlined to send students to the Islamic madrasas at Al-Azhar and Istanbul, but they were never implemented. Before the advent of Bibi Sahiba, every couple in the house had no more than two offspring. But Bibi Sahiba was blessed with eight issues in quick succession. Four sons and four daughters. The family that was craving for more children for generations received God's generous gift in the shape of these eight little blessings. Sheikh Altaf decided to call two maulvis from Delhi who would stay in his haveli and assume the responsibility of educating the children. He left little room for any amendment to his resolve. All affairs related to his children were arranged with great pomp and show, and their Maktab functions were so magnificent that they were a treat to behold.

Ben had everything that its inhabitants could need for everyday consumption, and if there was a particular need, the town was not far away, although it took the whole day or sometimes a day and night to travel the distance of about twenty miles between these two places. However, there was a particular exigency for which people often rushed to the town. It was the dearth of physicians in the village. While it had an unlicenced vaidya and a hakim, only the servants and poor relatives of the landlords visited them. Sheikh Altaf's family was fairly large anyway. Besides, guests frequented the house every so often. His four-horse landau trundled along the four-mile distance from the village to the bus stop, carrying the guests to and fro. On one occasion, Bibi Sahiba advised him to buy a house in the adjacent Biharsharif town. They had to go there often to see a doctor or for other needs and stay at undesirable places. Owning a home there would be good for the children too. He liked her suggestion and bought land in the town on which he built a house resembling his great haveli. It was named Ben House. A caretaker was appointed to look after the house, and in this way, the bond between the village and the town was further strengthened.

When the Khilafat Movement helped to transform India's freedom struggle into a mass movement, all the crusaders of the movement became soldiers of the Indian independence struggle. The spirit of the movement remained the same, its purpose changed. Sheikh Altaf took part in the independence movement with great enthusiasm. He was sent to jail for protesting against the visit of the Prince of Wales. A big chunk of the income from his lands was spent on the independence movement. The moneyless freedom fighters who were jailed had no one to care for their families in their absence. It was the moral duty of those who could not be imprisoned, accidentally or by any reason, to look after them. Besides helping them with his money, Sheikh Altaf also managed to send food to the distraught families, without differentiating between Hindus and Muslims. Even those who gave any importance to untouchability in their personal and social life overlooked everything in their fight for freedom.

It was not easy for an outsider to reach Ben. One had to undertake a ten-hour journey by bus or taxi, or board the train from Patna to Biharsharif and then take a bus or taxi to reach the crossroads from where a dirt road led to Ben. If the visitor happened to be a guest of Sheikh Altaf and he knew about his arrival, the landau would wait for him by the roadside. Others had to walk all the way to the village. The coolie boys were always available to carry luggage on their heads. Prominent political leaders felt considerable unease in going back and forth to the village. Two full days were spent only on the journey there and back, and they usually travelled with lots of people. It was obviously not possible to manage a ride for everyone, so they had to walk on foot. Sheikh Altaf initially did not want to leave his ancestral home, but when some leaders advised him to stay in Biharsharif, he decided to settle there.

2

After his arrival in the town, Sheikh Altaf's political activities increased greatly. Patna was the provincial centre of the struggle for independence. Every so often, the town bustled with a flurry of activities. Leaders from Delhi kept visiting the place. It was easier for Sheikh Altaf to travel to Patna from his new house in Biharsharif, where people frequently called in on him. The Indian independence movement in Biharsharif and around it gained momentum because of the presence of Sheikh Altaf. The last train from Patna reached Biharsharif at ten o'clock at night. So, dinner was laid out after the arrival of the train. Fortuitously, one or two guests always turned up at Ben House. The stove kept burning all day and night, and the kitchen constantly buzzed with commotion. There was no dearth of workers. Bibi Sahiba had also brought along with her many maidservants from Ben. No one who visited the house at any time of the day went out without being served up and taken care of. People who came there were never asked their names and addresses. Often, many people would complacently stay there for weeks in a row, which allowed them the opportunity of joining Sheikh Altaf's dinner table for two meals every day. But they were never asked their names, why and wherefrom they came and for how long they would stay. Because of his intense social activities, Sheikh Altaf had very little chance to meet his wife and children every day. Days passed without him being able to see even Bibi Sahiba. The haveli was huge and spacious. There was a fairly long distance between the men's and the women's quarters. If a man wanted to visit the female quarter, he would have to pre-inform his arrival. Bibi Sahiba was fully aware of Sheikh Altaf's feelings and needs. She made every effort to enhance his dignity and honour. Those who returned from a visit to the place always lauded Bibi Sahiba's cordiality and etiquette.

The education of the eight children continued after the family shifted to the town. A maulvi and a hafiz (person who has memorized the entire Quran) were always there in the house. When the oldest son, Sarwar Husain, completed studying the Quran, Persian, Urdu and mathematics lessons at a tender age, they themselves suggested that he should be tutored at home to prepare for the college entrance exam. Sheikh Altaf relented after some hesitation, and a tutor was summoned from Patna to teach the boy English and other subjects. After teaching him for three years, the teacher recommended that the boy was fit to take the entrance exams.

In those times, there was only one university for the states of Bengal, Bihar and Orissa—the Calcutta University, which administered the entrance examination for admission to the colleges. Sarwar Husain took the exams and topped the university. For the first time someone in the family had acquired Western education and earned fame. It was a new experience for Sheikh Altaf. He felt inspired by the importance of education. Without wasting any time, he got Sarwar Husain admitted into Presidency College at Calcutta and emboldened Asghar Husain, his second son, to prepare for the entrance test.

And just when the Khilafat Movement was gathering momentum in India, the Turkish Caliphate died in its homeland. Kamal Ataturk emerged as a symbol of the modern, twentieth-century Muslim. But a large segment of Indian Muslims flatly refused to accept him as its symbol. Hundreds of thousands of people had wasted their lives away in the Khilafat Movement, and it was now not possible for them to discard it all at once. However, Gandhiji's wisdom and intelligence came to their rescue, and with his keen quick-wittedness, he turned the focus of Indian Muslims towards the independence movement. It indeed gave a new course to their restive energies; a new era of national solidarity began in the country. Ben House had once been the centre of both the movements. But now all efforts there were targeted at the attainment of independence. The British government was already keeping a close watch over Sheikh Altaf's activities. Visitors to his house also came under close scrutiny. There was suspicion about informants at the various large gatherings at Ben House, but Sheikh Altaf encouraged them. He wanted the British to feel this unease.

As soon as Sarwar Husain arrived back home from Calcutta for a vacation, Sheikh Altaf decided to get him married. He had resolved to betroth his orphaned niece to his son, although she was four years older in age and Sarwar Husain always called her Apa, elder sister. Everyone in the family was against the marriage. Bibi Sahiba had herself expressed her disapproval in a subdued tone. But no one could prevail over Sheikh Altaf's stubbornness. His argument was that every Muslim should follow the tradition begun by the Prophet of Islam, who himself in the nick of youth married an elderly widow. This statement rendered everyone speechless. Sarwar Husain bowed down quietly to his father's decision. His only worry was how he could consider as his wife the girl whom he had always called Apa. The custom of involving relatives or friends to inform the parents about the likes and dislikes concerning the choice of a spouse and sitting in a quiet corner with fingers crossed had not yet become rife in those days. So, the marriage was solemnized, and the bride shifted from her prenuptial room to the room that was especially prepared for the married couple. A few days later, Sheikh Altaf's nephew Akhtar Husain arrived at Ben House after completing his bachelor's degree. Sheikh Altaf gave him his eldest daughter, Asmat Bibi, who was only twelve years old, in marriage. In the meanwhile, Sarwar Husain, the bashful new husband, left for Calcutta after staying home for a few days, with the wedding mehndi still brightening his hands and feet. When Sheikh Altaf's second son, Asghar Husain, completed his college entrance examination and returned home, Sheikh Altaf's elderly uncle summoned the young man to Islampur for a change.

The old uncle, a designated Khan Bahadur, was a big zamindar who owned sizeable portions of village lands in Islampur. He had sent his son to England to become a barrister and waited for his return while acclimatizing himself with the use of fork and knife. When his son came back, he got him married with great pomp and show into a prominent family. And for their accommodation a grand mansion was built, in a remote village like Islampur, in the style of White House, the official residence of the President of America. Those people who raised objections to such opulence in a village, when the son was almost certainly expected to practise as a barrister in a big town, were ignored. But it so happened that some months after his marriage, Khan Bahadur's son died suddenly and unexpectedly, leaving behind in the bleak and barren haveli his old, grieving parents and a pregnant wife. The widow, a few months later, gave birth to a daughter and joined her dead husband. Left in the haveli were now a bottle-fed infant, its senescent grandparents to look after it, with four trembling, shaky hands, and an army of domestic servants. The bottle-fed infant had now grown up into an endearing twelve-year-old girl.

As Asghar Husain arrived at the Islampur haveli for his holidays, he was ungrudgingly chosen to marry the young girl. He hailed from the same family, and the property would rather stay there. There was no need to ask or inquire anyone about him. Though Khan Bahadur loathed his nephew's resentment against the English rulers, which was why he had stopped meeting him, the bond of blood, nevertheless, had its own pull. So, a day before Asghar Husain's departure from Islampur, his nikah (marriage ceremony) was performed with Khan Bahdur's granddaughter in the presence of some village elders, and he was sent off to Biharsharif with loads of fruits, sweets, some traditional snacks and two helpers.

The moment the nikah sweets reached Biharsharif, it sparked a half-hushed tumult in Sheikh Altaf's house. The incident suddenly jolted the family, which had not yet recovered from the fatigue following Sarwar Husain's wedding. Sheikh Altaf had gone to Patna to receive Madan Mohan Malviya and Pandit Motilal Nehru, who were travelling to Calcutta, and their train was scheduled to halt at Patna for a few minutes. Owing to Sheikh Altaf's political views, his relationship with his uncle, the picky Khan Bahadur, had strained. When his uncle was awarded the title of Khan Bahadur by the British Empire, everyone except Sheikh Altaf visited the gratified man to greet him. In fact, on the very same day, Bal Gangadhar Tilak arrived at Biharsharif, defying the ban imposed on him by the British governor to enter the Bihar province. Obviously, the British police had made all plans to arrest him, and it was to happen in the meeting that was to be presided by Sheikh Altaf. When the news reached Khan Bahadur, he quipped curtly that it was by virtue of the British Empire that such an efficient postal system was established in India.

The hasty marriage of Asghar Husain deeply hurt Bibi Sahiba. She had not been consulted on either of her sons' marriages. She had sent Asghar Husain to Islampur to relish the healthy village food and environment before revisiting the tasteless food at the university hostel at Calcutta. Little did she realize that her son would not remain the same after his return from Islampur. She was also scared how Sheikh Altaf would react on hearing about his son's unexpected nikah, considering his uneasy relationship with his uncle, a relationship that had worsened to the extent that they had stopped visiting each other. What shocked Bibi Sahiba more was that Khan Bahadur did not even care to seek Sheikh Altaf's consent before marrying the latter's son off to his granddaughter. On Sheikh Altaf's return, everyone at the house kept the matter a secret from him. They left it to Bibi Sahiba to inform him about his son's nikah. So, when they sat at dinner, the time when family matters were usually discussed, she informed Sheikh Altaf about Asghar Husain's nikah. He kept eating with his head down. Sitting close by, Bibi Sahiba was waiting for a violent storm brewing within his awed silence. Sheikh Altaf finished his dinner, cleaned his hand and face, sank into an easy chair holding the hookah pipe in his hand, and only said, 'What more can I say in this matter? It was an uncle's right.'

It was only after then that the nikah fruits and sweets were distributed among the relatives, and the news of the nikah was announced.

3

Without any illness or lack of care, Sheikh Altaf suddenly passed away at the age of forty-five. The house filled up with sounds of weeping and wailing. The household was shocked to lose their head. The boys, though married, had not yet finished their studies. Bibi Sahiba was herself still in her youth. There remained only Akhtar Husain, her nephew and son-in-law, as the eldest in the household. After graduating from law school at Calcutta, he had come back to settle in the house and start his legal practice at Biharsharif. He comforted his aunt-cum-mother-in-law and took over his dead uncle's responsibilities. Ever since he could remember, Akhtar Husain was always interested in the two movements, the Khilafat and the struggle for Indian independence. Whenever political leaders visited Sheikh Altaf, Akhtar Husain tried to stay closer to them, discussing political matters with them, taking good care of them and sparing no effort to arrange conveyances for them. He also enjoyed wearing khadi clothes.

On the other hand, Sheikh Altaf's sons, like obedient children, did exactly what their father asked them to do.

They were not allowed to approach anyone unnecessarily. It often happened that when Sheikh Altaf sent one of them to conduct any of his guests to Patna, they did not converse all along the journey.

At the time of Sheikh Altaf's death, his two older sons were in Calcutta. The other two who were still young were tutored at home, learning the Quran, Persian and Urdu. His three daughters, other than Akhtar Husain's wife, were achingly young, and they had virtually no relatives, close or distant, other than Bibi Sahiba, to look after them. Upon hearing the news of his untimely demise, Sheikh Altaf's uncle came from Islampur to offer his condolences. During his stay there, some prominent local leaders of the Congress party also visited the haveli to offer their sympathies to the grieving family. Sheikh Altaf's uncle was so annoyed to see them that he left for Islampur the same day. When Sarwar Husain and Asghar Husain arrived from Calcutta, they found their father's resemblance in Akhtar Husain—their cousin and brother-in-law. His presence halved their grief. Sheikh Altaf had left such a coherent and well-organized administrative arrangement of his zamindari lands that a change of hands did not disturb its status. Everything in the house kept going as usual. However, the radiance surrounding the house had undeniably faded.

Sheikh Altaf had, in his lifetime, bequeathed to Akhtar Husain a piece of land in the premises of his huge haveli, and built a bungalow for him on the land. After starting his legal practice, Akhtar Husain met his clients in his bungalow, but spent most of his time with his uncle in the haveli. And though he was married, he, nevertheless, gave his aunt and mother-in-law, Bibi Sahiba, whatever fees he received from his clients, as he had no significant personal expenses other than his everyday needs. Sarwar Husain and Asghar Husain continued their studies in Calcutta. After completing his bachelor's degree with a first class, and receiving a scholarship, Sarwar Husain was sent to England for the preparation of the Indian Civil Service examination. He stayed there as a paying guest in the house of a kind English lady. Asghar Husain, on the other hand, was married off in the midst of completing his studies. Although he passed his final examination, he did not get a good grade. This didn't bother him; he inherited vast estates from his in-laws, of whom his wife and he were the only rightful heirs.

Though the Muslim League was established in the country long ago, it came to life when the Nehru Report was introduced in 1928, which disheartened and disappointed the Muslims against the Congress party which had ignored their interests. Wily and opportunistic Muslim politicians took full advantage of that opportunity, and playing on the despondency of the Muslim masses, they impressed upon them that since Muslims had ruled the country for more than seven hundred years, the Congress now wanted to gain independence and ensure their subservience in a Hindu India. It was, therefore, inevitable for them to form their own party, their separate slogan and an entirely different objective. The soil was being prepared for the seed that was going to be sown. And the Muslim League emerged as a powerful organization in no time. Its branches were established in small towns and large villages, and public meetings and processions were initiated from time to time. The Muslim League brought out its own newspaper which exaggerated facts beyond the pale. Those who were gullible were disposed to go with the tide, and they were the people who very easily became leaders of the Muslim League.

There were people even inside the Congress party who were waiting to discover which way the wind was blowing, and finding it congenial joined the Muslim League. Those Muslims who remained with the Congress owing to their ideology and belief, realized that their condition had worsened with the passage of time. During the British presence in India, caste and religious discriminations and dispute had penetrated into the politics of the country. The Indian National Congress was the most prominent party, but its members were discreetly ardent Hindus, Muslims, Sikhs or Christians. They were recognized in their areas on the basis of their religious identities. In the Hindu-dominated areas, nobody cared about the Muslims, and in the areas overshadowed by Muslims, the Hindus did not have any say. In the changed situation, the Hindu leaders were organized and strong in the areas where they were dominant. They not only had their people's sympathy with them, it was also constantly increasing as a result of political awareness. On the other hand, when the Muslim League declared that it was the sole representative of the Indian Muslims, most of the Muslims practically accepted its invite. Consequently, the influence of the Muslim Congress leaders rapidly waned in their areas. In less than ten years, the country saw two political parties appearing on the national stage. Although still ruled by the British Empire, the divisions were so profound that when the Muslim League demanded a separate homeland, the Congress party did not show any hesitation in accepting it.

Biharsharif had not only seen and heard national leaders of the time like, Maulana Shaukat Ali, Maulana Mohamed Ali, Bal Gangadhar Tilak, Madan Mohan Malviya, Sri Babu, Anugrah Babu, Professor Abdul Bari and others, in the wake of the Khilafat and freedom movements, but was also very familiar to them. Ben House was, however, the centre of political activities. Biharsharif's prominent people who frequented the place were immediately recognized as they appeared on the streets. Local leaders like Syed Mehdi Hasan, Mohamed Hasan, Mohamed Fakhruddin, Bansi Lal, Ajodhya Prasad, were often seen on the dais whenever there was a public gathering. Therefore, along with that of Sheikh Altaf's, the faces of these leaders were also imprinted on the mind of the residents of the town.

Political exigencies demanded that the Muslim League had to be accepted as the sole representative of the Muslims, which led to Syed Mehdi Hasan and the other Muslim leaders to bid goodbye to the Congress party, to become Muslim League leaders. Asghar Husain lived mostly in Islampur, with some stays in Biharsharif. When Gruning, the English subdivisional officer of Biharsharif, was transferred, he gifted his old car to Asghar Husain. The car made three or four rounds every week between Islampur and Biharsharif. Earlier, it was seen on the road when the English officer visited Islampur on a hunting trip. On such occasions, some other cars also accompanied it. Though Asghar Husain was the son of an ardent nationalist leader, he took to disliking the Congress party when he read the Nehru Report minutely, and heard, in a small meeting, the speech of a Congress leader who only a few days later joined the Hindu Mahasabha (the right-wing Hindu nationalist political party).

British commissioners and collectors frequently visited Khan Bahadur, Asghar Husain's wife's grandfather. Once when Khan Bahadur invited the governor to dinner in a remote village like Islampur, a red carpet was laid over the road to honour him. In those days a provincial governor was held in very high regard. Asghar Husain had seen that with his own eyes. He had studied at Calcutta's prestigious Presidency College, and some of his friends had successfully cracked the ICS exam. He loved pomp and ceremony. And fortunately for him, God had bestowed upon him the life he so passionately loved.

When Asghar Husain heard that the Muslim League was going to convene at a large public meeting at Biharsharif, he left for Biharsharif immediately in his old English car. One of the Muslim League leaders who was coming to attend the meeting was an old college mate from his Presidency College days, the son of a famous barrister of Patna. Asghar Husain hosted a lunch for him at Ben House and invited all those Muslim League leaders who were on a visit to the town. Akhtar Husain, at that time, was out of station on an urgent errand. Since a lot of people were coming for lunch, the preparation began a day before the party. Dozens of pullets were purchased, and sturdy, home-bred goats were delivered from the village. Liveried waiters were summoned from a big hotel in Patna. A huge shamiana (tent) was erected in the maidan, and hundreds of chairs and tables were laid out under it. The tables were set with a glass placed next to every plate, and a rolled napkin adorned every glass. In preparation for the party, Asghar Husain tried to replicate the same scenario that his grandfather had once created in the entire Islampur village in honour of the British governor of the time. He had inherited his family's sophistication; they were known far and wide for their etiquette.

The Muslim League leaders arrived at the party in a large procession. They were flanked by hundreds of people shouting slogans,

Muslim League zindabad, long live Pakistan, down with Congress, down with Gandhiji.

Mehdi Hasan's open-top Ford, carrying some leaders, was laden with flowers. And behind it was a cavalcade of horse-drawn carriages conveying the League supporters and workers. They yelled their rallying cry long after entering the Ben House courtyard. Then began a series of speeches, bearing in mind the exigency of the occasion, custom and expedience. Right at that moment, Akhtar Husain riding in a horse-drawn carriage entered Ben House and was dumbfounded by what he witnessed. Sitting in his carriage, he tried to comprehend the situation and when things became clear, he walked off directly to his living quarters. Clad in a khadi pyjama and kurta, and a topi on his head, he was looking quite strange against the bustling crowd in the maidan. He had not left his room locked, and found that the furniture was moved out from there, and laid out in the courtyard outside. His room had been occupied by two wooden bedsteads with white cotton sheets and large pillows on them, but there was nothing there now. A mat stood rolled in a corner of the room. Akhtar Husain spread it on the floor, changed his clothes, and lounged on it.

Just then, Asghar Husain entered the room, and finding his cousin there, asked him, 'Adab Bhaijan! When did you come? I didn't have the slightest inkling.'

'I've just arrived.'

'I thought you weren't coming today, so I took the beds out for the guests.'

'That's fine with me. There shouldn't be any flaw in offering hospitality to the guests.'

'I feel so blessed! Everything has been so well organized. I hope you know that Sir Matiullah's son was my classmate at Presidency College. He was here in town for a meeting and I threw a party for him. I couldn't help inviting other people who were associated with him.'

Akhtar Husain remained silent.

'Bhaijan! Why don't you come out and meet them? You are our oldest male relative in the house. Your presence at the luncheon is very important,' Asghar Husain asked him earnestly.

'What are you saying, Asghar? You know very well who your guests are!'

'What do we have to do with their political ideologies? They are my friends and I have invited them—that's all.'

'Would your father attend this party if he were alive today?'

'I'm sure he would. I have invited a close friend of mine.'

'But what about all those slogan-shouting fellows with him? What does that mean?'

'My friend is an eminent political leader. It's quite obvious, therefore, that his supporters will follow him wherever he may go. Besides, who can forbid them from shouting slogans? I haven't invited them, anyway.'

'Never mind. You should go and entertain your guests now. I'm sorry, I won't be able to attend.'

'Bhaijan, you're going to do that in your personal capacity. You will stay there as my guardian, on behalf of my dead father.'

'My dear cousin, I really don't feel inclined to sit and dine with people with whom we are at loggerheads in streets, lanes and fields.'

Asghar Husain tried his best and pleaded with him, but Akhtar Husain remained adamant. Finally, he had to entertain his guests and see them off, all by himself. Meanwhile, when food from the women's quarter of the haveli was brought to Akhtar Husain on a salver, he refused to accept it, feigning illness. It was the same food that was prepared for the party. It was quite unusual of Akhtar Husain to decline food unless he was really full. When Bibi Sahiba heard this, she asked for the purdah to be drawn and came out of the female quarter to see him. When she entered his room, she found him saying his Asr (afternoon) prayer. He greeted her after finishing his prayer.

'Why didn't you take your lunch, beta?'

'I'm feeling heaviness in my stomach and deem it better to get some sleep.'

'You might be feeling travel weary. I wish you had let me know. I would have prepared a light meal for you.'

'It doesn't matter. I'll have an early dinner.'

'I'm going to send a few light chapatis and soup for you. Dinner time is still far away.'

Akhtar Husain said nothing and Bibi Sahiba returned to the women's quarters.

When the furniture scattered inside the shamiana was being carried back to the house, Akhtar Husain asked the servants to take his beds to his bungalow rather than bringing them to his room in the haveli. His decision created a furore in the house. But nobody dared to speak anything. His wife was a quiet, uncomplaining woman. She simply waited for her husband's orders. Bibi Sahiba was not very happy with the new arrangements. Akhtar Husain had now started living in his bungalow. Apart from this there was no difference in his behaviour. He would come, as before, to the haveli for his breakfast and dinner. And on occasions when he found himself very busy, he had the food delivered from the haveli. He continued handing over to Bibi Sahiba whatever money he earned from his legal practice. Asghar Husain went back to Islampur after staying for a few days.

The news arrived, a few months later, that he had formally joined the Muslim League at a public meeting held at the Gandhi Maidan in Patna. But to Bibi Sahiba, it appeared no different from joining the Congress party. Her information about the Congress party was that it desired the welfare of both the Hindus and the Muslims. And she learnt of late about the Muslim League that it wished for the well-being of the Muslims only. She was a pious woman. In addition to offering the five obligatory prayers a day, she also took great care to say optional prayers. During Ramadan, in particular, the women in the haveli competed with each other in reading the Quran as many times over as they could. Among her late husband's companions, there were a substantial number of Hindus. Some of them believed in ritual impurity and refused to eat food in Muslim houses, so Bibi Sahiba had to make special arrangements for them. But even then, she did not harbour any adverse feelings for them. She could not tell much difference between the Muslim League and the Congress party. Both of them appeared to her as two sides of the same coin.

Asghar Husain visited Biharsharif every now and then. The road from Islampur to Patna crossed Biharsharif, and whenever Asghar Husain went to Patna for some reason, he made it a point to stay at Biharsharif for a few days. He never forgot to meet his mother on his return from Patna. He had become an executive member of the district Muslim League committee. And so, every time he stayed at Biharsharif, he received visits from lots of local Muslim League workers. Slogans were ceaselessly spouted and flower garlands were showered. But the Congress party workers who came to meet Akhtar Husain never chanted slogans. In any case, the tradition of holding celebrations and meetings of the Congress party in Ben House was no longer maintained. The Congress party office was housed in a separate building where meetings were held every so often, and police raids were launched off and on. Akhtar Husain was often imprisoned for his anti-British activities. He always kept ready one suitcase full of his clothes and other requirements, and never wasted time when the police came to arrest him. If there was no one from the house around him at that time, the news of his detention reached his family members late.

Akhtar Husain had a spacious, round chabutra (a raised platform) built in front of his bungalow. On summer evenings the chabutra was sprayed with water, and lawn chairs were placed on it. A round centre table with the latest newspapers stood in the middle. Lounging in an easy chair, Akhtar Husain ran the show. Ajodhya Prasad, Bal Govind Verma, Ratlal Prasad Sharma, Hakim Mohamed Asim, Maulana Mohamed Kazim and Ali Ahmed Rizvi, among others, gathered there almost every evening and stayed late into the night, fiercely debating over the political miscalculations of the Muslim

League, the Congress party, Gandhiji, Subhas Chandra Bose, Shri Babu and Anugrah Babu. Each time Asghar Husain came to Ben House, he felt bad about the evening gatherings held by his cousin. He would often complain to his mother about his cousin openly inviting enmity with the British government. But Bibi Sahiba failed to understand how it could invoke hostility of the ruling government, especially when Akhtar Husain's visitors always talked about the welfare of the country, of all the people living in it, as they had been doing since the time of Sheikh Altaf. Now if the British government misread it as an act of animosity no one could do anything about it. It was enough to convince Asghar Husain that his mother would not hear anything against his cousin Akhtar Husain.

Sarwar Husain returned from England only after failing twice in the Indian Civil Services exams. In those days it was obligatory to acquire a bachelor's in law in order to appear for the Indian Civil Service exams. And eventually that degree proved very useful to him. Since Biharsharif was a relatively small town, he started his legal practice at Patna, and rented a house there. But his wife, even after repeated insistence, flatly declined to stay with him at Patna. She was Akhtar Husain's younger sister, and had been living with her brother ever after her marriage. She had never formally lived with her in-laws. Besides, a strange coldness existed between Sarwar Husain and her. Perhaps, the very thought of them being first cousins had proven a barrier to conjugal intimacy. Sarwar Husain never wrote to her from England, and his wife also never sent her greetings to him, though whoever wrote to him, inevitably informed him about his wife's well-being. When she absolutely refused to budge from her stance, Sarwar

Husain started living alone at Patna. He summoned a cook from his village and hired an office clerk who stayed with him. He also called his four younger siblings—two brothers and two sisters—to Patna to live with him. Bibi Sahiba was not ready to leave the house where she had spent a lifetime with her husband. She, otherwise, occasionally visited Patna. Every week she sent her son bakarkhanis (thick spiced flat-bread), kulcha cookies, namak paray (crunchy savoury snack), different varieties of kababs and halvahs from Biharsharif. Sarwar Husain was an intelligent man, and had studied law in England. Soon he earned a good name in his profession and was counted among the sharpest lawyers in town. He was not interested in politics, and although he was fond of reading newspapers regularly, he never discussed political affairs. He valued Asghar Husain's affinity with the Muslim League, and never talked ill about Akhtar Husain's love for the Congress party. Appreciating the fact that Akhtar Husain was his wife's older brother, and the husband of his older sister, Sarwar Husain never spoke much before him out of respect. He came home on the occasions of Christmas and other government holidays, but the distance from his wife remained as usual.

Sarwar Husain was a new age man. He had lived in England as a lodger with a landlady for years. He used to wander around the city, picnicking, and swimming with the daughters and nieces of the woman. He brought home many pictures of him and his girlfriends, which his brothers and sisters saw with great interest and fascination. But when he showed them to his wife, she turned her face away without looking at them. Though Sarwar Husain could not make her understand, he explained to his mother, brothers and sisters that in England it was not unusual for young men and women to interact with each other. It was, in fact, a part of their culture. Bibi Sahiba recalled fondly that that was the reason why her heavenly husband was fighting against firangi (foreign) culture. *In our culture a woman's place is either her husband's house or her grave.* She, nevertheless, was very proud of her son that even after having lived long enough in England, he had not brought home any firangi woman, although people had inveigled her to expect the opposite. She was actually a woman of strong faith—whether it was in God, in her husband, in her children, in her son-in-law, in the Congress or the Muslim League.

4

It was the time of the national general elections. Patna and Biharsharif together constituted a large area with a significant Muslim population. The Congress party had, from this area, fielded the nominations of Khwaja Abdul Hameed who was not only famous, but popular among both communities. He was also the president of the District Congress Committee. He was jailed during the Quit India Movement of 1942, and was recently released. Even much before the elections, whenever the name of a possible Congress candidate from the area was considered, the choice largely fell on him. On the other hand, the Muslim League nominated Maulvi Abdul Ghani, a former member of the Congress party, known to be second only to Hameed in his popularity. But after the failure in 1936 of the combined Congress–Muslim League ministry, he resigned from the party and joined the Muslim League. He was a great orator. When he spoke, he would lambast Gandhi and Nehru so harshly that no one could gather courage to contradict him. When Muhammad Ali Jinnah called Maulana Azad a 'show-boy' of the Congress, Maulvi Abdul

Ghani took it upon himself to spread the derogatory epithet to the surrounding villages of the Patna district. It delivered the desired result, and even children started openly making fun of Maulana Azad. Each time that they saw a Congress leader they asked him jestingly about Maulana Azad.

Newspapers reported that when the Aligarh Muslim University students saw Maulana Azad at the Aligarh railway station, they loosened their pyjama strings and chanted, 'show-boy, show-boy'. It was the talk of the town for many days. Two of those Aligarh Muslim University students were from the villages neighbouring Patna, and when they came home for their vacation, they were much admired. These students were staunch, hot-headed Muslim League supporters and looked quite quixotic in their Aligarh pyjamas, sherwanis and Turkish fez caps with a moon and star woven into the front. They travelled around villages telling the Muslims the difference between Congress and Muslim League, talking about the importance of the Muslim League's call for the division of India, speaking on Maulana Azad's pro-Hindu and anti-Muslim stance, condemning the dirty politics of Gandhi and Nehru and commending Sardar Patel's frankness and sincerity. The students went door to door and collected enough donations to fund the Muslim League candidate. In this way, they significantly paved the way for his victory. The area had been for a long time a stronghold of the Congress party, and was much frequented by the national politicians. At the national convention held by the Congress party at Ramgarh, the maximum number of delegates was sent from this district. Many provincial Muslim League leaders were consistently working there. Asghar Husain had come to Biharsharif a few weeks before the elections.

The part of Ben House which contained Sheikh Altaf's living quarters and whose walls had witnessed the presence of famous Congress leaders, numbly watched the inauguration of the Muslim League election office within its precincts. The place bustled with activity day and night. Large arrangements were made for victuals for the volunteers. Breads were ordered from the traditional bakers, and curry dishes were prepared in the home kitchen. The election office of the Congress party was set up at the party office, but since Akhtar Husain was a powerful Congress leader, his bungalow swarmed with party volunteers round the clock. The constant presence of workers of warring parties at the same place raised fears of a looming conflict. The Muslim League volunteers were larger in number and talked loudly against the Congress. Every so often, Akhtar Husain stormed out in rage, but the party workers calmed him down. Since it was election time, not many Hindu leaders of the Congress party were seen in and out of his bungalow. Most of them who visited him were Muslims, and the Muslim League workers fumed with anger on seeing them. The Congress Muslims were caught in a curious situation. Though the Congress party candidate was a Muslim, his election campaign was mostly organized by the Hindus and in the Hindu-dominated areas. Aside from the provincial leaders, some national leaders had also toured the area. Nehru's printed appeal for votes had been distributed among the inhabitants. The most interesting thing was that the Muslim leaders and workers of the Congress party could visit only the Hindu-dominated areas, because when earlier they tried to enter the Muslim-majority areas they were attacked with sticks and spears. They were often severely beaten and landed up in hospitals. All prominent Congress leaders were now with the Muslim League. The Muslim workers of the Congress were still confident as Maulana Abul Kalam Azad was with them, but he also faced continuous disparagement from Jinnah. The Congress learders convened behind closed doors and left quietly.

Akhtar Husain worked day and night for the triumph of his party's candidate. The courts were open, but he had stopped going. His clients came to him but departed when they saw their lawyer inflamed with an altogether different passion. This had started to tell upon his well-established legal practice, and hardly any Muslim client visited him now. On the other hand, the advocates associated with the Muslim League were making hay in such a favourable situation. It vexed Asghar Husain deeply to find that his cousin was forsaking his family and his legal practice while working frantically for the success of the candidate belonging to a Hindu party. But he could not say anything to him since Akhtar Husain was older than him. So Asghar Husain poured his heart out to his mother and his sisters, and they listened to him quietly. They felt that Asghar Husain was quite correct. *How could people of a different religious group be accepted as one's own?* Nevertheless, they did not even consider Akhtar Husain at fault, and he too never complained to them about his younger cousin. One fateful day, the Muslim League volunteers assaulted Akhtar Husain's two close friends belonging to the Congress party. He brought home the wounded volunteers, got them checked by a physician and arranged milk and diet for them. Specially prepared food was brought to them from the women's quarter. The women of the house cooked food in cauldrons for the Muslim League workers on the one hand,

and rustled up prescribed diet for the wounded Congress party members on the other.

The election day was one of tumult, commotion and clamour. Cars ran up and down the streets of the town the whole night. There was a carnival-like atmosphere in the entire area. It was a very large constituency and only one member was to be elected from it. (But after Independence, the same area was chosen to elect one-and-a-half-dozen candidates.) An overwhelming silence seemed to drape over Akhtar Husain's bungalow. He had cast his vote in the morning, and was sitting on the chabutra outside his house. The Congress volunteers appeared at short intervals and brought him the latest election news. In contrast, Asghar Husain's haveli had turned into the centre of fire and fever. The Muslim League volunteers appeared in throngs and yelled slogans. Though it was prohibited to spout slogans on the election day, perhaps those who had imposed the prohibitory orders were sleeping.

Akhtar Husain had directed his wife to cast her vote on the Congress's symbol. He did not say this to anybody else in the house. His wife, like an obedient woman, went to the polling booth in burqa and tendered her vote. A cycle rickshaw was summoned to carry her to the polling station and back. All the other women in the house went there in Asghar Husain's car. At the very same time a sudden puzzling thought struck Akhtar Husain, and he sent for his wife's burqa. Incidentally, she had lent the burqa to another woman to help her go out and cast her vote. Akhtar Husain grumbled loudly at her when he did not get the burqa, and scolded her severely. The poor woman stood sheepishly silently shedding tears. When the burqa was returned, she sent it immediately to her husband. The town remained abuzz until four in the

afternoon. In the evening the news came in that the voter turn-
out was unexpectedly high. In fact, the contest was basically
between the Congress and the Muslim League. There was so
much of enthusiasm throughout the night that nobody in the
opposite camps could sleep. The counting of votes started the
following morning. A few maulvi-looking Congress leaders,
while travelling in a car, were waylaid by some young men
on the street corner of a mohalla. The delinquent youths
thrashed them soundly, shaved off their beards, smeared black
paint across their faces and danced around them with their
pyjama strings undone. When the beaten up men went to the
police station to lodge a complaint, they found that the police
already had a report against them. They were arrested then
and there.

The election results were announced and the Muslim
League candidate Maulvi Abdul Ghani emerged victorious
with a big margin. The Hindu Mahasabha candidate came
second and Khwaja Abdul Hameed, the Congress aspirant,
fell to the third position. The Muslim League supporters
were euphoric. They took out a huge procession and marched
through the town, abusing Gandhi, Nehru and Azad,
shouting slogans, chanting 'Qaid-e Azam Muhammad Ali
Jinnah zindabad.' The triumphal procession reached Ben
House, and the revellers thronged the big front maidan.
Asghar Husain was felicitated with huge floral garlands.
Maulvi Abdul Ghani, the successful candidate, was not there
at that time. He was away at Patna. But Asghar Husain's
presence made up for his absence. He was receiving greetings
and compliments in the place of the winning candidate. Then
started the session of speeches. Asghar Husain and other
speakers threw light on the importance of the Muslim League,

the benefits of the partition of India, and the anti-Muslim attitude of the Congress party. The meeting dragged into the late hours of the night. Akhtar Husain's bungalow stood still holding darkness and silence within. He was busy, trying hard to negotiate the release of his arrested party leaders. He was also worried the police might treat them badly, and saw to it that they were getting proper food in prison. The news of their arrest had already reached the prominent Congress party leaders from Bihar. Professor Abdul Bari, a prominent Congress leader and social reformer, wanted to meet them, but the government did not allow him to do so. So, after consultations with Akhtar Husain and other party leaders, he returned to Patna.

Apart from the impact that this election had on the provincial politics, it had certainly cast its sinister shadow over Ben House. Akhtar Husain was a taciturn and unforthcoming person, anyway. After getting freedom from the responsibilities of the election, he returned to his legal profession with renewed interest.

In England, the Labour Party had come to power. Its leaders had supported the Indian independence movement much before the party had held the office. Gandhiji had regular communications with the Labour Party leaders. They remembered their promises and assurances after acquiring power, and they issued positive statements in respect of the independence movement in India. This undoubtedly restrained the Congress party from displaying their usually aggressive behaviour. As a result, the Congress workers retired to their homes and tried to recover their lost self-confidence.

The Muslim League leaders' morale was bolstered after the elections. They had achieved their first goal, and were heading towards the other. Though an empty public platform lay open before the Congress party leaders, they were so engrossed in their struggle for independence that they could not draw their attention towards the issues of public relations and political exigencies.

Asghar Husain returned to Islampur. He was now vice-president of the district Muslim League party. He bought a bungalow at Patna and started living there. He asked Sarwar Husain, his elder brother, to come and live there, but was refused. Both the brothers had, nevertheless, so much love and affection for each other that they were regarded as role models. Sarwar Husain did not have children, which was perhaps why he showered love on Asghar Husain's children. He had brought his brother's two children to Patna to live with him, and admitted them to a convent school, arranging two tutors to teach them at home also. Though Asghar Husain's wife objected to sending her children off to live on someone else's money, Asghar Husain did not allow his wife to interfere in his personal matters. She was the granddaughter of a very prominent person, a fact which did not stop her husband to tell her in no unclear terms, 'Then go and take care of your properties! I'm not your paid clerk or agent. God has armed me with strength. I can earn my own living.' The threat stunned his wife to silence because she knew that it was not just a threat. Asghar Husain was a man of his word.

It had become very painful for Sarwar Husain to stay alone in Patna. He had entrusted all his money and the housekeeping to the hands of his clerk. And his affairs were being managed in a very sloppy and clumsy way. He also suffered from chronic piles. He sought treatment for the disease when he was in England, but it did not go away, and his piles would often bleed badly, sometimes right when he got ready for the court in his lawyer's uniform. On such occasions he desperately needed a comforter, a caretaker. Watching him so helpless and lonely, many families came forward to offer their daughters in marriage, but withdrew when they discovered that he was already married. Yet a few of them did not stop trying even after that. They believed that for such a wonderful young man of a high family even four marriages were valid.

Sarwar Husain tried once more to bring his wife to Patna. But now her behaviour had become even more erratic. She refused to come infront of her husband. Her accusation was that the last time he came, he cut off her locks and hired a sorcerer to cast magic spell on the severed tresses, and since that day she had been suffering from recurring illness. She was often wracked with sudden, violent convulsions— shouting and yelling, clenching her teeth, frothing at the mouth, followed by losing consciousness, remaining in that condition for hours together. Immediately after regaining consciousness, she would start abusing and cursing her husband. Sometimes she had seizures during sleep. No one stayed by her side during those nights save her old ayah, who was also her intimate confidant as much as she was her maidservant. But she also could not do much except crying bitterly and sprinkling water on her ward's face when she fell into spasmodic fits. Though her mother-in-law and her sisters-in-law were there in the house, Sarwar Husain's wife had stopped visiting their quarters. On the advice of her ayah, she went with her to various dargahs of revered ascetics, tied threads of hope on their tombs and visited fakirs and mystics who gave her taawiz (good luck amulets to protect her from evil). Some also wrote Quranic verses using saffron on china plates and asked her to wash them and drink the water. The fits, nevertheless, never ceased their assaults, and at the same time her hatred for her husband kept increasing. She was in one of her worst tantrums when Sarwar Husain came to fetch her. Her fury escalated into a furious outburst when she saw him from behind the curtain, and he could do little else than walk out on her. When he told his mother about the incident, she called for Akhtar Husain asking him to join her for evening tea, and narrated the entire occurrence to him. He thought for a while, with his head bent forward, and said, 'She is not well now. It's better to leave her here for some time.'

'Bhaijan, we have the best physicians in Patna. She can have her check-up and will get the best of treatments there,' Sarwar Husain uttered.

'But at the moment she is under the treatment of Hakim Asim, a known hakim here, and she is showing signs of recovery.'

Hakim Asim was a well-known Congress party member in town. A devotee of Maulana Azad, murid of Maulana Husain Ahmed Madani and an alumnus of Deoband, he was Akhtar Husain's great friend, soulmate, and constant companion. Everyone fell silent after listening to him.

News arrived the following month that Sarwar Husain had married the well-educated daughter of one of his lawyer friends. Hearing the news, his first wife smashed her hands against the wall, breaking her glass bangles, and covered her herself with a white dupatta. But the strangest thing that happened was that her fits and spasms suddenly disappeared. She started spending most of her time in observing prayers and fasts. The news had a very negative effect on Bibi Sahiba.

She had become the very living image of sorrow and anger. She saw her son's act as immoral and a direct consequence of his British education. She agreed with the people who said it hardly mattered that the son had not brought a firangi wife, he had nevertheless behaved like the firangis. She pondered pensively. *Has ever anyone in her own family or even in other noble families disregarded his wife and married another woman? It is not good if the wife is ill-tempered or she does not meet her husband and his relatives, but to desert her for those weaknesses is too hard a punishment. Above all, she was Sheikh Sahib's own choice for his son. She is his niece, his next of kin. His soul must be in pain.* Bibi Sahiba wrote to her son clearly that he was not allowed to visit Ben House, and that his association with that house was over. She also stopped sending traditional home-cooked delicacies to him, and called back those of his brothers and sisters whom Sarwar Husain had taken with him to Patna. However, Asghar Husain's children still remained with Sarwar Husain. Asghar Husain and his other brothers were privately very happy with the way their elder brother was behaving, but remained silent for fear of Bibi Sahiba. Even if she never reprimanded her children, they always stood in awe of her. Whenever she stopped speaking on any matter, everyone stayed quiet, and silence reigned the house.

Asghar Husain kept himself busy in his zamindari, farming and gardening, and had no time to visit Ben. He had nevertheless taken a few steps about his landed property at the suggestion of Sarwar Husain. But none of them knew as much about their family property and farmlands as Akhtar Husain. He had a little land of his own in the Ben village, and he often used to go there for its arrangement. He had never interfered in his uncle Sheikh Altaf's zamindari affairs except carrying out his instructions which he regarded as his moral duty. After severing relations with her son Sarwar Husain, Bibi Sahiba especially asked Akhtar Husain to look after all the zamindari affairs of the family. He tried to show his reluctance, but could not say no to her orders, and therefore, made it a point to take a trip to Ben on every Sunday and other holidays. Due to the lack of proper transportation, he bought a horse because all of Sheikh Altaf's horses had died. Every week, Akhtar Husain rode down to Ben in three hours, wrapped up all the work there and returned early the following day.

He maintained an accurate up-to-date record of the land yields and the income from them, and handed it over to the gomashtha (paid agent) to take it to Bibi Sahiba. He personally never took the account register to her. But if Bibi Sahiba sought any clarification or had any questions to ask, he showed up and explained things to her in such minute details that it fully satisfied her. Akhtar Husain's regular visits to Ben had breathed some life into the forsaken haveli. The house now stayed clean and tidy, and a few home servants were employed to stay there permanently. Akhtar Husain began spending his long vacations there. His regular arrival emboldened the villagers in Ben. Sheikh Altaf's migration from there had made the people feel very helpless and insecure. In the past, the villagers celebrated Sheikh Altaf's occasional visits to the village as Eid days. With Akhtar Husain's resumption of regular visits to Ben, they felt the same Eid days returning. Even when he went for just a few days, many local issues surrounded him. Sheikh Altaf had a raised cement platform built opposite his haveli in the village. Every evening the platform was covered with a spotless white chador (large sheet), and Sheikh Altaf sat there encircled by the villagers. Lanterns kept burning the whole night. The village had a mixed population of Hindus, Muslims and Harijans. Though majority of the landowners in the village were Hindus, the big landowners were Muslims. The landowners in the villages surrounding Ben were all either Rajputs or Bhumihars, but the peasantry working on their farms consisted of a substantial number of Muslims. Stories of cruelty of landlords had not yet reached that village. The farmhands were very happy with Sheikh Altaf. Even if the wages they were paid for their labour were not sufficient, they received the help they needed from the haveli, and if their gross annual earnings were calculated, they would be found to have earned more than their toil. The landlords in villages neighbouring Ben lived like their notorious counterparts recounted in stories about feudal atrocities. Stories of zamindars beating and bruising the farmers, pulling down the huts and getting them trampled by the bulls and abducting the village damsels reached Ben secretly from the nearby villages. As the tales travelled by word of mouth, spice and colour was added.

People used to give examples of Sheikh Altaf as an exemplary landlord. When Akhtar Husain assumed responsibility of the zamindari property after Sheikh Altaf's demise, he not only continued all his traditions, but also tried to strengthen and develop them. He was a man of the people, so he could not keep himself away from them. Akhtar Husain kept himself constantly informed about the worries and troubles that afflicted the people of Ben and tried to help them as much as he could. He charged no legal fees for cases he fought for the villagers. It was purely through his efforts that the entire village and its adjacent localities were drawn into the independence movement with open heart and mind, and Ben was the only village where its Muslim inhabitants had stopped the cars of Muslim League leaders from entering the village. When Asghar Husain tried to go there, the villagers fell at his feet, begged and pleaded and somehow prevented him from coming in the village. Emulating them, the Hindu villagers also did not allow the Hindu Mahasabha party leaders to step inside the village. Yet, despite these endeavours, the Hindu Mahasabha candidate from the area surprisingly garnered a lot of votes. This mystery remained unravelled for quite a long time. Congress party leaders, Muslims and Hindus alike, were always warmly welcomed in Ben. The villagers were very proud of the fact that they had seen the faces of celebrated national leaders like the Ali brothers, Gandhiji, Madan Mohan Malviya, Shri Babu, Anugrah Babu, Professor Abdul Bari and Maulana Mazharul Haque.

But after the elections, the atmosphere became tense. Division and distrust based on affiliations to either the Congress party or Muslim League marred each and every house in the village. The discrimination between Hindus and Muslims had raised its invisible ominous spectre everywhere before the people. In many regions of the Punjab and Bengal, Hindu–Muslim riots had broken out, which became a hot topic in Ben and around it. The Muslim League leaders had already shown the dream of Pakistan as a separate nation for Muslims. After their departure, the Hindu Mahasabha took charge of conveying a frightening interpretation of that dream to every Hindu house.

On his visit to Ben, Akhtar Husain saw that the people were terrorized. Very few Hindus came to meet him, and the Muslims he met looked stupefied and scared. He was observing the situation for quite some time now and was worried. He had had written communications with Gandhiji on that issue, but no one was doing anything to mitigate the situation. A conspiracy of silence had sealed their lips. Till that time the Congress party had not declared national solidarity as its political objective, although in all its meetings one could clearly observe persons wearing beards and skullcaps sitting on the dais with other party leaders.

5

A violent communal riot had struck Noakhali in 1946 causing fear and panic in the nation. The festival of Diwali was around the corner, but Gandhiji appealed to people not to celebrate it, commemorating the people massacred in the rampage. The nation did not observe Diwali, and the festival that particular year came to be called Black Diwali. Gandhiji toured Noakhali which defused the explosive situation to a certain extent. He went from village to village holding a lathi, his inseparable companion, in his hand. People saw him with their own eyes, listened to him with their own ears.

The nation had had not yet fully recovered from the horrors of the Great Calcutta Killings when a massive religious riot broke out in Noakhali, which the English newspapers reported as the organized fury goaded by revenge. Ali Suharwardy, a Muslim League chief minister, was in power in the province at that time.

A few Muslim villagers of Ben showed Akhtar Husain some scraps of paper which they had recovered from the shirt pocket of the village barber by inebriating him with village toddy. Some dates and days were scribbled on the scraps with names of some peoples and villages, and some unintelligible symbols and characters. Akhtar Husain failed to decipher their meaning. People said that the paper scraps were distributed vis-à-vis the communal unrest simmering in the country. They even alleged that they were circulated by none other than some of the Congress party leaders themselves. But Akhtar Husain did not believe them and gave no importance to those scraps.

He had been hearing and watching these kinds of things for the past twenty-five years. In those days when the Muslim League was not yet born, and the Congress party reigned, sometimes two groups of Hindus and Muslims stood up against one another. Rumour-mongers were never in short supply. Still, he went to Patna and talked to the collector and superintendent of police. The collector called the subdivisional officer of Biharsharif and gave him some directions. Akhtar Husain also held consultations with Professor Abdul Bari and Anugrah Babu in Patna. They formed a delegation of some provincial Congress workers, who were great followers of Gandhiji and worked at the spinning wheel for four hours every day. They would travel around from place to place carrying the message of peace and solidarity. Akhtar Husain and the other two leaders also accompanied the delegation. After travelling for weeks, they reached Biharsharif where a public meeting was organized at the courtyard of Ben House. It started with the recital of Quranic verses and Vedic mantras, very much like the prayer meetings of Gandhiji, after which eloquent speeches were delivered. The entire crowd took the oath of maintaining national solidarity, and quite contented and pleased with their accomplishments, the delegates left for Patna.

Despite all efforts to the contrary, communal violence eventually could not be contained. It flared up in hundreds of villages near Biharsharif. Scores of people were killed. Thousands were left wounded and homeless. They made their way to Biharsharif from all around it. The town's railway station, mosques, madrasas and dargahs were overflowing with refugees. Akhtar Husain walked restlessly in the corridor of his bungalow every night. He had abandoned his legal practice. He was getting minute-by-minute news of the riot-affected areas, and his distressed companions regularly visited him. Many people had warned him, but Akhtar Husain was not prepared for what he witnessed around him.

However, treacherous time had played its part, and the stories he had been receiving from his party mates had unfolded before him. He sat ensconced with his companions, ruminating about how to ease the situation, but they could not see any way out. Akhtar Husain wanted to visit the riot-hit areas with a delegation of the Congress party workers, although the local administration did not allow him to do so. At that time there was a famous Congress leader called Maulana Ayyub Ansari, who was a disciple of Maulana Azad and a follower of Gandhi and Nehru. By virtue of being a Congress party worker he had to endure scorns and abuses from friends and strangers alike. He, nevertheless, knew how to take all negative flak in one ear and eject it out of the other. A cheerful and kind-hearted man, he had stopped talking in public since the day the riot had broken out. He was Akhtar Husain's close friend. And when thinking glumly about the prevailing situation he found it difficult to fall asleep, he would come to Akhtar Husain in the dead of night—to find him, too, wide awake. Then, both of them would drift off in deep contemplation until daybreak.

Suddenly, one day the news came to pass that Maulana Ayyub Ansari was killed at Belchhi, a town near Patna. The Congress party all over India turned into a house of mourning. Akhtar Husain went and spilled out all his anger on the subdivisional officer. The leaders of the provincial Congress party leaders came to Biharsharif to offer their condolences. Gandhiji also regretted the death of Maulana Ansari. The tragic thing was that even his body was not found. The circumstances surrounding his death were revealed only when some Hindu friends of Maulana Ansari came to Biharsharif and gave an eyewitness account of the incident. They reported that when local authorities did not allow Congress party delegation to visit the riot-affected areas, Maulana Ansari quietly decided to go there alone. He was a diehard Congress worker, and was quite well known in and around Biharsharif.

When many years ago, Gandhiji had toured those areas, Maulana Ansari accompanied him everywhere. He was confident that no one there would dare to cause any harm to him. His family members and friends persuaded him to change his mind, but he refused to listen to them. And finally, when the rioters besieged him at Belchhi, he, quite unlike him, countered them with long arguments. Some Hindu Congress workers also appeared on the spot to help him, and appealed to the hooligans, apprising them of Maulana Ansari's secular credentials. But all their reasoning was in vain, and the insurgents killed him in no time at all. Maulana Ansari's barbaric murder terribly discouraged the Congress party. To encounter the alarming and embarrassing situation, Akhtar Husain and other Congress leaders set up a relief camp and reorganized and revived the party workers. They formed many committees and asked almost all their workers to keep themselves busy in relief works.

Asghar Husain had also come back to Biharsharif with his wife and children. Though his area was safe as yet, no one could anyway guarantee it would remain so in the coming days too. The Muslim League had also opened a relief camp in Patna. It had an office running in Biharsharif too. Carloads of party workers came every day from Patna to Biharsharif and returned early in the night. It was a great relief that the towns and cities were safe, and the frenzy had not reached there, otherwise it was impossible for people to flee for shelter. British troops were especially dispatched to the disturbed areas to control the riots. Riding on tall horses, the white soldiers reached the villages, and intimidated the Indians with their awe-inspiring presence and dreaded wild behaviour, which helped in quelling the riots.

As the situation gradually improved, the local administrative authorities permitted delegations of different political parties, with certain terms and conditions, to visit the riot-hit villages. Akhtar Husain along with some of his very close friends immediately left for a tour of the distraught villages. On reaching there, what he saw with his own eyes was quite different from what he had been hearing from his workers. Settlements after settlements were uprooted. The uneasy, deathly silence of the wilderness all around was telling its tale of misery and affliction. There were many wounded victims to whom medical help had yet not reached. Countless others had already died due to the absence of it. There were villages where entire families were wiped out, leaving no inheritor alive. Dead bodies lay scattered all around. The awful stench of rotting corpses hung heavy in the air. Several trucks had transported the dead bodies to the closest towns, but there was still a lot left to be done. The acrid stink was so overpowering that only people with strong nerves could go there. Some people had survived the massacre only because the Saviour had willed them to live, otherwise the killers had done their best to terminate their lives. They had countless tales to tell, but there was no one to listen to them.

The residents of the villages recounted that they had been listening to the sounds of the clinking of temple bells and the chants of *bajrangbali ki jai* for many nights in the past, before the riots had started. When they asked about it from their Hindu neighbours, they replied that it was usual to pray in the temples at night. After the severe drought that had devastated large areas of the village the year before, they were worshiping their gods, praying that the calamity would not strike again. The villagers also said that they saw some strangers entering the villages. They believed that since there were many grown-up girls in the villages, so people were coming from outside with marriage proposals. Suddenly, unbeknown to them, their village was surrounded by a screaming mob. The air resounded with the cry of *bajrangbali ki jai.*

When the growing clamour shook the unwary villagers out from their slumber, they mistook it as the war cry of dacoits who had invaded their villages. The hapless villagers quickly took out whatever weapons they had—swords, spears, axes and well-oiled lathis. But when no one entered their huts and cottages for long, and the riotous uproar swelled on and on, they then realized that they were besieged and would be killed any moment. Bedlam broke loose inside the houses.

All the men gathered on a raised barn roof. They embraced one another and cried mournfully asking forgiveness for their mistakes. Those who had become disciples of sufi saints, tied to their chests the paper that contained the genealogical lineage of their spiritual guides.

The ones who had performed Hajj, took out their shrouds that they had brought after rubbing them on the walls of Kaaba. The women were asked to collectively jump into the well. They were told that death was their sacrifice to save their honour. Small children were made to sit with copies of the Quran on the folding stands before them, and were asked to go on reading the holy scripture. And when all hopes were lost, they had to walk on blades of sword to present themselves before God. But there was still some hope, a little trust that the villagers had in the people with whom they had been living and eating for years. What if they were not related to them by blood, they were nevertheless closer to them than many others. Children from lower caste communities regarded as untouchables grew up in their houses along with their own children. They lived with them in their houses like blood relatives. And now these untouchables had been given weapons to attack their benefactors.

When the assailants saw that nobody had dared to come out in response to their threats and challenges, they felt emboldened and tried to break into the houses. Doors and windows were smashed. Those who were hiding had no option but to come out and meet their attackers head on with their weapons. They accepted death, fighting with whatever came in their hands: swords, axes, lathis, knives or even hand fans. The women jumped into deep wells to their deaths. Children were brutally murdered. The inhabitants of the houses whose doors and windows were not smashed saw with their own eyes that the lower-caste boys who had grown up in those houses not only opened the doors for the attackers but also showed them the places where the women and children were holed up. In almost every village, the story was repeated. But there were a few villages where the villagers without any bias against caste or creed put up a bold front and repulsed the attackers. They were few and far between, and Ben was one of them.

Concerning the communal riots, a report was doing the rounds that the Hindus of the riot-hit villages had disappeared on the occasion, but they did not participate in the local riots. In every village where riots took place, people heard about the mysterious appearance of the scribbled paper scraps, but when they rummaged about in search of those scraps, they discovered that they had disappeared after doing their job as mysteriously as they appeared. Akhtar Husain discussed about those slips with the provincial Congress leaders, although he felt abashed when they asked for proof, which he was unable to provide to them. When Gandhiji came on a tour of the affected villages, he informed him also about the mysterious slips of paper. Gandhiji asked him very sincerely to somehow recover those papers to get the true picture.

Akhtar Husain worked hard to get hold of even one of those scandalous pieces of paper to justify his statement. But all his efforts went in vain. They had simply vanished into the mist. He was sad he could not initially understand the importance of those bits of paper. He did not again meet Gandhiji out of embarrassment. A very honest, outspoken, and ardent leader of the Congress party at that time was one Professor Abdul Bari. He had played a very important role in organizing the labourers from Bihar. When Gandhiji, after making a tour of the riot-affected areas, was occupied in discussion at the Sadaqat Ashram with influential party leaders and respected people of the town, Professor Abdul Bari told him straight on that some big provincial leaders of the Congress party were involved in the riots. Gandhiji asked him to prove his allegation. He assured Gandhiji that he would submit a file with all the proofs in a couple of days. While he was coming back to Patna from his Jamshedpur head office, he was accosted by a Gurkha soldier posted at the Bakhtiarpur railway crossing. As the professor got down from his car in a rage and walked towards him, the Gurkha shot him point-blank. His dead body lay there all night. Some people recognized him the following morning and the news reached everywhere. After his death, some people came out with names of many Congress leaders whom they blamed for the communal flare up, but they could not provide any proof and were considered as lying in the absence of any evidence.

The biggest problem that emerged after the riots was that the refugees in the camps refused to go back to their villages, though their lands, orchards and houses were still safe there. The Congress workers tried their best to restore their trust so that they return to their places. Akhtar Husain and his party colleagues obtained the written statements and signatures of many people throughout the villages promising them to protect their lives and property with all their heart and soul. But the refugees stuck to their guns. The Muslim League leaders consoled and comforted them repeatedly that their sacrifices would not be rendered wasted. They assured them that no power in the world could now stop the formation of Pakistan. They should no more think of going back to their homes. Shortly, they would, by the will of God, go to Pakistan as citizens of a new country. Their comforting words mystified the refugees and made them vacillate. Whatever confidence they had regained was badly shaken.

The camps that the Muslim League workers were running were very well managed. The entire arrangement was very good, including good food and clean water, whereas the camps run by others were not half so well managed. The visits and sympathetic approach and statements of Gandhiji, Nehru, Khan Abdul Ghaffar Khan and other Congress leaders had started to ease the situation. In the villages where Gandhiji had organized prayer meetings, the number of participants had increased. But what was actually happening was that the Muslim League leaders patted the refugees to sleep immersing them in the dream of Pakistan, and the refugees fleeing from Punjab and other regions of Bihar recounted to them the horrible tales of bloodletting and murder which filled them with feelings of insecurity, and kept them from returning to their homes.

The Congress party formed an enquiry committee headed by Akhtar Husain. One particularly remarkable thing with the Congress was that even its most ordinary worker was well aware of his area and its people. It, therefore, made it very easy for them to prepare their strategies and programmes. There were eleven people in Akhtar Husain's committee, six of whom were Hindus and five Muslims. He started his work with sheer honesty and impartiality. The committee members were staunch followers of Gandhiji. Three of them had already stayed with Gandhiji at his Sabarmati Ashram, and had participated in his yagna for self-purification. The members toured each and every village, collected figures and statistics, and estimated the extent of loss and damages.

They observed everything directly, and grasped the true events and stories, arduously preparing a detailed report based on them. It carried a lot of information that spilled the beans. For instance, the report mentioned that people from the higher castes, mostly zamindars, whether belonging to the Congress or the Hindu Mahasabha, had played obvious roles in the planning of the communal carnage. Low-caste Hindu boys raised in Muslim households were tempted with money, goods and lands, and urged to spy on their benefactors. Though the Hindus of a particular village certainly did not take any part in the riots that broke out in their village, they, nevertheless, went to other villages and participated in the bloodbath wholeheartedly. The Harijans were drugged with liquor and stuffed with money, and were given the paper slips to deliver messages. On the other hand, there were various pleasant incidents where Hindus, on a personal level, put their lives in danger to save the Muslims, and provided them asylum in their own houses. These were the encouraging occurrences that had kept people like Akhtar Husain from falling apart. Their belief that they were going in the right direction was further strengthened.

When the meeting of the enquiry committee was called, four of its members absented themselves. They later sent messages tendering their resignation from the committee since they did not agree with the findings of the report. Akhtar Husain and his other colleagues were taken with surprise because the report was finalized with unanimity, and at the time of its submission no member had complained against it. If anyone had any objection, they ought to have raised it before its submission. They failed to understand what caused the discord. After serious contemplation, they postponed the meeting and decided to meet the dissenters and resolve differences. Incidentally, Akhtar Husain could not meet the four of them. After inquiring about them it was discovered that they had left the town. The deadline for submitting the report was approaching.

Ajodhya Prasad, Akhtar Husain's close confidant, met one of the dissenting members suddenly at the akhara (gymnasium) of Mani Ram. The man told Ajodhya Prasad that he had to stay in the same society, and could not leave for Pakistan like Muslims. He could not, therefore, authenticate and sign the report and earn the displeasure of his own people. Ajodhya Prasad remonstrated with him, explained everything to him, persuaded him and even rebuked him, but the man refused to budge from his stand. Finally, under obvious compulsion, the remaining members undersigned the report, and Akhtar Husain sent it to the president of the provincial Congress party. The president, on his part, promised to place the report before the central Congress party meeting.

The Muslim League had not formed any committees, but stuffed the daily newspapers with their columns peppered with passion-rousing stories. Young boys working as newspaper vendors made rounds of streets and lanes, shouting the headlines, selling their papers like hot cakes. The owners of petty newspapers became millionaires overnight. They opened their own presses and raised the sale of their papers many times over.

6

Asghar Husain had only temporarily come to Biharsharif, for he could not leave Islampur for a long time. Besides his landed estate, he enjoyed a special social status there. Though Islampur had remained unaffected by the communal violence that had jolted other villages, the feeling of insecurity grew stronger there with each passing day, as tensions pervaded the air.

The villagers realized their affections for Asghar Husain after he left for Biharsharif. When he returned, some were angry with him for leaving them alone when they needed him. A deeply emotional man, Asghar Husain was impressed by the love of the villagers. He had no desire to leave his people, but his family obligation and a special courier from Bibi Sahiba forced him to leave.

In the past, he had stood by his villagers in times of flood and earthquake. When news of an impending earthquake hit them, Asghar Husain got a huge tent pitched on the luxuriant front lawn of his spacious mansion and stayed there with them wide awake for the entire night. The earthquake, however, did not come. After the great Bihar–Nepal earthquake of 1934, it had, nevertheless, become an unconscious habit among the villagers to wait almost every year for yet another quake to strike. So, whenever in disarray, they always flocked to him, as Asghar Husain had endeared himself to the inhabitants by his kind disposition.

Prior to his decision to leave the countryside, he had been considerably hesitant. But the fires of religious fury were blazing all around Islampur, and any time a spark could reach there, turning the village into a wasteland. Sarwar Husain had written several letters from Patna and insisted that it was not right for him to be there with the children in such a tense atmosphere. He had himself witnessed that some people in Biharsharif were mercilessly massacred as they did not forsake their houses just because of their fowls, ducks and goats. Some others were killed for the love of a few mounds of grains stored in their clay granaries. Bibi Sahiba and others in the house still painfully remembered the brutal killing of the helpless woman who peddled eggs to local residents. Every week, she used to bring them a basketful of eggs from the nearby villages, and sat for hours talking about the world. When all her village folk ran for their lives, the poor woman could not accompany them for the sake of her fowls and eggs that were her only wherewithal, and as a result was burned to ashes along with her house. Bibi Sahiba wept over her death every so often. There were few Muslims in the locality in Patna where Asghar Husain had bought his house. A caretaker looked after it, and the house bustled with life only when Asghar Husain graced the place. In spite of his efforts, Sarwar Husain was not ready to leave the rented house. He was happy in his lodging and was convinced as well that it was a lucky house. He was considered among Patna's famous and prominent lawyers, and it was in the air that he would be made a High Court judge after Independence.

Asghar Husain had left his children in Biharsharif. The place had a significant Muslim population, and there was no risk of a violent uprising there. And no one was aware of what he had planned for his future. He did not disclose his plans to anyone, and people knew them only after he had executed them. He took charge of the relief camp set up by the Muslim League at Patna. With the efforts of the Congress workers, many people had returned to their homes as there was no food left in relief camps. Although the situation was calm now, fear and distrust still pervaded the atmosphere. Some people planned to sell their lands in the villages and buy houses in the towns. They accepted the value of their lands fixed by the buyers, despite knowing that the price was very low, because they had no other choice left. They had to buy houses in the towns in any case. The cost of houses in the towns was rising constantly. There were fewer houses and the number of buyers was increasing. It had become an intensely competitive situation.

Akhtar Husain and his friends were very worried about the prevailing situation. They knew that the entire Muslim population of the villages could not settle in the towns and an exodus would stoke the fears of a breakdown of the regional economy. Muslims felt cut off from their roots. No matter how well-off an Indian is, he is deeply attached to the countryside. He feels uprooted without it. After much deliberation, Akhtar Husain and his men decided to personally meet members of the two communities in the villages, and convince them that they should stay there and also let others live there by establishing an atmosphere of trust. Although many Congressmen took little interest in this endeavour, the result was, nevertheless, favourable. The sale of lands fell down as people decided to remain in the villages.

7

The Cripps Mission (also known as the Cabinet Mission, 1946) came to India with the British government's offer of transfer of power to the Indian leadership, to preserve India's unity and to grant her independence. The common man was ignorant of most of the clauses in the plan, but the educated Indian could talk of nothing else. Akhtar Husain's buddies gathered at his bungalow every evening and held long animated discussions on the sensitive subject.

Electricity had newly arrived into the town. Akhtar Husain had installed high-voltage light bulbs outside in the lawn, whose incandescence lit up the entire atmosphere. The pleasure that he and his friends found in talking in the electric light had been entirely absent in the sick yellow light of the lantern. At that time, it was generally believed that the Cripps Mission had arrived in India for the creation of Pakistan, because by then, it was quite clear to all that the British would benefit by doing so. But Akhtar Husain and his colleagues believed that Pakistan could never become a reality. The struggle for independence was not waged for the partition of the country, but for the foundation of a shared nationality. Gandhiji had said that Pakistan could only be possible over his dead body. When Gandhiji did not withdraw his statement, how then was it possible to create a Pakistan? Until now, Congressmen had had the experience that Gandhiji never lied. He had never gone back on his word. If he did not want to speak, he would take a vow of silence and not speak for days. Maulana Azad had to suffer abuses for his denial of the two-nation theory and friendship with the Congress party. He had, nevertheless, full confidence in Gandhiji, Nehru and the Congress.

Asghar Husain became the pivot of all political activities of his party whenever he came to Biharsharif. All the Muslim League fellows would gather around him at his mansion and discuss the political situation of the country with great fire and fervour. They were very happy that no power could stop the creation of Pakistan. Muslims had ruled India for seven hundred years and could not stay in a country ruled by Hindus. They had tasted the bitter fruit of Hindu friendship during the interim government and did not believe Hindus could be friends. Allah Almighty had already said that disbelievers could not be their friends. Pakistan was a reality now. The Muslims of Punjab, UP and Bihar had not shed their blood in vain. Maulana Azad had spoiled his future in his love for Hindus. Now even Muslims were calling him names. They believed that he would come to his senses only after the Hindus would pull his beard.

After wrapping up the meeting and finishing his evening meal and prayer, Asghar Husain would go to the women's quarters. Putting the brass betel box in front, he would draw a map of Pakistan with such absolute confidence that the womenfolk would become convinced that they would see Pakistan when they woke up the next morning. Asghar Husain's younger sister once saw the green flag of Pakistan in the rising sun of the morning. The entire household got up with feverish excitement and started chanting the Kalima.

Asghar Husain felt sorry for his cousin Akhtar Husain who he believed was destroying both his faith and the world, all for the kafirs' friendship. Pakistan was not going to be built by any human hand. It was to be created by God's indomitable will. He pitied Akhtar Husain, who was just as insignificant as Gandhi and Nehru, and even Maulana Azad, against the sheer power and will of God. His spoke eloquently past midnight with the women of the house listening to him.

Akhtar Husain visited the women's quarters only on necessity or when he was summoned. And he never indulged in any political discussion with the ladies inside the house. His wife knew that he did not like to hear anything against the Congress party. She also regretted that in his friendship with the Hindus, he had needlessly earned the enmity of all. But she was not ready to accept that her husband was wrong. And although Bibi Sahiba agreed with Asghar Husain, she felt offended when something bad was said about Akhtar Husain. She had found the heart and mind of her husband in him. No one in the house dared to open his mouth in front of Akhtar Husain. However, he was practically not on speaking terms with Asghar Husain. If they ever came across one another, the conversation did not proceed beyond formal greetings. Akhtar Husain was not, in any case, free with anybody in the house. He was somewhat frank with Sarwar Husain, but they had of late severed that relationship.

8

Finally, the much-awaited news arrived. India became a free country. Pakistan came into being a day before. Congress had approved the proposal for the partition of the country. In Biharsharif, the news created a strange atmosphere. All the Muslim Leaguers rushed to meet at a public square, congratulating one another, distributing sweets. Maulana Azad was mocked and mimicked. Asghar Husain was in Patna that day, but he returned home in the evening. A large crowd gathered at his house, and the air filled with cheers and greetings. The Congress workers who believed the words of Gandhiji and revered Maulana Azad were left in deep despair. They remembered Gandhiji's words that Pakistan would be created over his dead body. But he was alive and was now saying that its birth was indispensable. The most disgraced person in India on the eve of its independence was Maulana Azad. He had lost his battle to keep India and the Muslims united. But the Congress showered encomiums on the understandably crestfallen man which looked like celebrating the death of a revered saint. Akhtar Husain remained confined to his room that day. His friends too did not come to see him, although the bugle of India's freedom had sounded. The Hindu workers of the Congress were happy but the Muslim workers felt desperate and defeated. They had opposed the formation of Pakistan, and had taken a lot of abuses from their own people. And now Pakistan had become a reality. It was an open secret that India was going to gain freedom. The Muslims in the Congress party had been living for quite long on the belief that they would live together with a sense of pride alongside their Hindu brethren in an undivided free India and were not ready to accept any alteration or appendage to it. But that long-held conviction of theirs was completely overwhelmed. And suddenly they stood aghast, facing a reality that was impossible to deny.

9

Asghar Husain had realized that after the formation of Pakistan, it was no longer possible for him to stay in India. The enthusiasm and sincerity with which he had supported the Muslim League had certainly secured for him a place in Pakistan, but at the same time he had weakened his roots in India. He started making arrangements for his journey to Pakistan. Countless people were waiting in the wings to flee to Pakistan. The people whose confidence had strengthened owing to the sustained efforts of the Congress workers were shattered at a single stroke with the creation of Pakistan. They decided to go to Pakistan anyway, even when they received low offers on their lands and properties.

Asghar Husain sold almost all of his farms, orchards and even his villa at Patna. He had millions of rupees in his hand. The landholding rights were not yet abolished. So, he named his son, who was born deaf and mute, as his heir. He would have even sold 'White House', his mansion at Islampur, but no one was willing to pay the right price for the house. The name of the magnificent house was on everybody's lips in and around the village. And they knew it well enough that they could not afford to it.

He had never talked to his family about his estate plan. Bibi Sahiba was deeply shocked when she heard about it. She was indeed delighted to watch him drawing the map of Pakistan before her, but she had scarcely imagined her own children would ever think of going to Pakistan. She made every effort to stop Asghar Husain from doing so, but he had no choice. He was going to the valley of his dreams. He advised Bibi Sahiba, too, to sell everything and accompany him. It made Bibi Sahiba feel like someone was ripping her away from her husband, and it taxed her patience. She could not speak a single word out of agony and anger, and started crying helplessly. Asghar Husain tried to comfort her by telling her that though Pakistan was indeed far, people no more travelled by bullock carts. She was not forced to go with him against her wishes, and he would keep visiting her off and on. She did not need to worry about him.

Sarwar Husain was very upset on receiving the news of Asghar Husain's departure. He not only loved him, but was deeply devoted to him and his children. Though he himself had a daughter, his fondness for his nephews and nieces had never faltered. The thought that they would all leave him and his daughter alone was a constant source of vexation for him. Perceiving Asghar Husain's unbending determination and his travel preparations, he too took a firm decision to go with him. Bibi Sahiba's persistent resentment had already uprooted him mentally from his home. After reading his elder brother's intentions, Asghar Husain advised him, 'You have an established legal practice here. Someday you can be a judge. It's not fair to leave everything in haste.'

'But I can't bear losing you and the children.'

'Your nephew Nisar is going to stay here.'

'But he cannot be a replacement for all of you.'

'The children will continue to come from there.'

'But only once in six months or a year. How can I survive the rest of the days without them?'

'What will happen to our other siblings, our mother and the property if you, too, decide to leave?'

'Amma is annoyed with me anyway. Not willing to look me in the face. Other siblings are away from me too. Brother Akhtar Husain is already taking care of the property. Who's going to interfere with that?'

Asghar Husain fell silent when he saw his brother's doggedness. The problem for him was that he was going to Pakistan with millions of rupees, while Sarwar Husain did not have any money. He spent whatever he earned. He was a man who spent freely and had not ever thought of saving money. In Patna, he lived like an aristocrat. There were get-togethers and feasts day and night. Legal practice had become a child's play for him. He was thinking of setting up his profession in Pakistan too.

Asghar Husain could not stop him from leaving, but he persuaded Sarwar Husain to go a few months after him, so that he could go first and establish his foothold there. Sarwar Husain immediately advised him to leave his wife and children, whom he could later take along with him to Pakistan. Asghar Husain had no choice but to accept.

Before leaving, Asghar Husain met all his relatives, but he was particularly reluctant to meet Akhtar Husain. He knew full well that he would send him off in his usual courteous manner without passing any comment. Yet he deferred the meeting for several days. It was nevertheless important for him to say goodbye to his cousin. Finally, he gathered courage and bumped into him. Akhtar Husain showed no surprise when he heard about his decision. It looked as if he had anticipated the news. He did not talk to him much, and uttered just a few words as a farewell note.

'Be happy where you live. That's my only prayer.'

Images crossed before his eyes of countless Muslims, and not only Asghar Husain, selling their lands, properties and all, fleeing to Pakistan. He had tried his best to stop the disillusioned procession, but no one was ready to listen to him. Properties worth millions were being sold for a pittance, and the sellers were still happy and gratified.

In those days, people said it was very easy to travel to Pakistan. There was a direct train route. It was only after some years that the secret was revealed that it was actually a river of fire which travellers had to cross to reach there. But it was the pul-siraat (the bridge), the fleeing Muhajirs believed they must cross to enter their Paradise. Some people accompanied their relatives for some distance along the way, and reported on their return that the area was not very different from Biharsharif. They had entrusted their relatives to God. But the volatile situation created after the riots had now calmed down. Properties and lands of the émigrés were now priced fairly and sensibly.

Akhtar Husain sent a detailed report of the state of affairs to Gandhiji, Nehru and Maulana Azad. He did not receive their responses, but after a few weeks, Jawaharlal Nehru planned an official visit to Biharsharif. Extensive public announcements were made about it. Congress workers tried their best to ask more and more people from the villages to the attend Nehru's public meeting. It had not yet become a common practice at that time to pay and ferry truckloads of people to attend political rallies and meetings. When Nehru arrived at the rally, there was a vast churning sea of people at the venue. It looked like a buzzing country fair. Akhtar Husain chaired the meeting as he was the district Congress president. Nehru clearly said that what had to happen had already happened. It was neither the Hindus nor the Muslims who were responsible for the partition of the country. The British had divided the country, and they had used both Hindus and Muslims as their tools to achieve their ends. Those who wanted to go had gone now. Those who were left were citizens of India, and would live in their country. They had to live and die together. Anyone who thought of the Muslims who had stayed behind as traitors and foreigners was the enemy of the country. Nehru also reprimanded Congressmen for sitting enclosed in their houses. During his speech, slogans were raised several times. And when he finally concluded his speech with the chant of Jai-Hind, the entire crowd echoed thunderously with one voice.

Nehru's visit breathed new life into the Congress. Now that the doors of the Muslim League had closed permanently, the Congress (under Nehru) reigned the political arena. With Akhtar Husain as the party leader, the Congress encouraged and guided the traumatized Muslims who chose to stay behind. Although they had organized watchmen from among themselves who patrolled the streets at night, their fleeing co-religionists had instilled so much fear in them that they hardly seemed alive. Akhtar Husain had already known it and seen with his own eyes that those who had left for good had taken enough money to start a new life in a foreign land. And those who stayed back were people who worked in the fields and mills, made a living rolling and selling tobacco beedis and stopped worrying about tomorrow because each passing day brought them enough trouble of its own. They might have supported the Muslim League, but they could not at all dream of migrating to another country. Their fellow-Muslims who had used them for their own ends had now left them to fend for themselves. They appeared like a train waiting on the tracks with its engine well out of sight.

The Congress party found a golden opportunity in such a hapless situation. Those who were led astray could be guided, especially when they were no longer in danger of being misled by false promises. Akhtar Husain drew in front of him such a beautiful map of a free and secular India that they almost forgot about their dream of the kingdom of God. They had witnessed the worst communal riots, and had lost almost everything they had, but others from distant places like Punjab and Lahore had met the same fate, for that matter. Akhtar Husain promised the villagers that the government would take better steps for their welfare. They, too, were willing to compromise with the new situation. But whenever they heard sarcastic voices calling them traitors, asking them why they were still living in India as a constant source of annoyance, even after they had divided the nation and founded their own country, they seemed to look abysmally lifeless.

Even the Congress party had no panacea for their fears and phobias. These maladies had not only taken root in them, but were also getting stronger by the day. Even though a few among them talked kindly about Gandhi and Nehru, they were very different on the inside. Akhtar Husain was aware of the situation but there was little he could do to change it. The train had derailed, and it was not easy to bring it back on the tracks.

10

Asghar Husain left alone for Pakistan. He sent letters to Bibi Sahiba and Sarwar Husain which informed them that several Sindhis had fled Karachi, leaving behind their lands, houses, money and effects. The custodian of evacuee property had taken possession of all their unclaimed assets, and was acting in a very slipshod and arbitrary manner while making allotments. Asghar Husain's coffer was full, whereas the other Muhajirs had nothing with them except their own lives.

After much toil and trouble, he got himself allotted a cinema house, a three-storey building and a plot of land. Apart from the money, his proximity to the Muslim League also helped him to a great extent. He had a photo album that had him up close with Muhammad Ali Jinnah, Liaquat Ali and other Muslim League leaders which also made things easy for him.

No sooner had Asghar Husain received the allotment than he took possession of those places. The building was owned by a Sindhi businessman who had left in a hurry, leaving some of his belongings. There were three four-roomed flats on each floor of the building. Every room had small wall niches. Some of them were empty and some were adorned with statuettes of Lakshmi and swastika marks made with sindoor. Asghar Husain got rid of the swastika marks, but he liked the attractive clay figurines, and did not want to throw them away. So, he kept them as decoration pieces. But his real problem was that the entire building had a temple-like atmosphere that had to be given a mosque-ish look, and the task was not that easy. He summoned from the nearby Muhajir camp a few madrasa-educated young men who had come from India and wore beards. He asked them to recite the Quran, perform Fatiha, and call the five-times-a-day azan in the building. The young men and their families were staying in the Muhajir camps since they were not allotted any permanent accommodation. They felt tempted when they saw Asghar Husain's near-empty house and told their relatives about it when they went back to their camps. Consequently, one day all of them suddenly walked into the house, bag and baggage.

This was a new crisis for Asghar Husain. But he was a seasoned man, and a crisis such as this did not deter him. He notified the Muhajirs that his family would soon be joining him and refused to allow them to stay despite their many pleas.

He hung a large board over the building's main entrance with 'Asghar Husain Mansion' written on it in large letters. There were some articles of wooden furniture in the house that needed repairs and paints. He locked them all in one room. One room had a rusty iron safe. He tried hard to open it but failed. After setting his house in some sort of order, he planned to go to India and bring his wife and children. When an officer friend of his, working in the Allotment Office got word of his intentions, he dissuaded him from doing so for the time being, saying that whenever the Muhajirs saw an unpeopled house, they broke into it and occupied it. If anyone captured the house in Asghar Husain's absence it would be very difficult to evacuate it. The Muhajirs had nothing left to do except stealing and squealing. Widespread looting had broken out. Asghar Husain was confused. The passage between the two countries had become particularly dangerous. He passed several days in a dilemma.

During this sticky situation, he went through an unnerving experience. He was living alone in his new-found mansion. Some Muslim League leaders too acquired good bungalows in the vicinity. Jinnah and Liaquat Ali Khan were working day and night to strengthen the new state. The Indian government's refusal to hand over fifty-five crore rupees to Pakistan towards the second installment of arrears to be paid to it under the terms of division of assets and liabilities was released to Pakistan by force of Gandhiji's fast and strike.

At this time, Asghar Husain was invited to a dinner at a political leader's house. While returning late into the night, he found light streaming out of the windows of his house and sounds of voices emanating from within. Some Muhajirs had broken into the house. The first thought that occurred to him was to enter the house and face the situation. But realizing that it was not fit for him to go alone, he retraced his steps and went straight to the prime minister's residence. Incidentally, the prime minister had just returned home. Seeing Asghar Husain in the portico, he gestured to him to come closer. Asghar Husain drew near and told him the whole story. The prime minister ordered the army commander on phone to get the building evacuated immediately. He sent Asghar Husain in his official car to the commander at the military headquarters. It took some time at the headquarters to make necessary preparations. At about two o'clock in the night, several military vehicles rolled into the locality and on reaching 'Asghar Husain Mansion' ordered the occupants to leave the house within two hours. The Muhajirs were probably harbouring the delusion that nothing was going to happen since it was now their own country. They ignored the warning and did not move out. Within an hour, the commander ordered his soldiers to remove the illegal squatters. The troops started the operation as soon as they were ordered. They seized them by their arms, shoved them hard and drove everyone out of the building, and threw their belongings on to the road. On a frosty winter night, men, women and children stood on the road crying, protesting, beseeching the kingdom of God, the country of their dreams. Asghar Husain regretted their plight and wished to do something for them. But how could he be expected to allow them to usurp his property?

Asghar Husain became cautious after that incident. He was living all alone in a large building. There was no immediate threat of any illegal occupancy of his plot of land and the cinema hall, yet he slept very little at night, and that deprivation made him sleepy during the day. When the overall situation on both sides of the border improved a little, he wrote a letter to Sarwar Husain asking him to come to Karachi with his wife and children, or send them off to Karachi, if he had changed his plan to migrate.

Sarwar Husain was ready to leave immediately after receiving the letter in Patna. Asghar Husain's wife and children had been preparing for the journey for a long time.

But when news of Sarwar Husain's departure reached his friends, they tried their best to stop him from doing so.

Sarwar Husain had become a rich and famous lawyer. It was in the air that he was shortly going to be made a high-court judge. But Sarwar Husain had decided to leave anyway after thinking long and hard over the matter. He truly loved his brother's children. His relationship with other kinfolks was almost doomed. His marital life had been a disaster. He believed that he would do better as a lawyer in Karachi. Most of the Sindhi barristers and lawyers had fled the country. He had, therefore, a greater chance of becoming a judge in Karachi.

Before leaving, Sarwar Husain went to Biharsharif to say goodbye to all his near and dear ones there. Bibi Sahiba refused to meet him, since she considered him guilty of breaking the time-honoured family traditions, which was, for her, an unforgivable crime. Akhtar Husain was also unhappy with him at the misfortune he had wrought upon his sister. And for her husband's sake, Akhtar Husain's wife also kept away from her own brother. When Sarwar Husain's first wife heard about his arrival, she came up to the door and began cursing and screaming at him so aggressively that it was just short of battering him. Perhaps she would have satiated that craving of hers, too, had she found him within her hand's reach. Sarwar Husain's two younger sisters were still unmarried. They lived in reverent awe of their mother, Bibi Sahiba. They still met their brother secretly, clung to his arm and wept profusely. They quietly prepared and gave him different varieties of halvah to take along with him.

Sarwar Husain arrived in Karachi with his brother's family, his second wife and their daughter. At that time, the only valid document required for travelling between India and Pakistan was money. Sarwar Husain had also brought some money with him. Asghar Husain kept two flats for himself in his building, gave one to his brother Sarwar Husain and leased out the rest. He took special care to ensure that refugees were not allowed to enter the rented flats, otherwise it would be very difficult for him to evacuate them. He rented out one flat to a Muhajir family from Kerala, whom he considered to be gentlemanly people. The arrival of Sarwar Husain emboldened Asghar Husain and restored his self-confidence.

Soon, Sarwar Husain joined the Bar. There were a few Hindu lawyers who looked timid and scared. The nature of court cases he came across in Karachi was quite different. Bihar had been the hotbed for family and domestic disputes, but in Karachi criminal cases and property disputes were common. Sarwar Husain began studying the cases intently. He was a hard-working man, and he had come to Karachi with a zeal and a determination to succeed.

11

At about the same time, a new issue relating to the custodian of enemy property cropped up in post-Independence India. The government declared the properties of all those people who had fled to Pakistan as 'enemy property'. For those who had not made any alternative arrangements, their property was confiscated. Problems plagued those properties whose owners had pre-planned and nominated heirs to their assets before leaving. Some of these heirs were real and some were fake. There was chaos everywhere. Officers from the custodian department would swoop in unannounced and seize properties with the help of police. Many innocent people were trapped in the ensuing mess. The fact was that there were only a few Muslim families left whose one or two members had not migrated to Pakistan. It was this weakness of the Muslim community which was exploited to the fullest. Some people borrowed a lot of money from them and blackmailed them regularly.

Quite surprisingly, a few people from the Congress party itself submitted a fallacious report to the government against

'Ben House' property. They had been nursing their grudge against it since the time when Asghar Husain had planted the Muslim League flag there, uprooting the Congress flag. Consequently, a government ombudsman arrived there with an order to seize the property. Asghar Husain's mute son was presented as heir to the estate, but the government did not recognize his claim. There was no choice now but to file a lawsuit against that order. Akhtar Husain initially took no interest in the case. He believed that all of this was happening exactly as he expected. And Asghar Husain was, anyway, not going to lose anything because he had acquired a privileged financial status in Pakistan in lieu of his assets left in India. Waseem and Shamim, his other two younger brothers, rushed home from Aligarh after hearing the news about the case. They lived in a different world at their university and the disturbing news had shocked them deeply. Asghar Husain's clerk Mukund Lal filed a lawsuit on behalf of his master's son. If the family members did not take any interest in the case, the entire property would be confiscated, and the whole family would have become suspect in the eyes of the government. The young brothers of Asghar Husain could hardly do anything. Akhtar Husain was the only person who had any influence in the society. But he had disconnected himself from the matter. On the other hand, he had also now started giving more attention to his legal practice, and since he was the president of the district Congress party, he also had to focus on organizational tasks.

The Congress was no longer a movement but a ruling party. And everyone who wanted to earn two loaves of bread for his family, tried to join the party by paying the annual membership fee of four annas. Some party leaders had fallen into a state of disillusionment with this situation. They mistook this rush and crush for party membership as an indication of its popularity. But Akhtar Husain was well aware that the party's major responsibility now was to rebuild the nation, and it could not compromsie on its core principles. He was also fully conscious of his responsibility towards his family. But he knew he was not needed much at home.

Waseem and Shamim suggested to Bibi Sahiba that she should call and talk to him about it.

So, one day Akhtar Husain was summoned to her quarters to evening tea. When they had finished their tea, she spoke to him, 'Son, the prestige of this house is at stake. Being the oldest male family member, it is your duty to protect and preserve its reputation. Young people do make small mistakes, but if elders do not forgive them, these mistakes may become awful realities.'

Akhtar Husain listened quietly to her. He had never argued with her, and when she fell silent, he took leave of her and returned to his bungalow.

He had fallen into deep trouble. On the one hand, he had his own principles and sacrifices and the honour that he commanded in the society. And on the other, there was Bibi Sahiba's order which he dared not defy. His political beliefs were mocked to his face inside the house, and he was often ignored in spite of being the oldest member of the household. Abusive words were hurled at him, though indirectly. He was even labelled as an apostate and an unbeliever. But Akhtar Husain was an honest and righteous person, with a secular and nationalistic disposition. Bibi Sahiba's order, nevertheless, above everything else, stood before him like a big question mark. He kept thinking all night, hearing the howling of dogs and jackals. The sounds seemed alien to him that night because he usually slept early and did not open his eyes before dawn. But that night sleep had forsaken him, perhaps taking an umbrage against him.

The next morning, Akhtar Husain called Mukund Lal, who had come to Biharsharif for consultation. He found out the details of the case, gave some necessary advice, and sent a message to Bibi Sahiba through Waseem that he had spoken to the clerk complying with her wishes. The house was filled with joy and satisfaction.

The clerk's account had made it amply clear to Akhtar Husain that there was not much hope in the case. Several such cases were being brought to the courts. Akhtar Husain did not take custodian cases. The newspapers, however, were very interested in such cases. They had specified columns for printing the details of these cases which were read with great curiosity. Any reference to Pakistan would make the public watchful and alert. It had become commonplace to call Muslims 'Pakistanis', to which abuse they either reacted by picking a fight or shutting themselves off from society for weeks. In both cases the abuser's enthusiasm increased, and such calumny became routine.

In the early days after Partition, people migrated to Pakistan for fear of imagined troubles. Going to Pakistan was easy. They had to simply take the train, save their life on the way, and rest assured to reach Pakistan if they remained alive. But later, holding a valid passport became a fundamental requirement to travel, along with a transit visa. After applicants submitted their passport forms, the painful process of police verification commenced which spread utter panic among the hopefuls. The underlying cause for discontentment among young Muslims was that they were looked at with suspicious eyes when they went for a job interview. They answered all the interview questions quite comfortably, but sometimes when they were asked quite bluntly 'Why don't you go to Pakistan?' their heads drooped in embarrassment, and their lips tightened in response.

As time went by, they hesitated going to job interviews, and started thinking of setting up their own businesses, as Islam exhorted its followers to go into business. They believed that the main reason for the collapse of their economic stability was that they had fallen for jobs in large numbers. The nation that embraced trade became prosperous and successful. The Prophet of Islam himself was a merchant. He went to Syria with his merchandise and returned successfully. Whenever any educated young Muslim was asked about his vocation, he would proudly say that he intended to set up a business.

Some Muslims opened clothing and footwear shops, but for fear of paying sales taxes started keeping two account registers. This made them fight on two opposing fronts. In trade, they tried to be honest as required by their religion. But in the attempt to hide their income from the government, their integrity would shatter, and the Muslim inside them groaned with pain. They would spend all their energy in patting their honesty to sleep, an exercise that completely exhausted them. Whenever their double accounts were caught, they believed that they would be punished severely on account of being a Muslim. They lived in constant dread of getting caught and arrested. While dealing with the officers of the tax department, they were always greeted with distrust.

Besides, the competitive atmosphere in the market proved very bad for them. They also lacked enough capital to start

their business. The money that they saved for their businesses
by selling their leftover property or their wife's jewellry was
hardly sufficient, because big capital was needed to stay in
the competitive market. The result was that once they closed
the shop on the pretext of Eid or Bakrid holidays, they never
opened it again, and their long-time customers returned
disappointed. These distraught young men would then make
plans to migrate to Pakistan. Spurious travel agencies were
busy sending people illegally to Pakistan through tortuous
routes. The business was in full swing. It needed only a few
thousand rupees to undertake the journey. This recipe was
very efficient and easy in getting people to East Pakistan. Jobs
were easily available there. The traditional sluggishness and
sloth of the Bengalis decelerated and impeded the work in
the offices, factories and docks. Leaving their tardiness back
home, when these Bihari youngsters went to East Pakistan,
they proved to be very useful to their employers there. The
local inhabitants were also impressed with their hard work
and dedication. When Biharis wrote letters to their relatives
back in India, they seemed so happy and satisfied that their
relatives envied them.

As the Muslims started losing the custodian lawsuits,
they encountered the same situation that had destabilized
them in the recent years. It was difficult for them to prove
that the property they occupied belonged to them. The case
was different with people whose documentary records of
their migration to Pakistan were available. But how was the
presence or absence of people who moved there illegally to be
proved? Even though they tried hard to prove it, and struggled
to make their forged documents appear genuine, only half of
them succeeded. Those who persevered after losing the case,

appealed to the high court, some even reached the Supreme Court.

Asghar Husain's property implicated in the case was worth millions. Bibi Sahiba was convinced that her son would surely return and restore the land and property back to the family. She would spread her prayer mat and beseech God desperately for his return. She knew that if her case was lost, then her son's visit to India would also become a dream. The whole house was also praying for a successful trial. Only Akhtar Husain looked calm and unworried. He used to receive reports about the progress of the case every day from Mukund Lal, and advised him if any such need arose, otherwise sent him quietly away.

Eventually the case was decided; it went against Asghar Husain. The day the news arrived, Akhtar Husain was at a provincial meeting in Patna, but his family mourned. The womenfolk started to wail, and Bibi Sahiba cried her heart out. Waseem and Shamim sat mournfully lost in reverie, and the clerk stood aghast repeatedly wiping tears with his thumbs. If any outsider chanced to stop by the house and watch the entire scenario, he would be quite sure that a young man must have died in the family. But the family was saved from any such snooping and eavesdropping because the walls of the house were massive, and there were no neighbouring houses.

The family waited anxiously for Akhtar Husain's return from Patna. A servant was dispatched to the railway station when he arrived late at night, only to be taken directly to a visibly upset Bibi Sahiba. He consoled his family, assuring them that he would take the matter to the higher courts. But Akhtar Husain knew secretly that this was a lost cause. He just didn't have the heart to tell Bibi Sahiba so.

PART TWO

PART TWO

12

The country plunged into shock and sorrow on the 30th of January 1948. Gandhiji was assassinated by an extremist. For reasons best known to themselves, the majority community thought it to be the handiwork of the Muslims as soon as the news of the killing came in. Sardar Patel announced on radio that a mad man had put an end to Gandhiji's life. The doubt appearing in the minds of Hindus further strengthened by that announcement, until Pandit Nehru clearly revealed the name of the killer. The Muslims breathed a sigh of relief.

After Gandhiji's assassination, an atmosphere of grief prevailed in the country for months. People said that since that tragic incident there was a marked increase in tolerance and an improvement in the political and social atmosphere of the country. But perhaps the pages of history were presenting a different reality. What was clearly evident was that communal forces were constantly and surreptitiously reorganizing themselves, and were actively engaged in trying to finally break the illusion about the Congress party's secular credentials. There was a seething undercurrent of unease and intolerance flowing through the country, though the smooth and still water on the surface soothed and pleased the unsuspecting and naive people.

A big chunk of the Muslim League leaders had gone to Pakistan. Some of their followers were still in India, and were living without any party or leadership, facing the might of the Congress. Those who had stayed back in India for personal reasons became as unconcerned with politics and the world. They remained confined to their houses, scoured daily newspapers, listened to the radio and sat together to unravel their hearts. They waited for some days, anticipating that they might be hanged for the crime of assisting in the creation of Pakistan. When nothing happened for a long time, politics started to haunt them again, but their party, the Muslim League, had already closed up shop in India.

The Congress party never persecuted the Muslim League leaders who stayed back. It did not deport to Pakistan those Muslims who had voted for the Muslim League or, by implication, for Pakistan. After forming the government, the Congress party made no distinction between Hindus and Muslims in the Constitution that it drafted for the country. It always considered the enemies of Muslims as depraved people. Gandhi camps were set up all over India to help hundreds of youths to learn Gandhian principles of truthfulness, tolerance, non-violence and self-help, emphasizing teamwork and unity. Anyone who after attending the camp went to the government office to register for a job, returned successfully.

Muhammad Younus was a passionate, firebrand speaker of the Muslim League. At the Patna session of the Muslim League, he had delivered such a rousing speech that Liaquat Ali Khan got up and hugged him. That was the day when he was elevated to lead at the state level. He was all ready to move to Pakistan. But as he was unable to sell his property at a reasonable price, he was constrained to wait until conditions became favourable. He had read in the newspapers that Pandit Jawaharlal Nehru had asked people to forget all past differences and work together with all their resources to rebuild their nation.

The speech greatly encouraged Muhammad Younus, and he wrote a long letter to Pandit Nehru in which he sought forgiveness for his follies and foibles and requested his permission to join the Congress party. He received a letter after about two weeks in which he was asked to call on the District Congress Committee. The letter delighted him that at least the ice had melted, but the instruction to visit the District Congress Committee office was like beckoning him to the closed door that was never going to open for him.

Akhtar Husain was the president of the District Congress Committee. A very principled and extremely patriotic man that he was, Akhtar Husain had recruited new members to his party who were like-minded. They were regarded as enemies of the Muslim League, and never wavered from their principles even in the worst of circumstances.

In the past if by chance Akhtar Husain bumped into Muhammad Younus, it was the latter who was the first to offer greetings, to which the former would duly respond but never took the initiative to be the first to salute. Vexed with his behaviour, Muhammad Younus stopped greeting him. In such a situation he deemed it an insult to go to Akhtar Husain with his request for membership of the party. He, therefore, came up with a way to solve the problem. He went to Patna, met the president of the State Congress Committee with the Prime Minister's letter, and shared his dilemma with him. At that moment, Vidya Shankar Jha, a minister in the provincial government was also sitting there. Both promised Muhammad Younus that they would do their best to help him join the Congress party; it hardly mattered if the district president opposed his entry. It was decided that in the state Congress convention slated to take place in Biharsharif the following month, they would publicly announce his inclusion into the party which would also create a tremendous impact on the people. Muhammad Younus assured them that he would also bring many erstwhile Muslim League workers with him into the Congress fold.

In this way, Muhammad Younus returned happily from Patna and quite confidentially started convincing all his companions to join the Congress party. They were themselves waiting for such an opportunity, but for fear of Akhtar Husain dared not talk about it openly. After much consultation, they agreed to keep their intention of joining the Congress party a secret till the provincial party president and the minister visited Biharsharif.

Right when the meeting, presided over by Akhtar Husain, was under way, at its appointed time and place, the provincial president of the party suddenly announced the induction of Muhammad Younus and his men as new members of the Congress party. Akhtar Husain was taken by surprise at the startling news. Looking completely perplexed, he listened to the provincial president who was, after garlanding Muhammad Younus, addressing the public,

'We should make up all differences, and concentrate on just one thing, a single-minded goal on how to help Bharat towards progress, how to build a new Bharat. Some of our brothers have taken part in the division of our country, creating a new country. But when we were fighting for the freedom of our country, we had dreamt of a Bharat which was undivided, immense and great. But unfortunately, it could not happen. Now, our brothers who are here are sorry for what they have done, and they want to repent. What could be better, in such a case, than to welcome them into the Congress party, so that they work with us shoulder to shoulder in the service of our nation?'

The crowd erupted in thunderous applause, including an unwilling Akhtar Husain who had to do it as the district president of the party. He felt humiliated that he had not been consulted on the membership announcement in spite of being the president of the district Congress. Later, a closed-door meeting was held at the state dak bungalow which was attended by the provincial president, the minister, Akhtar Husain and Muhammad Younus. The president threw some light on the need of the hour, and the demands of the approaching national elections. The minister asked them to forgive and forget all previous mistakes and bitterness, and appealed to Akhtar Husain and Muhammad Younus to rise above personal prejudices and think about the nation which needed both of them. He took a pledge from them that they would resolve all their disputes, and help the Congress party emerge as a strong political organization.

The efforts of the provincial president and the minister somewhat mitigated Akhtar Husain's discontentment. In fact, it was the mistake of the regional leaders who did not consult him on that issue. Muhammad Younus could hardly be faulted for that. In any case, the provincial president of the party had more powers than the district president, and now when Muhammad Younus had joined the party, he had to be given full cooperation.

13

His multiple engagements were adversely affecting Akhtar Husain's legal profession. His clients went to other lawyers. Usually, people who visited him were those who knew him well or were members of his own party. And, his political commitments allowed him little time to focus on his profession. This was inevitably upsetting his whole family. Besides his political and professional concerns, he also had to manage Sheikh Altaf Husain's zamindari estates and his other personal effects, though he could trust the gomashtha and the patwari who were already there to oversee the lands. To add to all of it, Asghar Husain's evacuee property case had now fallen into his lap. The case was in the high court now. Mukund Lal, who handled lawsuits in the lower courts, had never been to the high court. It was Akhtar Husain who first took him to the high court, and engaged a competent lawyer there to look after the case. But since the clerk was still new to the workings of the place, he normally needed Akhtar Husain's help, who willy-nilly had to find time for him.

Akhtar Husain's wife was a naive, dutiful woman. She took good care of her husband and children when they were unwell, and prayed for their constant well-being when they were in good health. She had three sons and a daughter. Her oldest son Faiyyaz was intelligent, bright, and ready-witted when he was only four years old and sang nursery rhymes so sweetly that his voice held the listeners spellbound. When he grew up, Akhtar Husain sent him to study at the Jamia Millia Islamia University in Delhi. Faiyyaz did well at the university at the beginning, and his good grades in college pleased his parents and teachers alike. But quite shockingly, he soon became disenchanted with his studies. He began missing classes and stayed in his hostel room most of the time. It would not have mattered much had his attention shifted from teaching to something else. There could be many justifications for that. The problem was that nothing really mattered to him, and he would utterly spoil everything that he took on to do. The president of the university wrote a detailed letter to Akhtar Husain in this regard, and called him immediately to Delhi. Akhtar Husain had kept himself so occupied in various activities that it was not easy for him to leave them and travel right away. Incidentally, the meeting of the All-India Congress Committee was scheduled to be held in Delhi the following month, which enabled him to visit the university. He met the university president after the meeting and heard further details about Faiyyaz. The university administration was not in favour of continuing the boy's studies, and they thought it was useless to keep him there anymore. The president also advised Akhtar Husain that since he was there, he should get his son treated by a good physician, as there was no dearth of qualified doctors and hakims in Delhi.

It was a reasonable suggestion, so Akhtar Husain took his son to a physician the next morning. The man examined Faiyyaz thoroughly. He found him completely healthy, and could not identify any reason behind his abnormal activities. So, he referred him to a psychiatrist. Akhtar Husain visited the suggested doctor, who kept his son under twenty-four-hour observation and performed a full range of tests on him. He finally diagnosed that the boy was suffering from developmental disorder and his mental growth had stopped at a certain stage which was why he was behaving in an aberrant manner. The revelation disturbed Akhtar Husain greatly. The psychiatrist asked him to take the boy back home in the hope that familial love and care would augment his mental development.

Akhtar Husain returned home with his son but did not tell anyone anything about his ailment. His kinfolks thought that the boy had gotten sick because of distress caused by being away from home, and that was why his father had brought him home. But there was virtually no one there to shower love and care on him round the clock.

The menfolk of the family were either away or too busy with their callings. Waseem had got a new job in Calcutta. Shamim had gone back to Aligarh and had taken up law. Akhtar Husain was rarely at home, and even when he stayed at home for some time, he was surrounded by people and scarcely got any opportunity to pay attention to the household. The women in the house were not strong enough to control Faiyyaz's disorderly behaviour. As he grew older, he behaved ever more like a child, and became the butt of everyone's jokes. He was eighteen and looked his age, but would act like a child. Whenever he walked out of the house, the neighbourhood children pursued him, jeered and booed at him; their mischief sometimes irritated him so much that he would chase the kids with stones in his hands. But when at home, he sat quietly in the corner. If he was asked to do some chores, he would often drop and break lots of things which made the requestor regret. At his age it was not proper to be hard on him. It appeared as if an endless sequence of mental anguish had signalled its beginning for the whole household.

The other son, Hamid, did not pay attention to his studies at all. His focus was more on sports and bullying his classmates. So, Akhtar Husain hired a home tutor who spanked the boy so severely for not doing his lessons that it left welts and bruises on his body. Akhtar Husain had given the tutor a free hand in that matter, and it was his strict order that no one should, in any way, speak in terms of the boy's education. But despite taking harsh punishments, Hamid refused to change. The poor boy was helpless. What could he do? He could not put his heart into his studies. After all, he was going regularly to school, and was taking home tuitions in the mornings and evenings. So, what was his fault if he was still making no progress, whatsoever? Irritated and angry, the tutor complained to Akhtar Husain, who beat Hamid bloody one day. Everybody believed Hamid would mend his ways. But his old habits did not leave him. He continued his studies as usual but failed to clear the exams.

When the results came out he did not come home. People got worried when he did not return even in the night. Akhtar Husain came to know about his absence at nine in the night. He took a rickshaw and rushed to the deputy superintendent of police, who was well known to him. The police immediately moved into action, and searched every nook and corner of the town. Search parties were sent to the train station and the bus stand. They also scoured all the pools and puddles in the town. The boy's relatives and friends were questioned too. But Hamid was not to be found. The entire family remained intensely anxious throughout the night. Bibi Sahiba and Hamid's mother kept constantly and silently crying. Akhtar Husain paced restlessly up and down all night long. Nobody in the family took their meals that night.

Early next morning, the patwari of Ben village arrived at the Ben House in Biharsharif, holding Hamid's hand. On seeing Hamid, Akhtar Husain wanted to run to his son and hug him. But he instantly realized that Hamid had behaved very unconscionably, and he deserved punishment not love. So, he walked back to his room without saying anything. When Hamid entered the women's quarters, his mother and grandmother embraced him with fond affection and started crying. The patwari told them from behind the door curtain that Hamid had arrived at Ben village the previous evening. He was so afraid of his father that he was not ready to face him. When he came to know that Hamid had escaped from the house without telling anyone, he coaxed him into returning home saying that everyone in the house must be very upset. The patwari also requested them not to put any questions to Hamid, because that was the promise he had extracted from the boy as a condition for his return.

Now, everyone in the house feared Akhtar Husain's bad temper. Normally a cool-headed person, his anger, when it welled up, took over the household like a sudden, fierce storm. He remained in his room until late in the morning. Akhtar Husain had no work outside that day, so he had to stay home. Bibi Sahiba decided to keep Hamid with her in the inner mansion because she wanted to settle his matters in her presence. Akhtar Husain revered her so much that he never raised a hand against his children when she was there. When he did not come out of his room for so long that breakfast time had passed, Bibi Sahiba sent for him. Akhtar Husain came in after a short while. The breakfast was laid on the chowki. His wife and Bibi Sahiba were sitting on a charpoy in front.

Akhtar Husain saluted Bibi Sahiba and sat down for breakfast. In the meantime, Bibi Sahiba called Hamid out and gave him a hand fan. He began to wave it over his father. Akhtar Husain raised his head after a while and saw tears falling from Hamid's eyes. All his anger towards his son seemed to fade away. He asked him for a glass of water, which the timorous boy brought to him in a jiffy. Waves of satisfaction washed through the faces of the women. After breakfast, Akhtar Husain exhorted his son for quite some time. He impressed upon him the importance of education, and asked him to prepare for the competition he was going to face in life. Hamid listened to him quietly with his head bent forward, and, in the end, promised that he would work hard to uphold the family's good name.

Akhtar Husain's third son Sajid was very smart in his studies. He had just started his first year of school, but a precocious child shows early signs of promise, so bursts of his genius were beginning to appear. He never forgot the lessons taught to him. His tutor and the maulvi sahib were amazed at his intelligence. Akhtar Husain had even thought of sending Sajid to Jamia Millia, but Faiyyaz's incident stopped him from doing so.

Faiyyaz had gradually become a burden on the whole family. He had now started behaving like a mad man. Bibi

Sahiba took him to the dargah (tomb) of Hazrat Makhdoom Sharafuddin Yahya Maneri. And she retired there for a chilla (a forty-day mystic seclusion at the saint's tomb) for Faiyyaz's health. Whether it was the saint's blessing or God's mercy, the boy behaved very well at the dargah. He had also brought along some books from his college days. He would be engrossed in his books throughout the day. This was a great relief for the whole family. At the end of the chilla, a customary thanksgiving religious function was held in the house. But after a week, Faiyyaz again returned to his old ways. One day, as usual when he went out of the house, the neighbourhood children followed him. He angrily threw all the large stones that he had collected while walking on the unsuspecting children. Some of the children were injured. The relatives of these children surrounded Faiyyaz in a field and thrashed him so badly that he returned home bloodied. His mother and Bibi Sahiba cried when they saw him in such an awful state. There was a time when not only the villagers in Ben, but also inhabitants of Biharsharif exercised great caution when talking to Sheikh Altaf. And today, his own grandson was brutally treated by the same people. Akhtar Husain was not at home, and there was no point in telling him about the incident. He would have found fault with his own son. The problem with Faiyyaz was that he seldom stayed at home during the hours of daylight. He was often found absent at breakfast and lunch. He would appear in the evening and eat all the three meals together. He was a full-blown young man now, but the soul that was encaged in his youthful body was still that of a child, while his brain had come to stop its process of growth at a certain stage.

Akhtar Husain's daughter was very dear to her father. She was named after Khaleda Adeeb Khanum, the famous Turkish writer and leader of the women's liberation movement in Turkey's Ottoman Empire. Khaleda was a year younger than Sajid. They were tutored together at home, but she was more interested in mischief than studies. She painted her maulvis's beard a bright red, startling him out of his slumber. She deflated her tutor's bicycle tyre and generally kept everyone on their toes. But Akhtar Husain wouldn't hear any complaints against his darling daughter.

Hamid reacted very positively to his father's guidance and instructions. And he tried doing his best to give full attention to his studies, learnt his lessons well and did all his assignments. Everybody in the house began hoping that he would pass his exams this time.

14

India was a vibrant new democracy now, an independent country with a constitution. When its first general election was going to take place, the Congress party, which had helped the country to achieve independence from years of British rule, was destined to win a huge support of the masses. With an overwhelming support of the masses, the party launched a massive grassroots electoral campaign all over the country.

Akhtar Husain did not want to put himself forward as a candidate in the elections, though he was president of the District Congress Committee. His colleagues were pushing him to run as a candidate from the Biharsharif urban constituency which had a sizeable Muslim population. The president of the provincial Congress had indicated to the people that the party would put up a Muslim candidate from that constituency. And the Congress could not find a more suitable candidate than Akhtar Husain. Muhammad Younus had also applied for his candidature. But it was common belief that the Congress was not going to consider his nomination because of his Muslim League background. The Congress had adopted the electoral strategy that each constituency should have a candidate who belonged to the caste or religion of its majority population.

After the list of names was prepared at the lowest level, it was examined and deliberated with intense scrutiny at the district Congress meeting. In addition, the provincial and central Congress committees had to review the names. The Congress was going to the public for the first time to seek votes. It required a lot of caution. The district Congress unanimously recommended Akhtar Husain's nomination from the Biharsharif urban constituency. After the final list was prepared, it was sent to the provincial Congress office through the general secretary of the district Congress. Those who were on the list and those who were not, all rushed to Patna and began their toil. But Akhtar Husain stayed back in Biharsharif. He considered this kind of hustling and bustling around for mere political aspirations as ridiculous. In his view, elections were a challenge for the Congress that every party worker had to accept. He toured remote areas of the district, met party workers and encouraged them to mix with the public.

Everyone was convinced that no power could stop the Congress party or its candidates from a huge victory in the elections. But Akhtar Husain vividly remembered Pandit Nehru who had once said that after the Second World War, Churchill suffered electoral defeat at the hands of the same British populace who had once made him an all-time hero.

Ajodhya Prasad, the right-hand man and close friend of Akhtar Husain and vice-president of the district Congress, went to Patna for some important work. As he returned from there, he went straight to Akhtar Husain's place. It was late in the evening and Akhtar Husain had gone to his bedroom.

When he was told about his close confidante's arrival, he immediately came out to the drawing room. The arrival of Ajodhya Prasad at that hour certainly presaged that some serious matter was at hand. He was a serious man and had his finger on the pulse of time. Akhtar Husain asked as he saw him,

'Is everything okay, Ajodhya Babu?'

'I don't know what to say or where to start, Brother! I feel that the Congressmen have lost their minds.'

'What happened?'

'You haven't still gone to Patna, and people are playing games there.'

'Are you talking about the nominations for elections?'

'Of course, that's what I mean. You should have met the provincial president.'

'Oh, let's leave that for now! You already know, I put in my nomination on your request. Otherwise, I don't have any personal interest in that matter. The party is free to choose a candidate of its own choice. We've to uphold the party discipline.'

'That's quite fine, but do you know who the party is going to field as its nominee in the elections?'

'What can I say? The district committee has already sent my name.'

'No, they've selected Muhammad Younus!'

Akhtar Husain was visibly shocked.

'What are you saying? Hundreds of people have applied, but I haven't seen his name anywhere.'

'That's the real trouble. We'd have been happy if the party had chosen any ordinary worker. But they've gone for this man.'

'How did you know about it?'

'Ram Narain, the State Congress President, himself told me about it. He's Muhammad Younus's biggest supporter.'

This was a second shocker for Akhtar Husain. The Congress had sidelined him and proposed the name of an old Muslim League member. He just couldn't see himself believing Ajodhya Prasad's words, and spoke up after ruminating for a while,

'Well, in that case, what should we do now?'

'Listen, they haven't decided yet. Let's immediately rush to Patna. We may have to go to Delhi.'

'So, do I have to go and plead for my candidacy now?'

'Many people are doing just that. The situation is such that we've no other option left now. We must shore up all our efforts to stop injustice.'

'But this rough and tumble of politics is against my nature. It's quite impossible for me to even think of pleading my case.'

'Please! You've to forget all that for now. We are the priests, not of any temple, but of the goddess of politics. And this goddess keeps smiling even in the face of adversities.'

Ajodhya Prasad's well-timed counsel prompted Akhtar Husain to pause for thought. But it all seemed very strange to him. What he had never even dreamed about, was now unfolding before him, and he had to endure, even if he abhorred it. Had the Congress party nominated any candidate other than him, he would not have raised any objection. But he bitterly felt that preferring Muhammad Younus over him was like publicly disrespecting him. Was that the reward for his sacrifices?

Akhtar Husain sat there mulling over what he should say, and after a while, raised his head.

'I can go to Patna, but on one condition.'

'What's that?'

'You've to accompany me and speak on my behalf. I will remain silent.'

'I wholeheartedly agree.'

It was decided that the two would leave Patna the next morning. Ajodhya Prasad stayed at Akhtar Husain's house that night. Both departed for Patna early in the morning. Though it was difficult for the common person, the president of the district Congress, however, could meet the state president or chief minister at any time. At ten o'clock in the morning, they met with the state Congress president Ram Narayan Sharma, but they found him surrounded by many people. Akhtar Husain and Ajodhya Prasad waited until all had left, so they could talk to them in isolation. They could get that opportunity in the afternoon. Sharmaji was the first to speak.

'Sorry, you've been waiting for so long. What brings you here?'

'We have come here to tell you that you've done a great injustice in selecting Muhammad Younus from the Biharsharif constituency. He has just joined the Congress party, whereas Akhtar Husain has suffered brickbats for the sake of his party, abuses were hurled on him and he has been often humiliated. What is the justification for choosing Muhammad Younus over him?'

Sharmaji heard him patiently, and opened his mouth only after Ajodhya Prasad closed his.

'Do you want to say anything else on this matter?'

'No, Sir. Nothing. We just want to appeal for justice.'

'Then, listen to me now,' Sharmaji started his riposte. 'The first thing I want to tell you is that we should not dig into any person's past, but try to see who he is, and what he's doing now. Muhammad Younus has already entered the Congress party, so he's ours now. He is a brilliant speaker and has his finger on the pulse of the people. In the second place, we have to rise above our personal emotions, if we want to win the elections. Muhammad Younus can become an asset to the party, and there is no doubt about his victory.'

Ajodhya Prasad remarked as Sharmaji paused for breath.

'But what about the stepmotherly treatment being meted out to the old Congressmen?'

'To begin with, Akhtar Husain should stop thinking that he is being treated unfairly. He must put the party's interest first, before his personal good. Can you deny the fact that Muhammad Younus is more popular among the Muslims than Akhtar Husain? We had already witnessed it during the Muslim League days. And he's a better speaker than Akhtar Husain, and he has enough money to spend on elections. In the face of such facts, tell me where can we get a better candidate than him? You already know that many Muslim candidates from Biharsharif are going to stand against the Congress candidate. The contest is going to be tough, and therefore, we must select a strong candidate.'

It appeared from Sharmaji's utterances that he had ultimately decided to nominate Muhammad Younus as the Congress contender from Biharsharif and would not listen to any other argument. Nevertheless, Ajodhya Prasad spoke his mind

'Sir, it means that you want to impress upon the Muslims that the real leaders were, in fact, not the Congress Muslims, but the Muslim Leaguers. In this way you are proving Jinnah true who had said that the Muslims in the Congress are just for show. Now, just imagine what feelings you are going to arouse in those Muslims who have sacrificed or destroyed their lives for the Congress.'

Sharmaji had to stomach Ajodhya Prasad's unpleasant words, but he had a ready-made answer for him.

'What can I do now? The decision has been taken by the state Congress committee. The list of candidates has been sent to Delhi, and now the ball is in the high command's court. Its decision will be final.'

Akhtar Husain and Ajodhya Prasad had now realized that Sharmaji did not want to talk on that matter anymore. They came out of his residence.

Akhtar Husain said complainingly, 'You have made me feel humiliated without any rhyme or reason. I've lost whatever respect he had for me. Sharmaji always held me in high regard. And now he must be thinking that I too am begging for my nomination like all those common folks who are crowding the party offices.'

'You have vainly entered public life. You have to use all sorts of wiles and guiles if you are going to fight the wrong kind of people. You can't play the game of politics if you feel slighted so quickly.' Ajodhya Prasad replied bluntly.

Akhtar Husain made no bones about his resolve. 'Let them choose candidates of their choice. I have no interest in that. I have to obey the orders of the high command like a faithful soldier of the party.'

'I'm in complete agreement with all that you're saying. But we fought for the freedom of our country, not because those who were just spectators at that time would make us a laughing stock now. We will not allow that sacrifice to become futile,' was Ajodhya Prasad's final answer.

'Well, what should we do now?' Akhtar Husain said in a voice surcharged with disgust.

'What we have to do now is to catch the earliest train to Delhi. There's nothing left to do in Patna anymore,' Ajodhya Prasad offered his advice.

'But I don't want to go to Delhi,' Akhtar Husain declared.

'You're afraid of challenges, aren't you?' Ajodhya Prasad tried to provoke him.

'There's nothing to contest. What different is going to happen there? They won't go against the wishes of the state president.'

'But we can at least raise our voices there. We had taken up arms against the oppression of the British, and we should now, at least, protest against the mistakes of our own people.'

Akhtar Husain did not dispute his friend's reasoning, when he saw his firm resolve, but expressed his inability.

'But how can we travel in such a haste? I don't enough money in hand.'

'I'll manage the expense. You needn't worry about that. Let's travel today!'

Ajodhya Prasad's unyielding haste threw Akhtar Husain into confusion. He had come to Patna for only one day, and had just enough money to that end. Now, if it was incumbent on him to go to Delhi, he had to go home first to make some arrangements. But Ajodhya Prasad was insistent on making the journey the very same day, without any further delay. He went to see his son-in-law at a law college hostel to borrow some money from him. Incidentally, even the son-in-law did not have any money. But he somehow managed to arrange some money after much toil. When Akhtar Husain saw that there was no escape possible, he spoke out,

'But listen, Ajodhya Babu, I am not going to plead my case there too.'

'I know that very well, Sir. Just come along with me, and don't say anything. Just stay with me. Anything else?'

A sudden smile crept over Akhtar Husain's lips. They left for Delhi by the night train.

15

They reached Delhi the next day in the afternoon. There were Congress candidates from all over India in Delhi at that time. A Congressional nomination was a written warranty of victory at the polls, and everyone was scrambling to win their party's nomination. Delhi was overcrowded with party ticket seekers. All the hotels, ashrams, inns and guesthouses were full. Despite the plunder by the British Empire, Indians still had enough money to splurge on their happiness. Akhtar Husain had come to Delhi during his son's student days, and had stayed at the guest house of the Jamia Millia Islamia. He took Ajodhya Prasad there. Luckily, a vacant room was assigned. After resting there for some time, the two went to Pandit Nehru's mansion to try to find a way to meet them. He was told there that he could stand in queue the next morning and talk to the prime minister for a minute or two while he was meeting people on the lawn of his house.

They returned to the guest house. After dinner, Ajodhya Prasad and Akhtar Husain drafted a memorandum of appeal to show Nehru the next day. When they met the prime minister, they told him about the terrible injustice of Mohammad Younus's nomination against Husain's.

'Has Muhammad Younus joined Congress?' asked Nehru.

'Yes,' said Ajodhya Prasad. 'He was in the Muslim League and has recently joined the Congress. He is no match for Akhtar Husain who is an old guard of the Congress, and had suffered much abuses and aspersions for his loyalty to the party.'

'Have you brought a written submission?'

Ajodhya Prasad gave the typed memorandum to the prime minister.

'Please go and meet Maulana Azad, and tell everything in detail to the general secretary of the party. I will call him in a little while,' Panditji instructed them and went ahead.

Cheerful and emboldened, Ajodhya Prasad and Akhtar Husain immediately went to Maulana Azad's residence. There also they saw a sea of people. The two new visitors spoke to the secretary and requested an urgent meeting with Maulana Azad.

'It's very difficult, Sir. All appointments are fixed in advance. Sorry, I can't be of any help to you.'

'Please try to understand. It's very important that we meet him right now. We've been sent by the prime minister. Pass our names along to Maulana. He'd perhaps like to see us.'

'Sir, we've been given strict orders not to disturb him in any way, disregarding the visitor's status. Otherwise, what objections should I have in letting you meet him?'

'We have come from far away. Maulana knows us very well. Please send in our names to him, somehow.'

'Well, you can, if you like, wait for him in the portico. Maulana is going to come out in a short while. You can talk to him when he is about to get into his car.'

They went to the portico, as they now had no other choice. After a long while, Maulana came out to leave for office. The crowd was still there. His staff made way for Maulana, who walked down the portico steps, slowly, thoughtfully, his face inclined towards the earth. He suddenly looked up to see them standing down. Quickening his steps, he came near, and asked, 'How come you're here? Is there anything urgent?'

'Sir, Panditji has asked us to see you. We would like to draw your attention to a terribly unfair decision taken by our state president.'

'What's that exactly?'

'Sir, Muhammad Younus, an old Muslim League leader, has been nominated by the Congress party in place of the party's long-standing member Akhtar Husain from the Biharsharif constituency. You may well remember that Akhtar Husain is the son-in-law of the veteran Congress leader, Sheikh Altaf Husain.'

'Can I have a written representation on that matter?'

Ajodhya Prasad gave him the memorandum. Maulana deposited the papers in his sherwani pocket and got into his car.

From there, the twosome went to the headquarters of the All India Congress Committee, and sent their names to the general secretary who seemed to be awesomely busy that day. They were, therefore, asked to wait, and were called in after some time. Perhaps, Pandit Nehru had already directed the secretary general to see them.

'Come, come, please! What can I do for you?'

Ajodhya Prasad told him in detail all that he had said briefly to the prime minister and Maulana Azad. The general secretary listened carefully to his words, made some notes in his diary, received his memorandum, and assured him that the issue raised by him would be discussed and considered at the meeting of the Congress Parliamentary Board which was to be held after three days.

As they returned to their lodging, Akhtar Husain declared, 'Let's now go back to Biharsharif, Ajodhya Babu. We've now met all the important leaders.'

'Have some patience. Please wait until the day of the meeting. We'll return only after hearing their decision.'

'Now that's too much! What will we do here for so many days? We don't have to meet any important person now.'

'We still have lots of things to do here. We'll take a trip to the historic Qutub Minar, stroll around the Red Fort and walk through the ancient, sprawling bazaars of Old Delhi. No meetings now.'

'Have we come here on a sightseeing tour?'

'Of course not. But we will now walk around, unveil the wonders of the city. Is it such a bad thing to do?'

Ajodhya Prasad's humour gave Akhtar Husain nervous jitters, and he fell quiet. His nervousness amused Ajodhya Prasad for a while, but he appeased his puzzled friend, 'Brother, now it's not a matter of your prestige only, but of all of us, and of the District Congress Committee. We'll not leave halfway what we have so expectantly started.'

Ajodhya Prasad was not joking. For three whole days, they really roamed around in Delhi. They visited the Qutub Minar and the Red Fort, and offered their obeisance at the shrine of Hazrat Nizamuddin Auliya. Both friends must have seen movies in their youth, but had stopped doing so for quite some time now. Sohrab Modi's *Jailor* was running in the theatres in Delhi. They had not seen any of Sohrab Modi's movies after his blockbuster *Pukar*. It was a golden chance and a great fun for them to watch their favourite actor after a long gap. Later, they partook of the crispy gol gappas and chaat (savoury snacks) at Chandni Chowk, the hot and spicy niharis of the Jama Masjid and the cool and sweet barfis of Sadar Bazaar.

Three days passed riding on the wings of minutes.

On the fourth day, the meeting of the Congress Parliamentary Board was held. It started at eight in the evening, and continued until the early morning. The list of candidates from Bihar was finalized. The president of the provincial Congress committee and the chief minister of the state participated as special invitees. Ajodhya Prasad consistently pressed Akhtar Husain to spend the night at the Congress Committee office. The buzz and blare there had already robbed the night of its calmness. The place must be bustling with people, like a festival. But Akhtar Husain was not ready for that. He was already ill at ease in a surrounding where everything was going against his own principles. Ultimately, Ajodhya Prasad went to the committee's office, and somehow brought a clerk round to keep him informed of the meeting over the phone. The meeting was taking place in a closed room. The clerk could not tell him what was going inside, but he could, at least, inform him when it ended. And this he did with all honesty.

At six o'clock in the morning, the clerk reported that the meeting was over. Ajodhya Prasad, along with Akhtar Husain, reached the general secretary's residence after a short while. He had just returned dog-tired from the meeting, and was nonplussed to see them there so early. They sat together in chairs laid on the sunlit lawn.

'Brother, your candidacy has been decided, but only after a long and tiring battle.'

Waves of peace and happiness washed over their faces.

'The president and chief minister were quite uncompromising in their support for Muhammad Younus as their candidate. But Maulana Azad reprimanded them. Otherwise, Panditji appeared to have silently given in to their headstrongness. But nobody could say a word in front of Maulana Azad. You can comfortably go now and prepare wholeheartedly and energetically for the elections. The state president and the chief minister said that it is difficult for you to win the elections because the constituency has been the bastion of the Muslim League. Now, it's a challenge for you, so you have to win and uphold and defend Maulana's honour. The party will help you in every which way.'

16

Akhtar Husain and Ajodhya Prasad cheerfully returned from Delhi. By that time, the list of candidates had appeared in the local newspapers. When they arrived at Ben House, they found a large number of Congress workers waiting for them. They were chanting slogans like 'Akhtar Husain Zindabad', 'Ajodhya Babu Zindabad' and 'Congress Zindabad'. Akhtar Husain and Ajodhya Prasad were profusely garlanded. Just then, Muhammad Younus' motor entered the bungalow. He embraced Akhtar Husain and promised that as a Congressman he would fully support him.

Akhtar Husain's election campaign started in full swing. The Congress workers set about their tasks at once with great enthusiasm.

Akhtar Husain was going to face the masses for the first time after the country's independence. His party was going to form the government. There was no big party at the national level to oppose him. The Communist party had picked a Muslim candidate against him from Biharsharif. There were four independent candidates, too. One of them was a former

Muslim League activist. He came to the Congress along with Muhammad Younus but had now left the party and was standing as an independent candidate.

Congress candidates and party workers were working with great confidence. But Muhammad Younus was not seen anywhere. Whenever some Congress party member went to see him, it turned out that he was not at home. A few days later, troubling news arrived that he was working for Nasir Khan, an independent candidate. People reported that they saw him moving around in his car during the nights. Akhtar Husain did not believe them when he learnt about that. Whatever differences people had within the party, they never worked against it. So, one morning, Akhtar Husain paid Muhammad Younus an unannounced visit.

'Hey Akhtar Bhai, how come?'

'I've heard people saying that you're working against me. So, I've just come to see if that's true.'

'Those who say that are not only my enemies. They're your enemies, too. How can I indulge in this kind of betrayal when I have promised to support you?'

'Then please put your time into election work.'

'My apologies for that. I am deeply involved in tending to my domestic duties at the moment, and am not myself keeping well these days. Otherwise, I'd have never refused your call.'

Akhtar Husain returned assured and contented from there to find Ajodhya Prasad waiting for him with some old and new party workers. He had with him some of those who were eyewitnesses to the anti-party activities of Mohammad Younus. They swore to Akhtar Husain that Muhammad Younus was working for Nasir Khan at night. He had been sowing seeds of discord in the Muslim minds and creating misunderstandings against the Hindus. Akhtar Husain had never swallowed those rumours before. But he had to believe those who had spotted the man closely engaged in clandestine anti-party activities. He regretted the fact that Muhammad Younus merely pretended to support him, but was covertly working against him.

Ajodhya Prasad advised him, 'You are the president of the district Congress, so why don't you send him a notice and post a detailed report on his movements to the provincial and the All India Congress?'

Akhtar Husain fell into deep thought, and spoke after a little while. 'But I am myself a Congress candidate and Muhammad Younus has been my political rival, so my report can also be misinterpreted.'

'Even so, you also have some responsibilities since you are president of the district Congress. Breaking party discipline is quite unfair, and such activities must be countered, before others, too, start following it.'

Ajodhya Prasad's suggestion was reasonable. But Akhtar Husain was reluctant to take the initiative. He told Ajodhya Prasad, 'You, too, are the vice-president. Why don't you submit a report about his misdeeds? I do not like doing it myself.'

Ajodhya Prasad had realized by now that Akhtar Husain was never going to take any action in that matter. He had not yet learnt to understand the wily machinations of politics. Hence as vice-president, he agreed to send his own report to the party high command.

The Congress party was running an extremely successful campaign. The crowd in Akhtar Husain's public meetings was growing every day. He was hailed everywhere with great enthusiasm. All central and provincial leaders of the party were on the campaign trail. But Akhtar Husain asked them to pay their attention elsewhere, and not waste their time in Biharsharif, because he knew he was very popular in the villages and had an excellent rapport with the public. It was now for the people to respond to his love and compassion for them. Ben was a village, and it did not fall in his constituency, but still many youths from there started working for Akhtar Husain at their own expenses. Upon discovering that, he instructed them to work for their local village candidate.

Ajodhya Prasad had sent his report against Muhammad Younus in the wake of news constantly pouring in about his anti-party activities. But Akhtar Husain was convinced that Muhammad Younus could not do the slightest harm to him. There was a time Muhammad Younus was a fiery orator, fierce like a lion, but now the lion's teeth had fallen out and his claws were blunt. In addition to that, Akhtar Husain had great faith in the people of India.

Finally, election day arrived. The excitement of the voters was clearly visible at the voting stations. They stood patiently for hours in queue to exercise their franchise. People came to the polling stations in new clothes as if it was a day of festivity. A nation writhing under British oppression for long dark years was now beholding the morning rays of hope. People were gratified that they would ultimately choose their own government, which would work for their welfare.

Results were finally announced on the third day following the elections. The Congress had achieved grand success across the country. The party had struggled to liberate the country, and now the country had rewarded it immediately for its services. Akhtar Husain won by 8,000 votes, but the surprising thing was that Nasir Khan, the independent candidate who was not given much importance by the people in the beginning, had come second.

The Congress cadres were very happy at the victory. The day results were declared, a large number of people had crammed into the outer courtyard of Ben House. The place had not witnessed such a swarming crowd even when Gandhiji and the Ali brothers had paid a visit there. A good number of people had flower garlands in their hands, and each of them was jostling to be among the first to garland their leader. Akhtar Husain was so profusely garlanded that his face was covered with flowers. In the evening, a bullock cart gaily decorated with a huge flag on it, and Akhtar Husain mounted on top, wound its way through the streets of the town as a victory parade, followed by slogan-shouting party workers. At about midnight, when the procession came to an end, Akhtar Husain found an opportunity to go inside the mansion and receive the blessings of Bibi Sahiba, who recited prayers to remove the effect of evil eye on him, and scattered a fistful of rice to the winds as propitiatory offerings. Ajodhya Prasad stayed with Akhtar Husain all day. He left him only when Akhtar Husain went to the women's quarter.

Whenever anyone approached Akhtar Husain to adorn him with flowers, he would say, 'Look, the one who deserves this is Ajodhya Babu. It's his victory, so you should offer him these garlands.'

Ajodhya Prasad wore as many garlands on his neck as did his friend Akhtar Husain, and was as happy as if he himself had won the elections.

On the fourth day after the election, a meeting of the Congress Legislature Party was convened at Patna in which Dr Shri Krishna Sinha was elected leader, and was authorized to constitute the council of ministers of his choice. Legislators and other leaders started entering into the rat race for various ministerial posts. There was a continuous rush of contenders from Patna to Delhi to stake their claims. Ajodhya Prasad, too, advised Akhtar Husain to join the mad scramble, but Akhtar Husain strictly refused to do so.

'No, never! I filed the nomination papers only on your promptings. It had never been my desire, and it was no more than just a chance that I won in the elections. But I shall never allow myself to bow down to anyone for self-gain.'

'In that case, I'd go to Delhi alone, and try to work for you.'

'Let the matter rest now, Ajodhya Babu. Your hard work and love have helped me become a member of the legislative assembly, and I thank you for that. I shouldn't hanker after anything more, and am contented with what I have. I'd thank my stars if I could fulfil the responsibilities that have fallen upon me.'

Ajodhya Prasad fell silent when he saw that Akhtar Husain was not ready to talk on the subject. But eyebrows were raised that night when the chief minister's car entered Ben House to drive Akhtar Husain to Patna. Akhtar Husain took Ajodhya Prasad with him and departed for Patna. The state congress president and the secretary of the chief minister in Patna informed him that the chief minister had given final shape to his council of ministers, and was about to send the list to the Governor, when he received a call from Maulana Azad from Delhi who asked him to include Akhtar Husain in the ministry. The chief minister's hands were tight. He had already given the final shape to his list of ministers, and had informed all the nominated persons. But Maulana's wishes could not be ignored, so Akhtar Husain was being added to the ministry as a deputy minister.

As he heard the glad tidings, a shade of happiness crossed Akhtar Husain's face. Ajodhya Prasad felt overjoyed and relieved. He had not expected Akhtar Husain would get it without any effort. And Akhtar Husain was too dazed to believe that fortune had smiled on him. In the afternoon that day, the oath-taking ceremony of the new council of ministers took place at the Governor House. Akhtar Husain was not yet allotted an official residence, so he stayed at the guest house at Patna, and when he returned there after the swearing-in, he found an armed guard posted outside his apartment. A meeting was held in the evening where the ministers were distributed their portfolios. Akhtar Husain was given the charge of the Labour and Waqf departments. These departments were headed by Rameshwar Chowdhary who was the cabinet minister. It was decided that Chowdhary would look after the Ministry of Labour and Akhtar Husain would oversee the Waqf department.

17

The next morning, Akhtar Husain left for Biharsharif with Ajodhya Prasad. The people of Bihasarif welcomed them gloriously, lining both sides of the streets to greet them with flowers. In the evening, the procession reached Ben House. The courtyard was full to the brim with people. Muhammad Younus was already there with a thick garland in his hands. He hugged Akhtar Husain and congratulated him. Akhtar Husain, after his victory, had washed away all his resentment against him. He also embraced Muhammad Younus. Tears of joy were flowing in Bibi Sahiba's eyes in the inner mansion. Akhtar Husain's wife stood watching him from behind her mother's back, and happy tears welled up in her eyes, fell down and were absorbed into the earth.

Akhtar Husain left for Patna the next morning. He stayed in the guest house for a week, and moved into a furnished bungalow as soon as he was allotted one. There was no shortage of servants and peons, but he was accustomed to a family life. So, he went to Biharsharif, and requested Bibi Sahiba to move with the entire household to Patna. Bibi

Sahiba had not stepped out of Ben House after her husband's death. She did not outright refuse, but asked Akhtar Husain to take his wife and children to Patna. Akhtar Husain did not want to leave her alone for his own comfort, since Bibi Sahiba's sons were away in Aligarh, and she was living with her two young daughters, without any male member in the house. It was not possible for Akhtar Husain to make frequent visits to Biharsharif, and to take care of Ben House, while staying in Patna. He kept the issue on hold for some time, and started living alone in Patna, visiting Biharsharif every weekend.

When Akhtar Husain resigned as president of the district Congress party after becoming a minister, the District Congress Committee unanimously elected Ajodhya Prasad as its president.

One day, Akhtar Husain came home to find his wife and children waiting for him. They told him they had been sent forcefully, despite their protests. Husain immediately sent Hamid back to Biharsarif; he had no plans of using his influence to enhance his son's chances for the prestigious Patna College.

18

Many aspirants were participating in the hot race to fill up vacancies in the council of state. The legislators seemed to enjoy being in power. Seekers for the membership of the state legislative council had made a beeline from Patna to Delhi. A list of council candidates was sought from the state Congress committee, which was carefully compiled and sent to Delhi. The final decision was to be taken by the Congress Parliamentary Board whose meeting was due soon. Akhtar Husain had no interest in that. He was engrossed in his own world. It shocked him one morning, while he was looking at the final lists of Congress candidates in the newspapers, to find the name of Muhammad Younus there. He acknowledged that Muhammad Younus had powerful and far-reaching connections at all levels of the political hierarchy. Akhtar Husain remembered well his own recent travails in trying to get the assembly ticket. He would not have done that had Ajodhya Prasad not been there to set him in motion. But the thought calmed him down that Muhammad Younus was compensated for the loss of the assembly seat.

Muhammad Younus was held victorious in the election for the state legislative council. He was in Patna that day, so Akhtar Husain went to congratulate him and offered him a floral garland. Muhammad Younus came to stay permanently in Patna.

Six months after the elections there was a minor reshuffle in the state cabinet. Two ministers were dropped, and some portfolios were reallocated. Two new ministers were included in the cabinet, one of whom was Muhammad Younus. He was made a cabinet minister in charge of the same ministry in which Akhtar Husain was just a deputy minister. This further unsettled Akhtar Husain. The distraught man felt outraged and disheartened at being slighted right under the nose of Muhammad Younus, and as a result did not go to the office for two days. On the third day, Ajodhya Prasad came to him. He too was obviously saddened by the new changes. Finally, after staying at home for two days and thinking diligently Akhtar Husain decided to resign. Muhammad Younus was much junior to him and there was a time when he was among the applauders when Akhtar Husain and other Congressmen were being abused and browbeaten by all and sundry. Now he had to work in the ministry under Muhammad Younus. And this was something he just could not swallow. He consulted Ajodhya Prasad and, after some deliberations, forwarded his resignation to the chief minister. The chief minister accepted his letter but invited him and Ajodhya Prasad for discussion. Akhtar Husain was not ready to meet him, but on Ajodhya Prasad's advice reluctantly agreed to see the chief minister.

The chief minister met the two in private and asked the real reason for Akhtar Husain's resignation. Akhtar Husain had written to him that he was resigning for some personal reasons. But on the chief minister's continued insistence, he clearly told him what prompted him to quit. The chief minister urged him to withdraw his resignation in the best interest of the party and the country.

He explained to Akhtar Husain, 'Look Husain saheb, you know that many Muslim League workers in the province have joined the Congress. They have repented for their past misconduct and have promised to follow the secular principles of the Congress. So far, no complaint has been received about them, but there is anxiety among them that the Congress is ignoring them. Frustrated, they can go to the opposition and create problems for the Congress. It cannot be denied that these people have a significant impact on Muslims, and they can prove to be an asset for our party.'

'But what about the Muslim leaders and workers who have been serving the Congress for years, and who are still passionate about their services without any sense of greed? The old Muslim League people are encouraged to become leaders of the Muslims, and this is eventually going to eliminate the influence that the Congress has among them.'

The chief minister did not accept his argument, and said, 'We should not promote leadership on communal grounds. Our leaders follow the great principles of Congress on the basis of which the struggle for independence was fought. And they have to build a new country on that very basis.'

'But the Congress had itself laid the foundation of nominations for the polls on the basis of caste and creed. Why were these principles not considered at the time?'

Ajodhya Prasad had been questioning the attitude of the All-India Congress Committee from the beginning.

'Listen, we are politicians, not priests in temples. And it is important to win elections in politics because it gives us power. It gives us the opportunity to serve the people according to our principles.'

Akhtar Husain and Ajodhya Prasad fell silent. The chief minister eventually persuaded him to withdraw his resignation, and assured him that he would be given cabinet status once there was another reshuffle.

19

Hamid continued to persevere with his education and with some effort, passed his Bachelors in the third division around the same time that the government abolished the traditional zamindari system. This affected a large number of Muslims in Bihar. Zamindari was a major source of their bread and honour. That was the reason they were less inclined towards farming and trade. It had offered ease and stability to their life. So, the confiscation of their lands left them with the only option of looking for a job. Although there was much talk about abolition of zamindari and redistribution of land, it was made fun of and taken lightly at the time. But when that cause of joke turned a bitter reality, a great uproar ensued. People vented their spleen by cursing and abusing the Congress government. And when the storm subsided after quite some time, it was discovered that most Muslims owned no lands, and those who did could not cultivate them. From now onwards, those who owned farms must be the tillers of the soil—with their mothers, sisters and wives working on the farms. This situation created an atmosphere of sadness and frustration. The educated Muslim youth started looking for jobs, but only one in a thousand could get one, while for the rest there was utter hopelessness. It was at this time that Ibn Safi's detective novels began to flood the market, which at times gave much relief to disillusioned youths. Some of them dreamed of becoming central characters of these novels—Faridi, Imran or Hameed.

It was a difficult time for Hamid. After passing his BA, he repeatedly asked his father to get him a job now that zamindari had gone, and there was no option left. But Akhtar Husain refused to use his position to get any favour for him. However, he gave him the details about any post that fell vacant in various government departments. He also advised him to sit in the competitive exams for jobs, and promised to fully help him in the matter. But to Hamid all his talks appeared just hollow. He was a shrewd, educated young man. He had not only heard, but seen with his own eyes that many of his peers had obtained jobs through nepotism and recommendations. Their degrees did not help them. His colleagues envied his fate that his father was a minister, and so he lacked no backing or support to get a job. Hamid knew that Akhtar Husain could place him anywhere he wanted. But Akhtar Husain was not ready to give up the stand that he had taken on principles.

Because of his political and ministerial engagements, Akhtar Husain was unable to pay attention to his village, Ben. As a result, all the business there was left to be overseen by the patwari, the gomashtha and other employees. Although they were all trustworthy people, the atmosphere of the village had become such that the absence of the owner could at any time bring bad news. They used to cultivate with great wisdom, and deliver the grain on bullock cart to Ben House at Biharsharif. From behind the thick curtain at the door of the women's quarter, they would always plead with Bibi Sahiba to send someone from the house to inspect the lands, since bad times were in the offing. Once Bibi Sahiba sent Hamid there, but he could not understand anything. Looking at the far-flung fields and the lifeless faces of farmers working on it, he did not see any confusing problem. As a result, Hamid returned home after eating pond fish and hunting a few birds with his air gun. Akhtar Husain strongly urged that the mansion at the village should always be kept clean and whitewashed even if it cost a lot. The two-room outhouse of the mansion was occupied by the gomashtha and the patwari. The rooms in the mansion were opened once every week, and were cleaned. The cushions and the mattresses were exposed to the sun. There were dozens of mango, guava and lemon trees in the garden. Their fruits were packed in baskets and sent to Biharsharif. Hamid did not take to the bungalow though, and on the third day, fled to Biharsharif.

Meanwhile, Asghar Husain's case was opened in the high court and the lower court verdict was upheld. When his munshi reported this to Akhtar Husain in Patna, he strictly warned him to keep the matter a secret, and the news never reached Bibi Sahiba. He told the munshi that the case would be taken to the Supreme Court, and he would personally go to Delhi to do that. He asked the munshi to come back to him the following month for the purpose. But a few days after returning home, the munshi suffered a stroke and passed away. It triggered a new crisis for Akhtar Husain. Munshiji had been handling the case since the start, and he was familiar with all its ins and outs. After Munshiji passed away, he took out the relevant file relating to the case and put it on his desk for perusing it in his leisure hours. But whenever he intended to read the file, urgent official engagements got in the way and occupied his mind. The result was that the file was lost in the mess of other office files stacked on his desk, and when all the files were taken off the table for review, that file too went with them. After several months, the deputy secretary of the department came to Akhtar Husain with the dossier complaining that even after careful study, he could not understand what was there to review in it. Akhtar Husain discovered that it was the same file that had been missing. Perceptibly embarrassed, he apologized to the deputy secretary, and put it in a cabinet near his desk.

Akhtar Husain's financial condition was constantly deteriorating after becoming a deputy minister. He was getting a monthly salary of fifteen hundred rupees, whereas earlier, as a lawyer, he was earning much more than that. He got his younger son admitted to an English school, and sent his daughter to another school. Faiyyaz's psychiatric consultation fees were very high, and with so many expenses, there was no money left for Hamid. He had his small needs, however, for which he was always worried. He was a smoker, but could not ask for money to buy cigarettes, though he was always given extra money on demand in the name of laundry and postage charges for sending job applications to different places. Bibi Sahiba gave a fixed amount of money to Asghar Husain's mute son Nisar for his pocket expenses every month. The boy did not know what to spend on, so Hamid sweet-talked him into lending him the money. Nisar was very fond of watching films, and Hamid regularly wheedled money out of him, fulfilling Nissar's passion and meeting his own expenses.

20

Asghar Husain sent a lengthy letter to Bibi Sahiba from Karachi. He wrote that he was very happy there, and his cinema hall was thriving. He had built on the land allotted to him, a delightful, cozy bungalow which was leased to a foreign embassy at a reasonable monthly rental. All his children were studying in upscale schools and colleges. He had also acquired an import–export permit from the government and was soon going to start his own business. His information about Sarwar Husain was, albeit, very disturbing. His legal practice was going downhill, and the local inhabitants were preferred whenever an opportunity for his elevation to high court judgeship arrived. And whatever positions remained vacant were secured by the Punjabis. He had no other sources of income, and was just surviving somehow.

Asghar Husain did not mention a word about his court cases, though he expressed his grief at the death of Munshi Mukund Lal. About Nisar, his suggestion was that he should be trained in a skill and put on a job. He could not ask him to come to Karachi because that would be detrimental to him. He needed someone to look after him permanently and ended the rather longish letter sending his salaams and duas to everyone.

Bibi Sahiba felt very unhappy and ill at ease to learn about Sarwar Husain. He was quite well-off at the time when she had felt offended and stopped talking to him. His legal practice was at its height, and everybody believed that he would make his mark wherever he would go. But his recent awful condition brought tears to her eyes. In an instant, she wiped out all her anger against him, and asked Hamid to scribe a letter for her asking Sarwar Husain to leave everything in Pakistan, and return to India as soon as he could. There was still much left in India, and he would not be worse off even if he did nothing there.

Sarwar Husain's reply arrived after two weeks. First, he begged her forgiveness for all his sins, intentional or unintentional. Then, he clarified to her that since he had become a Pakistani citizen he could not return to settle in India. However, he could still come to India on a visit visa for a month or two, and he promised to do that soon.

It was astonishing for Bibi Sahiba to learn that he could not come to live permanently in India. She could not comprehend it. Many people from her village Sheikhpura worked in Calcutta and Bombay. They came back to their village after staying out for a decade or two, and then spent the rest of their lives there comfortably. They lived on the money they had saved and the grains from their farms. Their wives enjoyed buying gold earrings and bracelets every year. Bibi Sahiba could not believe Sarwar Husain's words, and when Akhtar Husain came to Biharsharif, she asked him about the matter. He remained silent for a while, and then responded.

'Yes, Amma! He is correct. He cannot now come here forever.'

'But how can that place be his home? He was born and brought up here. He has his houses, lands and farms here. His parents, grandparents are all buried here.' Bibi Sahiba became emotional.

'Amma, the truth is that Pakistan has now become a separate independent country. It has its own frontiers which do not overstep Indian borders. Those who live that side of the border are Pakistanis, and those who live this side are Indians. Pakistanis can't become Indians, and Indians . . .'

Bibi Sahiba stopped asking questions but could not reconcile herself to accept his logic. Whenever she tried to believe what he said, her heart refused to give in. She had never ever thought that her sons would leave her and settle in a foreign land, and what she heard from her son-in-law agonized her. There was no one in the house with whom she felt she could share her agonies. On occasions such as that, she was reminded of her departed husband. She would not have faced a trying situation like that had he been alive. He was a very influential Congress leader who could never allow his country to be divided and a new nation sliced out of it. She cursed those people day and night who caused her sons to leave her forever.

21

At the end of the year, Sarwar Husain paid a visit to Biharsharif. He looked old and too skinny. After alighting from the rickshaw, he went straightaway to the women's quarter, and fell at the feet of his mother. Bibi Sahiba pulled him up to his feet, embraced him and wept long and bitterly. When the dust had settled after a good long while, she asked him to come back with his family and manage his property. A simple and domesticated lady of the house, she could not understand Sarwar Husain when he said that as a Pakistani citizen, he could not now acquire Indian nationality. She directed her ire against the Muslim League when she came to learn that it was the Muslim League which had played an instrumental role in the creation of Pakistan.

'Why didn't you get a job there, my son? You had gone there to become a high court judge.'

A sudden blush swept over Sarwar Husain's face. 'Delays can happen in such cases, Amma. They have promised me, nevertheless.'

Sarwar Husain had brought some gifts for everyone in the house, apart from packets of pine nuts, almonds, walnuts and raisins. Asghar Husain had sent a leather bag for his son Nisar.

After he had distributed the gifts, Bibi Sahiba asked him in a quiet undertone if he had brought anything for his first wife. He told her that though he had brought gifts for her also, he was unsure if he should offer them to her because she had avoided to even see him. Bibi Sahiba made it clear to him that her agony had compelled her to refuse to see anyone, not even her own brother.

'You've done the right thing, my son. She is after all your wife. Conjugal relationships are made and decided in heaven. The mistake has already been made. Men can have four wives. Take her gifts out. I'll put them in a gift basket and send it to her. Go and see her if she accepts it, and try to win her heart anyhow.'

Sarwar Husain was feeling hesitant while taking out the gifts he had brought for his wife. But he could not override his mother's order. He had brought a few things: a saree, some bangles and a pair of sandals for his wife which he hoped to give her behind closed doors, if situation favoured him. Bibi Sahiba packed all the gift items in decorated boxes, arranged them on a tray covered with an embroidered cloth and asked a maid to take it to Sarwar Husain's wife.

When the maid returned after some time, she had two trays on her head: the one that she was sent away with, and the other, a new one. Both were covered. She laid the tray down on the table and darted away before saying anything. Bibi Sahiba lifted the cloth covers from the trays one by one. The first was the same tray that had the gift boxes. All the boxes were intact there except the one that had bangles in it. The other tray was filled with ashes from the hearth, and shards of broken bangles lay scattered on the powdery residue.

Bibi Sahiba hurriedly covered the trays. No one spoke a word as if the sight had suddenly cast a chill over the whole house.

The section of the house where Sarwar Husain's wife lived was an isolated area. She had confined herself there, and never moved out or met anybody. No one had seen her for years. On occasions, when she was suddenly seized with violent fits of hysteria, she would let out loud curses against everybody in the house except her husband. Everyone in the house heard her swear words but preferred to keep silent. Bibi Sahiba had strictly prohibited them from responding to her expletives. An old housemaid was the only human being who saw the hysterical woman every day, cooked her food, looked after her and updated the outside world about her. Akhtar Husain paid all the living expenses of his sister.

On the second day of Sarwar Husain's arrival, during the last part of the night, people in the house suddenly heard his wife's hysterical screams, shouts and loud curses. They did not pay much attention to her frenzy as it had become a normal occurrence for them. But her continued rantings and ravings jolted them out of their deep sleep. They could do precious little, however, because they could not go near that part of the house. It was like a forbidden area for them. Nevertheless, they could see, in the dark of night, Sarwar Husain walking out of his wife's dwelling with his head bent. The dazed wakers quietly hurried back to their beds.

Akhtar Husain had certainly called on Sarwar Husain, but he did not bring his children with him, and his comportment towards him was markedly cold. He advised Sarwar Husain that now that he had arrived, he should go to the village and look after the matters concerning his lands and farms. It was a reasonable suggestion. So, when the gomashtha came to see him, Sarwar Husain asked him to tell him everything about the lands in detail. He was himself a very brilliant lawyer and had handled many such cases successfully. Therefore, he pursued the matter further and went to Ben with the gomashtha, where the villagers welcomed him very warmly. He also found a few of his father's companions still living there. Sarwar Husain stayed there for three days, with the villagers flocking around him all the time. After his return home, he discussed in detail with Bibi Sahiba about the village properties.

They talked about the management of their farmlands and orchards as none of the family members were residing in the village. She told him that the man who looked after their village property regularly sent grains and fruit. Sarwar Husain advised her that since their farms were not all in one place, they should sell them and deposit the money in the bank to help meet the marriage expenses of his sisters. His mother considered it improper for noble families to sell their ancestral lands.

'Times have changed, Amma. Everything is in a state of flux. Landlordism has gone away now, taking away all that was glued to it.'

'Even then, my son, the earth is like a mother.'

'Muslims do not believe in that. They own the land wherever they go to settle, and it becomes their homeland. Besides, lands do not stay with one person forever, Amma. The way in which the Hindu government here is mollycoddling the lower-caste people, time is not far, and you will see it, when these plebeians will capture the seat of power.'

'What's new in that, my son? Whenever time takes a turn, the smaller pebbles float up and the bigger ones sink down. But my heart doesn't allow me to sell the farms.'

'Love of land is not the sign of faith, Amma. I also want to take some money to Pakistan, from the sale of the land. I badly need it there.'

Bibi Sahiba fell quiet for a while. It seemed as if she felt ashamed of the arguments she had given against the sale of the ancestral properties.

She eventually spoke up, 'It's your father's property, my son. You have a right over it. What's the use of such a property if you cannot use it? You can certainly dispose of a part of it and take the money with you.'

As for the property, Altaf Husain had bequeathed all his farms to his children but had made Bibi Sahiba the custodian of his estates. Nobody could sell any part of his property without her written permission. On getting Bibi Sahiba's assent, Sarwar Husain summoned the patwari and gomashtha from Ben and presented the proposal before them. Both of them stood stunned, unable to believe their ears. The land was of course not theirs, but they had served it with so much care and dedication that the feeling of love for it was deeply embedded in them. They were pained to hear that the same land would now be put on the market. But as it was their master's instruction, they could not do anything else. Sarwar Husain asked them to look for buyers. In those days there was no dearth of people eager to own farmlands. It was always considered a matter of honour and dignity to buy lands in the villages, and to buy Sheikh Altaf's lands was an act of self-esteem.

Many buyers came forward. A few of them were so excited that they wanted to talk directly to Sarwar Husain in that regard. But the patwari and gomashtha stopped them from doing so. As long as they were associated with the family, they believed they had to preserve its honour and dignity. Their own social status was also dependent on their association with the family. Otherwise, they were getting the same small salary that they used to get during Sheikh Altaf's times. The patwari gave more than that every month to his servant who fetched water for his household, and massaged his legs. The oldest son of the patwari was a deputy collector, and the second one was studying law. His cows and buffaloes were tied to the door of his house, while the patwari seldom left the outhouse of Sheikh Altaf. One of the sons of the gomashtha had become a sub-inspector of police, and his two other sons were studying in a local college. The patwari and the gomashtha each had a kilo and a half of milk and jalebis (coiled fried sweet) for their breakfast every day.

When the patwari's son heard that Sheikh Altaf's land was available for sale, he offered to buy it. But his father chided him for his arrogance and impudence. 'I have lived on this family's patronage all my life and will sacrifice my life for their honour. As long as I live, I cannot muster the courage to stand before our master as a buyer,' he said.

'But these lands are eventually going to be sold, and someone will surely buy them . . . what then?'

'Let a buyer come and our master sell the lands to him for a pittance. We are not going to say anything. But we cannot muster courage to stand before our master as buyers. It cannot happen as long as I am alive.'

'I've no idea what times you are talking about, Babuji. We also oversee issues related to the zamindari properties. Almost 90 per cent of the lands belonging to the zamindars are bought by their erstwhile servants and this upholds and saves their masters' honour and self-respect. They keep taking money from their patwaris and gomashthas and quietly register their lands in their names when they are unable to pay their loans. No one comes to know about it. This way they save their honour and their retainers are able to get some lands at a cheaper rate.'

'There might be other masters and servants elsewhere on the globe. But I've never dared to raise my head before my master. I have always considered them as my masters and will continue doing that. Therefore, I would never, in my life, allow what you wish to happen. Go away! God will give you a lot. But please don't interfere in this matter.'

'It's all right, Babuji. I'll do as you like. But please bear it in mind that ultimately, we are the ones who are going to live in the villages, and not your masters.'

'I know that, but I, too, am not going to live forever. Do whatever you want to, once we are no more.'

After some effort, the patwari at last found a buyer in compliance with Sarwar Husain's order and took the earnest money in advance. He got the land sale papers ready, and the registration of the sale deed was done at the lower court. The patwari had received all the money from the buyer before signing, and gave it to Sarwar Husain. It was 40,000 rupees. Having accomplished the sale, as Sarwar Husain was going to sit in the rickshaw, two men came rushing towards him.

'Huzoor, your men have got your land sold at a very low price. We were ready to give much more than that. But he did not let us reach you.'

'Brother, what has happened has happened now.' Though the men left after his curt reply, their words made Sarwar Husain uneasy. He came home and complained to

Bibi Sahiba against the patwari and the gomashtha. But she immediately stopped him from speaking anything more against them.

'Seek God's forgiveness, my son. Had these people been dishonest, everything would have finished up till now. They are better than some of our own people. You have been misled.'

Sarwar Husain said nothing in reply. The news of the sale of their land soon spread through the town. He had not sold all the farmlands, however. Only the dispersed lands were dealt with, and they still had a lot of land left under the family's possession.

Maulvi Shamsuddin, who had been his father's friend, and had maintained a cordial relationship with the family even after his friend's death, came to meet Sarwar Husain one day, and taking him aside, asked him, 'I've heard that you have sold all your lands.'

'Yes, Uncle. I've sold my share of them. I needed the money. Moreover, after my departure from here there was no one to look after them.'

'What was the urgency that pushed you to sell it so quickly? How could you take such a liberty? You should have asked me if you were really in need.'

Sarwar Husain knew that Maulvi Shamsuddin was not financially sound himself. He was just surviving, somehow. So, he asked him, 'How can you help me, Uncle?'

'I could not have personally helped you, Beta. But I have some good social connections which could have made things easier for you.'

'How could they be of use to me? Tell me, please, so that I may ask you if I need it in future.'

'My dear young man, I would have got you a loan, and it would have been a very secret affair. Nobody could have a clue about it.'

'But then how is the loan to be paid off?'

'It's only God who creates the ways of paying off the debts. We are his slaves and we need to seek His help.'

'In that case, what else can we do than to keep borrowing secretly, and when the lender finally demands payment, pay him off by selling valuables for a pittance? This is exactly what happened with Fazlu Chacha and Qamruddin Mamu. I can give you the names of many others victims like them, if you like.'

'But son, selling ancestral land openly is disgracing family honour. It is a million times better for a man to fulfill his needs by taking loans in secret.'

'What wisdom is that? Why hide the fact when people are going to know about it sooner or later? It has to be announced in order to get the proper price.'

'You do not speak like your father. We are not petty shopkeepers to keep count of profit and loss. We are people of noble descent. Our destiny has indeed brought us to a time when we have become indigent. But our family dignity and nobility has yet not waned a little.'

'Uncle, we have forgotten these impracticable bygone realities after going to Pakistan. The most pragmatic realities for us are to earn money and keep the family going. So, we are very careful about losses and gains.'

Maulvi Shamsuddin expressed his regret at the unbecoming behaviour of the offspring of ancestral noblemen, and departed considering that the disease had become untreatable.

In Biharsharif, most of Sarwar Husain's time was spent in moving in and out of the house settling family matters. It was now only twenty days before his departure to Karachi. He had deposited half the money from the land sale in Bibi Sahiba's bank account, and transferred the other half to Pakistan. One of the long-standing working staff of his family had migrated to Pakistan. Sarwar Husain sent him a letter asking him for a sum of money equivalent to 20,000 Indian rupees when he reached Karachi. He informed him that he would pay the same amount of money to the man's poor relative in Biharsharif. Now this man had become a millionaire in no time in Karachi. He had started his own contracting business and had earned both name and wealth, but was always very respectful whenever he met Sarwar Husain. Much later, Sarwar Husain came to learn that the man had declared that he was related to him. Sarwar Husain neither denied nor confessed. In Karachi, keeping friendly relations with the man was considered a matter of social status. He used to send money to his poor relatives in India, and often carried out monetary exchanges for those in need. He immediately wrote to Sarwar Husain that he was ready for the transaction. He also sent him the names of his relatives in India who were to be given the money. Sarwar Husain sent the money to those people through his gomashtha, and as a precaution procured their signed receipts. Throughout the course of events, the gomashtha constantly realized that he had to communicate with people whom he had never thought of meeting but for his master's order.

The next matter of importance was the marriage of Sarwar Husain's siblings. After consulting with Bibi Sahiba, he sent out marriage offers for his two brothers and two sisters. The offers were approved and the marriage dates fixed. Waseem had a job and Shamim was in the last year of his LLB. As regards the husbands-to-be of his two sisters, one was a prosperous farmer who was not much educated, but had a lot of money; the other was a graduate and was the owner of a shoe store. Sarwar Husain fixed his third sister's marriage with Nasiruddin, the son of the famous Congress leader, Imamuddin. The young man had no job, but was very active in politics. He had very close relations with many ministers and members of the legislative assembly. He also had very close contacts with Akhtar Husain. People used to say that the guy would achieve eminence in politics, and it really paid him handsome dividends.

Sarwar Husain sent telegrams to Waseem and Shamim asking them to come immediately. And when they arrived, the two brothers and three sisters were married with little fanfare. Among their close relatives, only Akhtar Husain could attend the marriages. Bibi Sahiba favoured a simple nikah for her five unmarried children, and an elaborate wedding ceremony to be held later so that Asghar Husain could also attend the functions, but she gave in to Sarwar Husain's insistence on getting them married without any delay. He knew well that it would be very difficult to come to India again in the near future. And in his absence, no one else could solve those issues so easily.

On the third day after the wedding, Sarwar Husain left for Pakistan. His visa was to expire in a couple of days. The extension he requested for, was rejected. So, he had no choice but to leave immediately.

When he left, Bibi Sahiba cried and a large crowd of people came to bid him farewell. They had now understood it full well what it meant to migrate to Pakistan. The rickshaw had arrived. Sarwar Husain had to stop at Patna and register his departure at the district police headquarters. Before reaching the rickshaw, he walked closer to his mother, kissed her hands, closed his eyes, and recited the Surah Fatiha.

With tears welling in her eyes, Bibi Sahiba uttered, 'Go, my son. May God take care of you. Come soon again, and come after you become a judge.'

Sarwar Husain could not say anything amidst the rain of tears. And the rickshaw took him away to the railway station.

22

When Akhtar Husain met Sarwar Husain in Patna, he told him, 'Bibi Sahiba is left all alone now, but she isn't ready to come to Patna. The girls have gone to their in-law's houses, and the boys are back on their jobs. Please, think what we can do for her.'

The matter was urgent. Asghar Husain's son Nisar, who lived with her, was physically deaf and mute, and could be of no help. Bibi Sahiba had a great affection for him. She had his bedstead placed beside her bed to take him into her constant care. He was a grown-up boy now, but she treated him like a child. She also bought a sewing machine for him, and hired a tailor to teach him tailoring every day of the week. Nisar did not take long to learn the skill of sewing, and began stitching small items.

Akhtar Husain's son Hamid was still hunting for a job, waiting to leave Biharsharif the day he got one. Bibi Sahiba's loneliness had become agonizing for Akhtar Husain. She was not ready to leave Biharsharif at all. Everyone was tired of pleading with her. Sarwar Husain had asked Akhtar Husain to get her a passport, and he would try to take her to Pakistan anyhow. He knew it well that she would neither go to Pakistan nor acquiesce to move to Patna. So, finally Sarwar Husain left for Pakistan. He felt he had accomplished much in his short stay.

Because of his many engagements in Patna, Akhtar Husain found little time to visit Biharsharif, and therefore, was not consulted on many matters regarding the marriages and the settlement of properties. He felt shocked at being ignored by Sarwar Husain and others. As a wise man, he recognized that he was not the titleholder of Sheikh Altaf's estate, but he had been looking after the property and was keenly aware of all its ins and outs. He could not make a decision about it, yet he felt he still enjoyed the right to offer his advice about it. The news of the sale of the land came very late to him, and it filled him with a pang of regret. Akhtar Husain had an uncanny ability to absorb his emotions. In his belief system, generosity was an article of faith. So, he continued going to Biharsharif every week, as before.

Whenever Akhtar Husain visited Ben House, his presence brought life and cheer to the place. A posse of policemen was posted to guard his bungalow. And visitors thronged the place to see their admired leader.

Muhammad Younus, though a cabinet-level minister, did not enjoy that popularity. He preferred to be surrounded by bureaucrats and policemen, and went only to parties hosted by some of his chosen people. He never met the common people directly. His secretary would collect applications and petitions from needy people. And no one knew what happened to those papers thereafter. However, upon his arrival, his old Muslim League friends and new Congress companions would get a welcome gate erected in the town, and bring truckloads of people in his rallies. A lot of money was spent on these arrangements. But no one seemed to worry much about it. After all, Muhammad Younus was a cabinet minister in the department of irrigation and power, and the people of these departments showed great alacrity on the occasion of his visit to Biharsharif.

Hundreds of vacancies were advertised for jobs in the irrigation department. As Muhammad Younus was the resident of Biharsharif, it created hope for the youth there. Everyone tried to reach him. Hamid also applied for a post. And Bibi Sahiba sent a missive to Akhtar Husain asking him to press his case to get him the job. Akhtar Husain promised her that he would find out about it. He did not promise her to lobby for him.

He learnt from Ajodhya Prasad that those posts were purchasable for 10,000 rupees each. In some cases, they were auctioned to the highest bidder. Akhtar Husain did not believe his ears, because such rumours were often fuelled in the realm of politics. One day, he incidentally went to the chief minister on an official visit. He saw there a delegation of the opposition parties who had come to submit a memorandum to the chief minister, demanding an investigation into the corruption taking place in the irrigation department. The chief minister assured them he would personally look into the matter. But the appointments were carried out unceasingly in the department. Hamid's colleagues who spent money got the jobs while Hamid could not secure any. The day his friends received their letters of appointment, Hamid stayed in bed. Bibi Sahiba came over to him several times to ask for food but every time he excused himself on the pretext of a stomach ache. She got painkillers for him, which he threw quietly out of the window. When evening arrived, and Hamid did not stir from his bed, Bibi Sahiba pulled the blanket off his face. The pillow was filled with tears. And the bed was moist. Hamid's eyes were red. He was probably crying all day long.

Bibi Sahiba was shocked to see his pitiful state. 'Now, what's this, my son? Come on, stop crying. You're a young man now.'

'Grandmother, I did my Bachelor's several years ago. All my friends have got jobs. And I am still not working. What's the use of living such a life?'

'How can circumstances so dishearten you? How are you going to face the world, then? The whole world is spread out before you right now. There are lots of people who don't work. They aren't dying hungry, are they?'

'Those who don't want to work have a lot to eat and drink in their homes, Grandmother. What do I have? I've to spend my life begging if I don't get a job on time.'

'God has promised us our daily bread and He will keep His promises. Why should we let ourselves worry about it? Besides, what's there that you lack here? You'll surely get a job any time soon.'

'Grandmother, my friends often mock me for my failure, saying how couldn't I get a job even when my father is a deputy minister. They say that my father has no influence. Nobody listens to him. Tell me now, how I should respond to them?'

'Your father is a very honest man. He cannot do anything unfair. He doesn't want his son to get anything by any unethical means. Where is the question of influence? He doesn't like to seek anyone's favour even for himself.'

'He doesn't want to see me doing a job, Grandmother. He is happy to see me jobless. You'll see it, Grandmother. If I don't get a job, I will migrate to Pakistan.'

She put her finger on his lips to stop him talking more. 'You shouldn't say those words. What do you know about Pakistan? It's a very different world from ours.'

'What should I do then? It's better than dying hungry here.'

'No one is going to die hungry in this house. We still have so much by God's grace that it can be more than sufficient even for your children all their life.'

'Grandmother, our lands, these farms are not hens that lay golden eggs. They can't sustain anyone for long. They are going to be taken away one day. You know, the government has planned to grant a lot of rights to the workers and farm labourers. The peasants will grow richer than their masters. They'll get both jobs and farms.'

'These are all fibs and fables, my son. What masters are going to surrender their lands to the peasants? Only granting of rights doesn't matter much. The real thing is the right of possession.'

'But what am I to do now, Grandmother? After all, I have my own needs and wants, and . . .'

'Come to me whenever you require anything. I will meet your needs. But for God's sake do not again utter the name of Pakistan. You don't know my son, what I myself have lost with the creation of Pakistan. Look how much your uncle fidgets and flounders to come here. What has Pakistan given to Sarwar? It is his ancestral property which has eventually been able to salvage his plight.'

Bibi Sahiba's wise utterances somewhat eased Hamid's tension. He felt relieved that if he did not get a job he would not die of hunger. At least as long as his grandmother was alive. He began job hunt vigorously and finally found a few part-time teaching jobs, which fetched him a good amount of money every month, fairly more than the jobs for which he had already applied. But home teaching was not a round-the-year job in those days. The busiest and most preferred months for tuition were when exams were around the corner. Parents believed that their children must receive tuitions if they had to pass exams.

An old bicycle was lying useless in the house. The brand name Raleigh engraved on its handlebar had not yet worn off even after years of rubbings. When he had some money, Hamid spruced up the broken bicycle and got it repaired. It was now practical and usable.

One day while returning from tuition, Hamid stopped at the roadside paan shop to pick up some sweet paans, and bumped into Chamo there. Clad in churidar pyjama, crisp kurta and a khadi waistcoat, Chamo was looking perfectly like a political leader. He was wearing eyeglasses. His hand automatically rose in salutation. Chamo also responded with great affection. His mother had in the past served as Bibi Sahiba's maid. In his younger days, Chamo used to wash the dishes at Ben House. He fled from the house when his mother died. He was reported to have gone to Calcutta where he was still living. No one knew what he did for his livelihood there. He dropped in at Ben House once in a while on his intermittent visits to Biharsharif. As a mark of respect, he never sat down in Bibi Sahiba's presence, and asked the children,

'Tell me, who am I?'

'Chamo . . . Chamo!' The children used to shout.

Bibi Sahiba called him Chamua, as the servants' names were always twisted by their masters in olden days.

'No, I'm Chamo Mamu. Those who call me mamu will get toffees.'

'Chamo Mamu . . . Chamo Mamu . . .' What objection could the children have in calling him mamu (maternal uncle/a title of respect), when they were going to be rewarded with sour–sweet Calcutta candies.

Once when Waseem saw that Chamo was enticing the children to call him mamu, he reported it to Bibi Sahiba.

'What's wrong in that, my son? He belongs to Ben House, after all. Calling him mamu will not raise or lower anyone.' She admonished him. And from that day, Chamo became the children's acknowledged mamu. Hamid too addressed him with that title of respect.

Chamo came nearer to Hamid and asked about everybody at Ben House. He then asked him, 'What are you doing these days?'

'I'm jobless, Chamo Mamu. Vacancies are rare these days.'

'That's strange! Your father is a minister, and still, there's no job for you.'

'Abba asks me to get a job on my own strength. He is against any backing or favours.'

'I don't know which world your abba belongs to. These days you can never get a job unless you seek someone's favours.'

'I'm now giving tuitions.'

'That's regrettable. How could a man from a noble family like you worry about getting a job?'

'You know Abba doesn't want to hear anyone utter the name of Pakistan before him. And Grandmother starts crying the moment someone mentions Pakistan.'

'That's okay. But what will you do if you don't get a job here? There's an age limit beyond which one can't get a job. Will you continue giving private tuitions your whole life if you cross that age limit? If someone like you with such an influential father cannot get a placement, then think about those who are not so lucky.'

Hamid listened to him; his eyes glued to the ground.

'Had Pakistan not been there, young men like you would have either died starving, or in the absence of any hope, indulged in robberies or other criminal activities. They have to do something to live. If there's no job for you here, it's not the end of the world. May God keep Pakistan safe and secure. For whom was it created, anyway? There's no dearth of either money or jobs there. You still don't know, dear Hamid, that when a man has money with him, strangers also become his own relatives, but if he is penniless and times are bad, even his near and dear ones behave like strangers. Think, how long will you go on wasting yourself on other's counsels?'

Chamo's words got into Hamid's head and were firmly embedded there.

'But, Chamo Mamu, how can I obtain a valid passport? Abba will never allow to get me one. And then the issue of visa and . . .'

'My boy, if you travel on an Indian passport, how long would you be allowed to stay there? You can't find a job there with your Indian passport. They will chase you away. Do you understand that?'

'What to do then?'

Chamo held him closer and spoke in his ears, 'Have you heard about the "gardania" passport?'

Hamid had heard a lot, but did not know anything about it. Many of his friends had used the gardania passport to enter Pakistan. It was an illegal immigration activity adopted by some undercover agents who in lieu of some money helped individuals or groups to cross over to Pakistan through illegal routes. When they reached the Pakistan border, they grabbed their client's neck—gardan in Urdu—and pushed them across the Pakistan border. Therefore, the nomenclature of gardania passport.

'I've heard about it from many people, Mamu, but I still don't know what it is and how it works.'

'You need not know anything more about it. I have sent to Pakistan thousands of young men like you through the same means. They've all got good jobs now and are living happily.'

Hamid understood that those who had gone there were working and happy. Chamo's encouraging talks awakened hopes in him.

'What should I do then? Tell me please, Mamu. I don't have any money with me at the moment.'

'Generally, it takes 2,000 rupees per person to get you to Pakistan, but we have served you and so will uphold the salt-forged bond. I can never forget Bibi Sahiba's kindness to us. You're her grandson. I cannot ask anything from you. Just give the man who takes you there some money for his sustenance.'

Chamo assured him that he would send him a letter once he reached Calcutta, and asked Hamid to arrive at Calcutta soon after getting the letter. He also went to Ben House with Hamid, and touched Bibi Sahiba's feet. He stayed there for some time, but did not tell her about the talks he had with Hamid. No one could get any hint of the glint of pleasure that shone on Hamid's face.

23

Hamid waited restlessly for Chamo's letter. He forbade the postman to hand over his mail to anyone else except him directly. A few days after that the mailman brought him a letter. The sender's address on the envelope was smeared and unreadable. But his secretly cherished hope flared up inside him. The only mail he received were interview letters and regret letters after interviews. His friends who had migrated to Pakistan never wrote to him. All these thoughts encouraged him to believe that it must be from Chamo. Hamid opened the envelope with nervous hands and as he read its contents his pleasures faded away. It was a regret letter from a firm about which he had almost forgotten after appearing in an interview months back. Perhaps the letter was kept neglected in its office for long. In sheer anger he tore up the paper into pieces. Utter helplessness brought tears to his eyes.

Waiting for Chamo's letter had become the purpose of his life. He had saved some money from his tutoring jobs. Chamo had still not given him any idea about the expenses needed for the journey to Pakistan. Hamid had worn a gold ring on his finger, which he had insistently secured from his mother, in spite of her persistent reproval that wearing gold was forbidden for men in Islam. His clothes were all arranged and ready to be packed for travel, and his books were stored in a wooden box. He was all set to undertake the journey at a short notice.

The second general election was approaching, and the race for those who pined for power had begun. Until that time, it was a formal rule that the central committee of a political party sought the lists of potential candidates from the provincial committee, which then asked the district committees to send in their choices of aspirants. There was a much longer list of nominees in the second general elections for government formation in independent India. Everyone had now become fully aware of the fruits of joining the legislature, and the political leaders craved for it.

Muhammad Younus was a member of the legislative council. He did not even apply for nomination to fight the general elections. Only one name was recommended by the district committee from the urban area of Biharsharif. And that was the name of Akhtar Husain, who was already a minister. His nomination, therefore, was decided. He was not running around, like other people. Muhammad Younus had gone to Delhi with a list of names of his followers. He had been in Delhi for fifteen days. When, after the meeting, the Congress Parliamentary Board released the last list of candidates, to everyone's surprise, Akhtar Husain's name was not on it. Muhammad Younus was nominated in his place. Ajodhya Prasad who was also the president of the district Congress rushed to Akhtar Husain's bungalow, and asked him to go to Delhi immediately. But Akhtar Husain refused.

He did not want to interfere with the decision of the party.

Ajodhya Prasad felt insulted, though, and decided to visit them.

'As you wish,' said Akhtar Husain, 'but please spare me.'

Ajodhya Prasad went to Delhi the same night. He returned in exactly two days after meeting some people. His face appeared colourless and tired when he called on Akhtar Husain. His deportment convinced Akhtar Husain that he had returned unsuccessful.

'What's the news, Brother? Good that you've returned. Didn't I request you to calmly accept the party's verdict?'

'No Sir, I can never accept that. The votes of the diehard workers of Congress, like us, cannot go in favour of those who had always in the past acted against the Congress party.'

'What will you do, then?'

'I'll leave the party, and so will many district Congress party workers. Tell me about your decision. We have already resolved what to do.'

Akhtar Husain looked deeply shaken.

'What will you do after leaving the party?'

'I will join the Socialist party. Acharya Kripalani and Jayaprakash Narayan are not strangers to me. They are our own people.'

'No, Ajodhya Babu, that's not fair. I will never advise you to leave the party. This will be a rebellion. Entering the Parliament or the state assemblies is not the ends and means of politics. Politics is the best means to serve the people. And that is what we have been doing for long.'

'Politics is not what it used to be, Akhtar Sahib,' said Ajodhya Prasad.

'Whatever it may be, but I request you with folded hands to not leave the party for my sake. I cannot join you, and I will remain working as an honest soldier of the party.'

'Okay, don't come with me, then. But I am going to call a meeting of the district Congress and I will place my resolution there. Won't you resign even from the ministry?'

'No, why should I? My resignation would be taken as my protest against being denied the party nomination. And I am not going to do that. Besides, it's now only a matter of few months.'

Akhtar Husain went to attend the district Congress meeting, leaving all his important engagements. There was so much anger at the meeting that many people were willing to leave the party. Akhtar Husain calmed them down and appealed to them to stay in the party. His lengthy speech mollified their fury, but Ajodhya Prasad resigned from his post as president, and the other office bearers also quit their posts saying that there must be some kind of protest. How else would the leaders finally realize how they had hurt the feelings of the district Congress and its workers? Akhtar Husain could not convince them on that issue.

During the election, Muhammad Younus came to him with a procession and sought his support. Akhtar Husain answered him, 'You should not worry about my support. I am a small Congress worker, which I will continue to be.'

He also showed Muhammad Younus the election plan of his campaign strategy for undertaking a tour of the entire region. He made an all-out effort for the victory of Congress candidates, and tried his best to put Ajodhya Prasad and other party workers, who were unhappy with the party's decision, on the election campaign. A few of them yielded, though half-heartedly, to Akhtar Husain's counsel, but Ajodhya Prasad excused himself. He promised his loyalty to Congress but would not participate in the elections.

The opposition party had put up a very strong Muslim candidate. They were taking full advantage of the turmoil and unrest within the Congress. Muhammad Younus was spending money recklessly on the election. He got many mysterious faces involved in his election campaigns. A whole army of vehicles was under his disposal. The election now was a lot different from that which was held in the past. Electoral standards had taken a vicious nosedive.

The general election at last took place, and Muhammad Younus was defeated by a margin of 10,000 votes. The defeat from Biharsharif was a big jolt to the Congress. Biharsharif was considered the stronghold of the Congress. Muhammad Younus resigned from the ministry on moral grounds. But his resignation was not approved. The ministry, anyway, was also near the end of its tenure.

Muhammad Younus was appointed as the chairman of the state transport corporation. The post was equivalent to that of a minister. He had his official bungalow and cars restored. The chief minister wanted to keep him in the ministry, because he was still a member of the legislative council. But this was not allowed by the high command. With regard to the formation of ministries in the states, the central high command of the Congress party had now started making the final decision.

24

Akhtar Husain vacated the official bungalow as soon as he relinquished office, though the chief minister had personally asked him to continue living there if he so desired. But his conscience did not allow him to do that. He started living in a rented flat in Patna. He wanted to stay in Patna because his son Faiyyaz was under the treatment of a psychiatrist there, and he did not consider it proper to disrupt the education of his other children, Khalida and Sajid, who were studying in a local college. He planned to rest for some time before resuming his legal practice. His days of busy official or social commitments were almost over. If he had made some efforts, he could have found a position that compensated for the loss of his ministry. But he did not consider it proper to do that.

After about a year, Hamid suddenly received a letter from Chamo asking him to leave for Calcutta without any delay, and to bring all the money and other belongings with him. Hamid had almost lost hope. But he had very wisely not spent the few thousand rupees that he had saved. Though, he was thinking of making some use of that money—in opening a small shop or an agency or running a small business. When he received Chamo's letter, he was elated. He cancelled all his plans and started working on only one master plan. Although it disheartened him to think of leaving Bibi Sahiba, he repeatedly convinced himself that he had to make some sacrifices if he wished to achieve something. He was soon going to cross his age limit for employment. And he could hardly see any bright future for himself at Biharsharif. There was no question of seeking permission from Bibi Sahiba or Akhtar Husain to do what he was going to do. They would never permit him to do that. And then he would be forced to disobey them. With much thought, he wrote a letter to Bibi Sahiba.

'My dear Grandmother,' he wrote, 'I deeply regret to tell you that, without your or Abba's permission, I am going to Pakistan. I find myself compelled to do that because I am left with no other option. I have been without any job for long, and there's no hope that I would get one near future. If you consider my case, keeping your feelings and emotions away, which are surely inspired by your love for me, you will support my decision. Anyway, I'll write to you once I reach there. Please ask Abba to forgive me if he can. He couldn't do anything for me, and if he could only forgive me, it would be his act of benevolence that I would never forget.'

He put the letter into an envelope, wrote the Ben House address on it and dropped it in the letter box in the dead of night on his way to the railway station.

Hamid did not have much difficulty in finding Chamo's house in Calcutta. His eyes flew open in surprise to see Chamo's elegant lifestyle. Chamo lived in a luxurious four-bedroom flat.

A Bengali family had migrated to Dhaka at the time of Partition. Much of their property was taken over by the Custodian of Evacuee Property in Calcutta. When they learned about this in Dhaka, the whole family returned to Calcutta via the gardania passport. And then started their legal fight against the West Bengal government. Chamo who had settled in Calcutta, worked as the representative of the dependents in lawsuits in exchange for a fee. He represented cases where people did not have time to attend the hearings. So, Chamo started pursuing the cases of such Bengali families, but did not take any money from them. It was a landmark case which dragged on for quite some time, and ultimately the government lost the lawsuit. The Bengali family was very grateful to Chamo, and married their daughter, who was a well-educated girl, to him. They sold some of their vast properties and bequeathed some to their daughter, including the flat. After that they returned to Dhaka. And from here started Chamo's well-heeled life. Though an illiterate when he left Biharsharif, Chamo had learned to speak and write English and Bengali in the company of people he came across in Calcutta. In social functions hosted by Urdu-speaking people, he used to speak Urdu with such a flair that everybody believed he must be from Lucknow.

He extended warm hospitality to Hamid and gave him a separate room. He introduced Hamid to all his visitors and friends as his nephew who was going to Pakistan. He told the same thing to his wife. Chamo was mostly absent, but his wife took Hamid on a tour of Calcutta. She took him to the Victoria Memorial, the Zoo, the Hooghly River and other important tourist spots at Calcutta. In the evenings, Chamo took them exploring Calcutta's famed eateries where they enjoyed mutton chops from Royal, or kheer (rice pudding) from Amjadia.

After several weeks, Chamo brought a man home. The man was wearing crimson lungi and a round cap on head, and sported a bushy mustache on his face.

Chamo introduced the stranger to Hamid. 'Look Majju, this is my own nephew. He wishes to cross over to Dhaka.'

'Master, if he's your nephew, he is my own too. Don't worry. Come on, son. Get ready, you must leave tomorrow morning.'

After that, Hamid went to his own room. Chamo and Majju stayed there and kept talking, ensconced in the room until late at night. Hamid's heart was filled with joy and excitement for his new life. He had his suitcase ready. At about four o'clock in the morning, a big wagon stopped near Chamo's flat. On hearing the sound of the horn, Chamo went out, and asked the driver,

'Is everybody ready?'

'Yes, Sir.'

'Where is Majju?'

'He's inside with the others.'

Hamid hadn't slept a wink all night. He quickly readied himself to leave, and his luggage was placed in the wagon.

Chamo called him near, and said, 'Take this letter, son. It's for your aunt's elder brother. He is a big man there, and I'm sure he'll find you a job. Here is 500 rupees for you. Keep it safe, for it will help you in need. I've explained everything to Majju. He will make you very comfortable.'

Chamo's wife was also awake. They bade Hamid a warm farewell. The wagon wound its way, twisting and turning through unknown streets. It stopped, after a long drive, on the outskirts of the city at a place dotted with a row of huts. The sun had climbed higher in the sky. Several men, women and children came out of a dark hut where the wagon had pulled up, and boarded the vehicle, filling it to capacity. There was nowhere for Hamid to sit, so he stood up. When the wagon was about to start, Majju asked Hamid to share the passenger seat with him. The vehicle again hit the road and continued to roll on until it reached a checkpost. A boom barrier made up of a bamboo pole was installed to block vehicular access through the check point. The wagon screeched to a halt on reaching near it. The checkpost officials remained frozen in their chairs. Three policemen came near the wagon.

Majju shouted to them, 'It's a baraat party (a wedding group),' and slipped something into the policemen's waiting palms. They went back, shaking their heads.

The bamboo barrier was raised, and the wagon sped off, clearing on the way three other checkpoints in the same manner until the day melted into night. The vehicle eventually stopped at a quiet place, close to a little straw hut. The occupants of the wagon were herded into the hut and fed with rice and fish. Then, Majju collected money from each of them, but he did not ask anything from Hamid.

After completing the pecuniary operations, Majju addressed the passengers, 'From here you must go on foot. My men will lead the way. Before dawn you'll cross the border. Pick up your luggage and start the journey.'

Everyone loaded their belongings on their backs and heads and started to walk. Four men were leading them. They had large flashlights in their hands. Those walking behind were following the beams lighting their path. They were strictly forbidden to speak on the way and stopped only when their four escorts sat down to take rest or smoke their bidis. Those moments brought relief to the weary travellers too. Many a times on the way, Hamid heard shrill sharp voices booming out in the darkness.

'Who's there?'

Every time flashlights beamed in their direction, their escorts would gesture everybody to stay still, and run towards the source of the lights. The journey resumed when they returned.

Just before dawn, they reached the bank of a narrow and shallow river. The four escorts asked the travellers to pay them. They searched their belongings and took away whatever they easily could—money, jewellry and even clothes.

They also asked Hamid, 'What do you have?'

'Five hundred rupees.' The words slipped casually out of his mouth. He had kept 500 rupees in the side pocket of the trouser he was wearing and the rest of the amount was deposited in its hidden pocket.

When he was handing over the 500-rupee note, the gold ring in his finger flashed.

'Take off the ring.'

The ring was very dear to Hamid. It was a souvenir he had kept as a reminder of his mother whom he knew not when he would see again.

Seeing him hesitant to slip the ring out of his finger, one of the escorts spoke sternly,

'Give me the ring, quick! You're our master's man, that's why we're not asking for more, otherwise . . .'

He quietly took off the ring and handed it to them. Then one of them said:

'Wade across the river to the other side, and walk ahead for about two miles to reach a bus station. Then go wherever you want from there.'

The water came up to their waist, so they all crossed it without any glitch. It was almost morning when they arrived at the bus station. A green flag with a white star and crescent on it was fluttering atop the bus station building. Hamid instantly recognized the flag. *So, we have reached Pakistan.*

Hamid took a deep breath. Buses were shuttling in and out of the terminal. His fellow travellers were running frantically after the buses. But Hamid pulled out a clean lungi from his bag, spread it on the verandah of the terminal building and offered a prayer of thanksgiving and gratitude to God. The bus for Dhaka was about to depart. He quickly got up and boarded it. Dhaka was his destination.

Dhaka was a big city. But Hamid was coming from a bigger city, Calcutta. On reaching Dhaka, he took a rickshaw and opened the letter that Chamo had given him. It read,

'Dear Badr-ul-Islam Bhai!'

I am sending my sister's son to you. He has a bachelor's degree and is a promising young man. He has moved there hoping to land a job that suits his interest. I'm sure you can help him find work that's right for him.'

Hamid put the letter into his pocket and talked inside his head. *So, I've come to Pakistan as Chamo's nephew. It hardly matters for me now, if my ancestry stands tainted from being the son of a Sayyid to one related to an underclass guy when my country, my nationality has all changed.*

The rickshaw stopped at the given address, at the gate of a large bungalow. The sun was setting as Hamid climbed down his seat and walked inside. He saw a house boy removing garden chairs from the lush green front lawn of the building.

He approached him and asked. 'Mian. I want to see Mr Islam.'

The servant could not understand his language, and looked askance at him. Hamid said immediately, 'Sorry . . . Mr Badrul Islam.'

The servant nodded his head and went in. Soon, a middle-aged, dignified looking man appeared at the door, wearing kurta and pyjama. After formal greetings and introductions, he took him to the drawing room. The drawing room was a perfect blend of simplicity and elegance. Beautiful and delicate sofas, ornate bookshelves, amazing display of musical instruments on the wall and heavily carved photo frames of Rabindranath Tagore and a few Nazrul Islam songs . . . Hamid liked that elegant simplicity.

After going through the letter, Badrul Islam said, 'So, you are Saminullah's nephew?'

It was only at that precise moment that Hamid learned that Chamo was also known as Saminullah.

'Yes,' Hamid responded calmly.

'You've come too late, my dear. There were jobs aplenty a few years ago. But the swell of migrants has generated more job seekers than jobs here. It has become difficult for even residents to find work now. Well, stay with us, and feel at home. I'll try to do something for you.'

A room was tidied up for Hamid. He spent three days there, most of which he spent sleeping. He was called to the dining room for meals, where he found Badrul Islam waiting for him with his wife and daughter. The atmosphere so alien to him at the beginning was giving way slowly to familiarity.

In the evening hours of the third day, Badrul Islam informed Hamid, 'There is a vacant position in the Adamjee Jute Mills. They are offering a monthly salary of 300 rupees and a residential flat. I've talked to them. Go and join the job tomorrow.'

Hamid felt the glad tidings were coming to him from the world of dreams. Badrul Islam had so easily succeeded in securing something for him which was quite unattainable in India. He looked up at Badrul Islam with tears of gratitude in his eyes.

He joined Adamjee Jute Mills the next day, but did not move into the mill's housing unit. Badrul Islam had advised him to first understand the new country, the new city and the environment there, and then move into a separate home. As a result, Hamid continued staying with him. Badrul Islam had a permanent export and import permit on account of which he had established a flourishing trade. Hundreds of people worked in his office which was already overstaffed. He lived with his wife and a grown-up daughter. Although Hamid had not yet become accustomed to the atmosphere of the house, he began to like it. Hamid had become mesemerized by Badrul Islam's daughter, Nazia. He watched her dance and sing and was completely smitten. Often after dinner, Badrul Islam and his wife, along with Hamid, would sit in the drawing room and listen to her sing. In addition to their love for dancing and singing, the family never forgot to honour their religious commitments of fasting and prayers. In the beginning, Hamid was unable to follow their conversations. He tried hard to understand them, and communicated with them in broken Bengali. Nazia studied in a local college, but in spite of being the daughter of an influential father she had no arrogance at all. She displayed no misplaced modesty either. Hamid talked to her once or twice almost every day, but rarely got any opportunity to strike longer conversations. As Saminullah's nephew, he was considered a family member.

25

Hamid had spent a long time living in the house of Badrul Islam. During all that time, though he had not formed any intimacy with Nazia, a wonderful warm feeling, nevertheless, had grown for her in his heart. Some overwhelming but nameless emotions were springing up inside him. He had saved enough money from his income, and now wanted to move to his own flat. Dhaka was not a strange place for him now. He met scores of people every day. Among them, some were from his hometown. They had left Biharsharif when he was still there, and it was said that they had gone to Calcutta or Bombay to earn. He also came across Azimuddin, a distant uncle of his, who had migrated there during the partition of India. The poor man had starved in India, but was now living a life of luxury in Dhaka. He had his own printing press, two cars and an elegant house. He had come to visit someone at the jute mill and speaking to Hamid had discovered that they were somehow related. He pulled a face at him when he learnt that Hamid was staying at Badrul Islam's house. Badrul Islam was one of the leading personalities of Dhaka, and he had a formidable reputation among the majority of the Biharis and Bengalis there. Hamid's distant uncle took him to his own house, and introduced him to his wife and children. His son worked in the press, and one of his two daughters was married to a man who was working in West Pakistan. The second daughter was studying in Dhaka. The family enjoyed enormous wealth and material pleasures.

He took Hamid into his confidence and said, 'You've arrived here very late, my son. The ample opportunities available here have already been seized by those who came in the early days of the Partition. You would have revelled in riches had you been here before.'

'Uncle, I trust my abilities to achieve my goals here,' replied Hamid, but his uncle could not get him clearly.

'But your abilities won't help you much here. You've to know the tricks of the trade. We are lucky that the Bengalis, fortuitously, are not so clever.'

Hamid did not like his argument. He had developed some empathy for the Bengalis while living with Badrul Islam.

'Wow, Uncle, what are you saying? Bengalis have the brainpower that we cannot attain in a hundred years. Haven't you heard the slogan that what Bengal thinks today, India will think tomorrow?'

'My boy, you don't know much about them. These Bengalis are so lazy that they would have been left far behind had we not come here. They have little education, and they follow the Hindu culture. Go to their villages and you'll find nobody saying they are Pakistanis. They think theirs is a Bengali country.'

'Well, that's not something bad! They have indeed a strong feeling of belonging to their community. But, despite that, think how these Bengalis have embraced the Biharis, sheltered them, treated them with love and respect. Why should we look down on them?'

'Hamid Babu, you came here late, so you know nothing. The Bengalis are so obsessively in love with their ethnic identity that they have no interest in Pakistan. The Urdu–Bangla language conflict still blows up every day. May God be kind to Jinnah Sahib who did not know Urdu, except for the word 'Pakistan', but made Urdu the country's official language. The Bengalis did not dare defy him in his lifetime. But after his death, they raised hell and spat fire.'

'But where is the problem if they want to preserve their language? After all, Urdu is not the religious language of Muslims. You speak Urdu, they speak Bengali. The dispute is over.'

'Young man, you won't understand it right now. Pakistan was not created to promote Bengali, Punjabi or Sindhi languages, or to foster the Hindu civilization. In this country, the same language will be spoken and the same civilization will be espoused for which Pakistan was brought into being. The founding fathers of Pakistan formed the country for us Biharis, who were persecuted by the Hindus. What difference did the creation of Pakistan make to the life of the local inhabitants here, except that the new ways of development and progress were opened for them? They got people like us to help them.'

Hamid found his words ridiculous. He remembered his father Akhtar Husain. What a well-balanced mind he possessed! He believed in mutual love and respect for one another. Hamid felt that Akhtar Husain's thoughts could be acceptable here too as they were in India. He did not think it worthwhile to argue with his uncle who had brought up his children in a very money-oriented environment, talking always about cars, sofas, beautiful houses and the wealthy lifestyles in Japan, America, Germany or Saudi Arabia. Hamid was not interested in those subjects, and therefore, he was considered a very boring person there. Every weekend they would plan an outing or a picnic and invite Hamid. But he had little time for those things.

Badrul Islam and his household were not only interested in music and dance, they had a very chaste literary taste. They had an excellent collection of literary works. There were complete English anthologies of Tagore and Nazrul Islam's compositions, which Hamid tried to read but failed to understand. Though when Badrul Islam explained the poems line by line to him, he started taking interest in reading them. He read the songs many times and every time they gave him a different pleasure. There was a time when such books and topics appeared very dull to him. He would very reluctantly cram expected portions of the coursebooks before the final exams, only to forget all afterwards. His mind would become a tabula rasa. But now he often had discussions with Badrul Islam on various topics. It was, rather, a one-way conversation which provided him, on every occasion, a chance to hear Badrul Islam and attain knowledge and information in the end.

One day, he said to Badrul Islam, in a suppressed tone, that he wanted to move to the staff housing.

'But why? Do you feel any discomfort here?'

'No, no . . . Uncle! It is more comfortable here than back home. But why to leave the flat when it is already allotted? Your affection is gratifying. But how long should I trouble you with my stay here?'

'Look, Hamid, troubles and worries hurt mentally and spiritually. Physical trouble is short-lived, and ends with time. Your presence gives us delight. Why do you want to take that away from us?'

Hamid had no answer to that. He had thought that he would leave from there only after Badrul Islam's assent. But the arguments that he had thought would convince him had just fallen flat.

26

A few days later, his distant uncle Azimuddin came to see Hamid at Badrul Islam's house. Hamid had gone out for some work, but Badrul Islam was there. When he learnt that Azimuddin was Hamid's distant relative, he treated him warmly, and asked him about Saminullah, hoping he might know about him since he was also related to Hamid. But Azimuddin could not say anything about Saminullah. After staying there for some time, when Azimuddin finally took leave of Badrul Islam, and drove out of his house, he saw Hamid's car entering at the gate. He called him out and they met outside the house.

'It's quite surprising for me, my son. I thought you were living here as a refugee, but Badrul Islam says you are related to him.'

Hamid ignored his scorn, and said, 'Please tell me, Uncle, are all relations blood-related? Aren't some much more than that?'

'Young man, blood is thicker than water. Do you know that?'

'But just imagine if there's only blood and no water. Could you have a relationship in such a case?'

'You possess a ready gift of repartee. But remember it well that Bengalis are quite ungrateful people. They have never been true to us nor will they ever be. Jinnah made a big mistake in taking them into Pakistan. He would have gained a lot had he taken the whole of Punjab. Fie on these indolent Bengalis!'

'Uncle, please control yourself. At least get away from the gate of the house of the person you're abusing.'

'Okay, Hamid. But don't forget my words. Don't ever trust the Bengalis. They are all Hindus, in fact. Try to probe any Muslim Bengali, you'll find Hindu blood in him.'

'So far, no such device has yet been invented that could distribute blood according to religion and caste. If ever invented, I would definitely think of following your advice.'

'Believe it or not, you have the option. I've been watching these people for a long time. And I know them well. Though citizens of Pakistan, they are only loyal to their own Bengali culture.'

'They don't live on anyone's charity. They earn their living by the sweat of their brows, and are loyal to their country.'

'Anyway, may God bless you! I came to tell you that your sister Shahnaz has passed her Bachelor's. To celebrate that, your aunt has invited you to have lunch and sweets with us.'

'Congratulations! Why didn't you tell me that earlier? We got uselessly involved in political arguments. I'll certainly come. But which day?'

'Next Friday,' Azimuddin answered, and drove away with such speed that the car would have hit anyone who happened to be in front.

Badrul Islam had seen Hamid talking to Azimuddin at the gate of his house, but had not heard their conversation.

He spoke to Hamid when he came in, 'Your relative had come to see you, Hamid. Why didn't you bring him in? Why did you send him off from the gate of the house?'

'He was in a hurry. Just talked a little and went away.'

'My dear boy, I have something important to talk to you about.'

Hamid shuddered, fearing Badrul Islam might have overheard his conversation with Azimuddin.

'What's that?'

'In fact, a family of refugees has arrived here after crossing the border. These people have fled from Muzaffarpur to save their lives. There has been a communal riot there. And many people have been killed.'

'Oh, that's too bad!'

'Yes, it is. Now those hapless migrants have been given lodging on the verandah of my office. But that is not a proper place for them. We cannot accommodate them inside the office rooms, because there are important documents and files there. And the open verandah is quite unsafe for them, in case they get caught in monsoon rain. Why don't you let them stay in the flat that is allotted to you? They will move out when they find a place for themselves.'

'You need not ask me. The flat is yours. You can use it as you wish. But since that is the Mill's property . . .'

'I will tell the general manager of the Adamjee Mills. I only wanted to get your consent.'

So, I am going to live permanently in this bungalow, Hamid thought. He had no objection in staying there, but could not just feel capable of shouldering the burden of anyone's excessive favour. But he had no other choice.

When Hamid went to Azimuddin at his invitation, he found the dinner table laden with a variety of Bihari dishes—spicy bachkas (vegetable fritters), crispy potato-chops, phulkis (savoury muffins), besan ki roti (gram-flour flatbread), pickles, ghee, sweet mangochis (dumplings), phirni (rice pudding) and a lot more. Azimuddin had also invited a few more Biharis who were working in Dhaka. After the meal, they plunged into conversation which focused on abusing the Bengalis.

'If these Bengalis were left to have way their ways, they would start reading the Quran in Bengali.'

'And their prayers are nothing but pretense. You know, once a Bengali thief broke into a Bihari's house. On hearing some noise, the owner of the house got up and rushed towards the kitchen. The thief realized it was too late to escape, so he started offering prayers. When the owner reached the kitchen, he saw that the thief was busy offering prayers.'

'I wish somebody should have asked him why he chose to break into the house to pray, instead of going to a mosque.'

The joke provoked laughter from all.

'The Pakistani government is pampering these people by giving them so many concessions. You'll see, a day will come when these Bengalis will become hot-headed and imprudent.'

'Hands and sticks must be used to teach them Islamic culture. They expect us to learn the Bengali language and civilization, without which we cannot work here, whereas they themselves hate to learn Urdu which is their official language.'

'They are a nation of dancers and singers, which is what they call civilization.'

'They are obsessed with the misguided belief that their Bengal is of gold.'

'Go and talk to any Bengali officer. He would hardly speak in Urdu. Whether you understand it or not, he will speak in Bangla. They are crazy about their language.'

Hamid quietly listened to their harangues against the Bengalis. Having lived there for quite some time, he had now clearly understood what people usually talked there and why. He was surprised to find that the servants who worked for Azimuddin were all Bengalis. And almost all of them were popping up from time to time in the room where the conversation was taking place. He himself did not participate in the conversation because his thoughts and opinions did not match the views of those people. Azimuddin and his guests talked late into the night.

And when everyone left, Azimuddin's wife asked Hamid, 'I've come to know that you are living with Bengalis, aren't you?'

'Yes, you've heard it right! The Bengali with whom I'm staying is dearer to me than my own relatives.'

'Hamid, you must understand that Bengalis can never be your true friends. They are deeply connected to their own community. You don't know what we have suffered here. After all, we came here after having lost everything back home. And we thought we had come to Pakistan. But here there's no Pakistan. It's Bangla and just Bangla everywhere.'

Finding him not responding to her, Azimuddin spoke to Hamid, 'Look, the Biharis who migrated to West Pakistan are very happy there. The place is like heaven for them. They got everything—jobs, houses, lands, properties . . . everything.'

'But, Uncle, there is a big difference between the two places. There were thousands of people who fled from West Pakistan leaving their lands and properties, which was appropriated by millions of refugees who came to Pakistan. But no one has gone away from here. Then why do you expect that refugees coming here would easily acquire properties and jobs as they did in West Pakistan?' Hamid tried to spell out the facts to him.

'Young man, migration has a very special place in the history of Islam. You must know how the Ansars of Madinah treated the Makkan refugees when our Prophet migrated from Makkah. They gave half of their properties to their refugee brothers in faith. Every Ansar had a Makkan refugee as his guest. What do the Bengalis know about these things? All they need is their golden Bangla desh.'

Hamid could not understand what they were talking about. He had met thousands of Biharis there, and all of them nursed seething grudges against the Bengalis. They had grievances against the Bengalis that they did not provide them with readily available jobs, houses and other facilities when they arrived in East Pakistan to save their lives. They had worked hard here and only then achieved whatever they had now. They felt humiliated when they compared their situation with that of the migrants living in West Pakistan. And perhaps this feeling of inferiority was growing inside them like a festering sore, oozing out as scorns and disdain against them. The night had worn on. Hamid asked Azimuddin's permission to leave.

'It's quite late, my son. Why don't you stay here for the night? This is also your home.'

When Hamid called Badrul Islam to inform him that he would not be home, Badrul Islam told him he need not inform him ever—after all, he was staying with his own kin. When Hamid repeated the words of Badrul Islam to Azimuddin, he remained silent.

The room adjoining the drawing room was opened for Hamid. It was clean, airy and decorated. Hamid was given a lungi and kurta to change for the night. So, he changed his clothes and fell fast asleep.

While still in sleep, he suddenly became aware that there was someone there in the room. His eyes opened. In the faint green bed light, he saw Azimuddin's daughter Shahnaz standing in front of him. He got up with a jerk.

'You . . . here . . . at this time of night?'

'Sorry, Bhaijan! But I've come here to talk about something very important.'

'To me?'

'Yes, to you. I haven't had a chance to talk to you in person before. Luckily, I've found the opportunity today, and gathered courage to come to you.'

Hamid was stunned at her courage. After all, her parents and servants were all there in the house. Anyone could wake up any time. And at that moment, who would wait to judge why Shahnaz had come to his room? He was very nervous.

'What do you want to tell me? Say it fast, before anyone gets up.'

'Don't worry. No one will come in this direction. Their rooms are far away on the other side. And then, once they sleep, they get up only in the morning. They don't get up frequently at night.'

'Alright. But, speak your mind, quickly!'

'Bhaijan, do you understand why my father is showing so much hospitality to you?'

'How could I know his mind?'

'He's laying a trap for you. He has tricked my brother-in-law in the same way into marrying my elder sister.'

Hamid was surprised at the girl's boldness and frankness. He could not say anything in response to her revelations.

She then said, 'But, Bhaijan! God bears witness that I have not considered you less than a brother. I cannot even imagine what my parents are thinking about us.'

Hamid wondered how to respond to this. She was creating her own problems. What then does she want from him?

'Tell me clearly now, what's that you want me to do? After all, I see no meaning in what you are saying. What can I say in this regard, what can I do?'

Shahnaz took Hamid's hand in hers. 'Only you can help me,' she said.

Hamid felt utterly perplexed and started to get suspicious of her.

She continued, 'Bhaijan, I am in love with a boy. We've been in a relationship for four years now. The problem is that he is a Bengali. And you know well how bitterly my parents hate the Bengalis. But I can't live without him. I can even lay down my life for my love.'

Her love story appeared interesting to Hamid. Her parents abhorred the Bengalis, and here was their daughter who was ready to sacrifice her life for her love.

Hamid asked her, 'What does your boyfriend do? Does he, too, love you with the same intensity?'

'He's second lieutenant in the army. He's prepared to do anything for me, for our love.'

'Now tell me what you want me to do?'

'When my father comes to you with a proposal to marry me, you just refuse. Tell him that you consider me as your own sister, and that you can't even imagine taking me as your wife.'

'That's fine. I'll exactly do that.'

'Bhaijan, God will reward you for this support. I'm too frail to return your favour.'

Shahnaz kissed his hands out of extreme gratitude, and ran out of the room.

Hamid could not stop laughing at the situation. He didn't know much about Azimuddin. In his childhood days, he had of course seen him visiting Ben House off and on. Bibi Sahiba used to meet him in the inner mansion of the house, and ask him about the well-being of people in her village. She introduced him to the children as their uncle, and asked them to say salaam to him. And now he had met him in Dhaka after a long gap. Little could he realize why Azimuddin was trying to show so much affection and closeness to him. Now that the Shahnaz had told him the truth, he was somehow feeling lighter. Azimuddin's activities and conversations seemed nothing more than a facade to him now.

27

It was more than a year since Hamid had left Biharsharif. Coincidentally, the day he ran away from there, Akhtar Husain arrived at Ben House along with his wife and other children. No one noticed Hamid's day-long absence as that was his usual routine, his normal tuition hours. But when night fell and he did not come, everyone started to get worried. Servants were sent to a few places where he gave tuition. It turned out that he had not gone to those places. The women began sobbing and the children fell quiet.

Akhtar Husain's wife beseeched him with tears, 'Do something, for God's sake! I've never asked you for anything, but today I'm pleading with you. Please bring my child back from anywhere. You are sitting there so quietly as if you have sent him somewhere.'

'What can I do? He's a young man now. No one can lead him astray. Wherever he has gone, he must have gone of his own free will.'

'Search his room and clothes, at least!'

When the room was searched, they found that his clothes weren't there, and neither were his bags and books. It seemed clear that he had left the place with prior preparation. No letters or notes were found in the room.

Akhtar Husain explained to everyone, 'I think there's nothing to worry about. It looks obvious that he has gone from here in a planned way. In a few days, it will become clear where he has gone.'

But his words could not console anybody in the house. Bibi Sahiba sent a man to Ben. Close and distant relatives were queried. Many letters were sent here and there. But nothing came to light. The next day, they received Hamid's letter which he had posted in Biharsharif the day he left the place. The news of his departure to Pakistan raised concerns. Where could he be? Under what circumstances? What if he had been arrested? Akhtar Husain's silence grew deeper. He was sad that his son did something he had always condemned. How bad it would be if he were caught? To how many people would he go on giving clarifications? His wife requested him to send a man to Pakistan so that he could find out about Hamid.

Akhtar Husain finally broke his silence, 'Thousands of people have fled to Pakistan. How many people were ever sent to look for them? Besides, I don't have any sympathy with someone who has deliberately broken the law. He could have left legally and properly if he wanted to go.'

Akhtar Husain spoke in such a tone that there was no room for further talk on that matter. His wife knew his mind very well.

The most distraught among them was Bibi Sahiba. Earlier, her idea of Pakistan was what Asghar Husain had

imbedded in her mind before he had gone there—an El
Dorado, a la-la land. But with her two sons deserting her
and migrating to Pakistan, and now Hamid leaving her too,
there was no one who knew Pakistan better than her. She had
raised Hamid since his childhood and loved him like her own
child. Grandparents tend to love their grandchildren more
than their own children. She felt Pakistan had taken him
away, too, and had once again shattered her peace.

Akhtar Husain's younger son Sajid had clinched
the first position in the university intermediate exams.
Somebody advised him that if he did his Bachelor's from St
Stephens College in Delhi, he could succeed in the Indian
Administrative Service (IAS) exams. Akhtar Husain wanted
him to continue his studies in Patna University. But his son
was adamant about going to Delhi. It was not financially
possible for Akhtar Husain to bear his significantly high
educational expenses in Delhi. After he left the ministry,
he had become ineffectual and practically inactive. His legal
career had also suffered significantly. Politics was his sole
interest and the only profession, but now young people were
entering politics. Its old time-honoured ideals were being
forsaken, and new values promoted. The Congress party had
now members who held divergent opinions. There was only
one thing common among them, though. They would all
take Gandhiji's name and praised him loudly, but looked at
old Congressmen with contempt. However, when a Central
leader visited any provincial town, and wanted to meet his
partymen in a closed room, the old Congressmen were fished
out from their confines and invited to the meeting. Akhtar
Husain was also now counted as an old Congressman. And
the young Turks of the party seldom remembered him.

Sajid feigned illness in protest when all his persistent pleadings were in vain. Akhtar Husain did not know what to do. He had no money. His son Faiyyaz was still under the supervision of a psychiatrist, and his daughter Khalida was in the fever of adolescence. He was also worried about her marriage. In such a situation, it was not possible for him to send Sajid to Delhi. When Sajid saw that nothing happened even when he refused to join Patna College, he was consumed with the fear of wasting a complete year. He stopped eating and drinking, and remained quiet all the time. Akhtar Husain had suffered the misfortune that had befallen Faiyyaz, and now trembled with fear to see Sajid's desperateness. He did not want to be hard with Sajid at that critical moment. After failing to persuade him to take admission in Patna College, he left him with his desperation and went back to Patna. Sajid's sheer obstinacy prodded him to embarrass his father, and so he enrolled at the Nalanda College in Biharsharif. When the news reached Akhtar Husain, he was caught in a real dilemma. He was staying in Patna only for his children, and especially for Sajid's studies. In the midst of a career slump, his daily visit to the high court proved to be waste of time. It had now become useless for him to stay at Patna. He once again tried to convince Sajid to enroll in Patna College, and assured him that though it was too late he would get his admission there with the help of the minister of education. But Sajid refused, and said that if he could not study in Delhi then it hardly mattered if he went to any college anywhere. Helpless and upset, Akhtar Husain packed his luggage and returned finally to Biharsharif with his family.

Ben House was once again all agog with hustle and bustle. Akhtar Husain's old friends and colleagues met there every evening. Many of them had withdrawn from active politics, because they could not support the rapidly changing face of politics. They openly and passionately deliberated on the fast-emerging trends in national and local politics, and left for their homes when they had vented their spleen. Ajodhya Prasad's interest in politics was limited to the extent that he would attend the party meeting only to see the old Congressmen. Otherwise, whatever suggestions he gave at the meeting would go in from one ear and out of the other. The country was facing many problems other than politics, which were not seen by anyone except the old stalwarts of the party. These old guards discussed these exhaustively but were unable to do anything. They needed political power and office to deal with these problems. And those who possessed the power to act had surrendered their conscience to power. Therefore, power compelled them to act as it willed.

Akhtar Husain started his law practice in Biharsharif. Some old, familiar people started coming to him. He had come back to where he had started from, but did not have enough work to keep him as busy as he was during the freedom movement. For the different development programmes that the Congress government drew up for the districts, it was necessary to consult grassroots leaders like him. Invitations for different events were sent to them because their names were still there on party list.

28

Hamid wrote a few letters from Pakistan which on reaching Ben House brought a wave of happiness and elation to those staying there. Whatever impact his departure had created, tidings of his well-being made everyone happy. Akhtar Husain also saw the letters and remained silent. Hamid addressed his father in all his letters, but only his mother replied to them. Akhtar Husain could not forgive his son's defiance.

India's third election was approaching. The Congress had lost its Biharsharif seat in the previous election. Now the provincial Congress wanted a very suitable candidate from there. Ajodhya Prasad and other friends suggested that Akhtar Husain should try again as Muhammad Younus was removed as chairman of the state transport corporation on corruption charges. He had earned a notorious reputation. Even though he was in the Congress, he was not considered for any political nomination. So, Akhtar Husain, at everybody's request, applied for the party's nomination to contest the elections. When the district Congress chief learnt about it, he came with Ajodhya Prasad to meet Akhtar Husain, and expressed his pleasure at his decision. He also offered him some money from the party fund to help him fight the election since it had become necessary to spend on campaigns. But as the party could not afford to pay the full amount needed for it, he requested him to put in at least fifty thousand rupees from his personal fund. Akhtar Husain was a politician who had always embraced integrity, correctness and honesty in his public as well as private life. He could not reconcile with the Congress chief's contention that politics had now become a thriving business which encouraged capital investments, and told him frankly that he had no money to do that. Ajodhya Prasad stood by his long-standing friend and refused to move with the times. But after much persuasion and exhortations, Akhtar Husain eventually agreed to the Congress chief's suggestion of receiving donations from business houses to fund his election campaign.

29

Akhtar Husain, did not want to fuss around for the party ticket. He hated bootlicking party bosses for favours. In the last elections, he had gone to Delhi only at the insistence of Ajodhya Prasad, and to appease him. But now, realizing the exigencies of the situation, he went to Patna with Ajodhya Prasad, and met with the party leaders. The number of aspirants for the Congress ticket had overwhelmingly increased. But for Biharsharif urban constituency, the Congress party sent only his name and started collecting funds in his name. Akhtar Husain kept himself unconcerned from the matter of donations. He was, in any way, not in favour of collecting financial contributions before the decisions of the party tickets. But the president wanted the district Congress to keep its funding strong. They had already opened several fronts of the election, and were busy working on all fronts.

The final list of candidates arrived after the electoral board meeting in Delhi. Akhtar Husain received the party ticket from Biharsharif. He became actively involved in electoral activities. Ben House was abuzz with campaign activities day and night. Akhtar Husain had placed all the financial responsibilities on the shoulders of the district Congress. He did not have any money with himself to fight the election, so the provincial Congress gave him ten thousand rupees. He left that money, too, in the custody of the district Congress. Whoever came to him asking for election expenses, he would send him to the president of the district Congress. He received lots of complaints that the district president of Congress was squandering the election money and was not spending it properly. He also personally saw that the opposition candidates had opened camps everywhere, where they were running regular langars (free kitchens) to provide meals to the poor, while the Congress party had just put up posters all over with the picture of a pair of bulls, which was the party symbol. Even Ajodhya Prasad had a grievance against the district Congress president: that he was acting unconscientiously in connection with the election money. Akhtar Husain heard everyone but said not a word, and busied himself with the election work. He had a group of sincere workers who worked unconditionally spending their own money. But they were not too many, and they had a huge lack of resources, because they did not strive to get them. For them, politics was not a profession but a service to people.

However, Akhtar Husain lost the election by several thousand votes. Although he graciously accepted defeat, it left his followers demoralized. Despite the lack of resources and money, these people had worked together day and night. They strongly believed that it was next to impossible that Akhtar Husain would lose by several thousand votes. But his defeat was a reality, and there was no choice but to accept it.

One evening, when Ajodhya Prasad came to Akhtar Husain, he brought an interesting piece of news, 'Have you heard the latest gossip in the air in your town, Brother Akhtar? The baniyas (grocers) of the town are nowadays making rounds of the house of the president of the district Congress.'

'But why?'

'They want to ask him to render the account of the donations that they had made towards the election fund.'

'But isn't that strange? After all, donations are usually given without any conditions.'

'In fact, they had given money to help the Congress party candidate win the elections. And the president had promised that after winning the election the Congress candidate would work for their benefit. Now the Congress has lost from here, and they want their money back.'

Akhtar Husain was briefly stunned into silence. He spoke after a while, 'Ajodhya Babu, we should leave politics and take sanyas (renunciation of the world) now. Politics has no longer remained our cup of tea.'

'We are not, in any way, in active politics now. But I still do not consider it a dirty business, though people have undoubtedly stained it.'

'I feel as if politics has become like a coal mine, and whoever enters it emerges begrimed. So, it's better to keep away. Just imagine, what would have been my position had I directly taken donations from people?'

'Yes, that's true. I've now realized what it means to give generous donations to political parties. It is a ploy resorted to by wily donors to obtain a license to get all their illegitimate work done by the politicians in power. Those in power cannot refuse these business houses as they have vast resources at their command.'

'I wonder if there is a secret like that hidden in my defeat too.'

'You are right. I did not believe it when I first received the news. But now that the matter is out in the open, I have to accept it as true. Elections can be won now by capturing booths, and not with the support of the people. That is actually what has happened here. The opposition party overtook us in power and money, so they won. Otherwise, there was no question of our losing—if we, too, had accumulated power and money.'

Akhtar Husain already had a hunch that something had gone amiss in the elections. Ajodhya Prasad's words confirmed his fear. Anyway, he was absolutely free now. He had stopped looking after his village lands since a long time ago, partly because of his demanding political and professional duties, and partly because he was upset that Sarwar Husain did not consult him when he sold some land and kept the account of the money to himself. Waseem and Shamim were on their jobs, and even when they visited the village on their yearly trip, they knew nothing about the length and breadth of their land. They believed what the patwari and gomashtha told them. Bibi Sahiba always asked Akhtar Husain to pay attention to the village land at Ben. And now that Akhtar Husain had plenty of time at his disposal, he went to stay there for a month. Much had changed in Ben during his long absence from there. Life in the village had completely transformed. Old people stayed confined to their homes and spent their times in prayers. Most of the Muslim boys had fled to Pakistan, looking for jobs. And those who had stayed back, were engaged in farming and petty trades, and were inextricably involved in village politics. They had no separate identity, and were known as members of groups led by the Rajputs, Bhumihars or the backward classes, the constituent caste groups to which they owed their allegiance.

Akhtar Husain heard a lot of disturbing news when the elders of the village came to meet him. The incidents of theft and robbery in the village had increased alarmingly. After seven o'clock in the evening, no villager dared to step out of his home, unless there was a desperate urgency, in which case they ventured out in groups. The police would not take any action if any crime was reported to them, and even when they did, they would demand heavy bribes. An overwhelming feeling of insecurity and distrust had seized the entire village.

Muhammad Yasin, an elderly villager, also came to see Akhtar Husain when he heard of his arrival at Ben. He was an old acquaintance of Sheikh Altaf's, and so Akhtar Husain called him uncle. Muhammad Yasin had actively helped some young boys from his village to study at the college in Biharsharif. When these boys did not get a job, he went to Akhtar Husain to request him to use his influence. But when Akhtar Husain failed to get jobs for them, they bought tractors and used them to plough their fields. Narendra Singh, son of a nearby village landlord Babu Surender Singh, advised Muhammad Yasin to buy a tractor too. People could now borrow money from banks to buy tractors. Muhammad Yasin owned large tracts of farmland. He liked the suggestion. He was spending large sum of money every year on his herd of cattle for ploughing his farmland. Sometimes the oxen died from snake bites, and oftentimes they became so ill that they were no longer capable of pulling the ploughs. Owning a tractor could relieve him of those constant headaches, and also like Babu Surender Singh, enable him to sell his grains for thousands of rupees. But his two elder sons dissuaded him from buying a tractor and fled secretly to Dhaka, one unassuming morning. Their misdemeanour so pained Muhammad Yasin that he discontinued his two younger sons' education after their high school. Both of his sons stayed in the village but had no interest in farming. They loafed around the village, went fishing in the river, played cards and indulged in all kinds of village sports and mischief all day long.

The narrow track that branched off from the main highway and led to Ben was divided into several similar dirt tracks right and left of it, leading to other villages. One evening, a person arriving in the village from Calcutta was looted and stabbed. He had a providential escape as the dagger wound was not deep, and his loud scream brought many villagers rushing to him, providing him with timely medical help, which saved his life.

The man was not only a rich businessman but also knew how to use his money. He paid off the local policemen, and several police vehicles began roaming the villages, launching a massive hunt. Azhar, one of Muhammad Yasin's sons, was arrested under suspicion along with one of his close friends who had also been arrested earlier, after some stolen goods were recovered in his possession. Azhar was detained only because of his association with the other fellow. The police took him to the police station and beat him so badly that he was rushed to a hospital. Azhar's friend was a Hindu, and the man who was waylaid was also a Hindu. Azhar was a Muslim. Ben had a mixed population of Hindus and Muslims. Azhar's battering by the police caused unexpected discontent among the villagers that ultimately erupted in sectarian tensions in the village between the Hindus and Muslims. The Hindus gathered every night and chanted slogans like 'Jai Bajrang Bali', and the Muslims answered by shouting 'Narai Takbeer Allahu Akbar'. The atmosphere of the village had changed in no time. Akhtar Husain was present in the village in those days, and he saw all that with his own eyes. He felt intensely that fires were simmering inside everyone waiting to flare up by an errant spark. He spoke to the Hindus and Muslims of his village, and tried to pacify them. He was surprised to find that no one liked that kind of tension. Everyone wanted a peaceful atmosphere. Despite that, slogans continued throughout the nights. Occasionally, the sound of a bomb explosion echoed through the night. Akhtar Husain returned to Biharsharif after staying in Ben for fifteen days. He had gone there to oversee his farmlands and relax. But he could do neither.

When he came to Biharsharif, he talked to the subdivisional officer and the deputy superintendent of police about the tense atmosphere in the village, and they assured him of sending the police force to the village to calm the situation.

Two weeks after his arrival in Biharsharif, many people from Ben came to meet Akhtar Husain. They informed him that the police had filed countless cases against both Hindus and Muslims. The villagers, therefore, were so wholly engrossed with their court cases that they had put behind them all their differences. They spent money like water, because the matter concerned their life and honour. Akhtar Husain regretted asking for police to be sent there, which turned the people further away from each other. He lobbied hard for the settlement of the cases belonging to both the communities, and also went to the village to make all the people sit together and pacify the atmosphere. Despite his efforts, the Muslims expected him to be with them as a Muslim, while the Hindus believed that he would support the Muslims in all situations. Akhtar Husain was an old Congressman, and was among those who had vowed to keep Gandhiji in their hearts forever, even though he had long since died. When he realized what people were saying about him, he had only two options in front of him. He could either sit quietly in his house or come out and stick to his principles. Obviously, he was going to be branded with what he had opposed all his life. As he had never learned to compromise, he decided to stay in Ben. After hearing the news of his decision, Ajodhya Prasad and his few old Congress colleagues also came to the village. They all met with each and every villager at Ben, and tried to find out their standpoints. The advantage of this was that whenever a meeting was called, people of both the communities came to it. After doing some spadework at the village, Akhtar Husain along with his friends went to Biharsharif and met the top officials. After much persuasion he prevailed on them to visit the village, withdraw the court cases and ask both the communities to forget their differences and embrace each other. Their visit to Ben was marked by a huge public gathering at the village maidan which reminded everyone of Sheikh Altaf's time. The subdivisional officer and the superintendent of police also arrived there. When people of both the communities started to hug one another, it seemed as if it was an Eid day. The cases were also withdrawn. Akhtar Husain was relieved that his efforts had borne fruit, but was left wondering how long such efforts would last and who would continue to do so when he wasn't there.

30

Communal riots broke out in Calcutta, and the flames of violence swept through the distant cities of Rourkela, Jamshedpur and Ranchi. The whole of eastern India was hit by this blazing sectarian fury. People said that since the minority community in East Pakistan had been uprooted and thousands of refugees had fled to India, so the riots in India were a natural reaction to that. The mayhem and massacre continued for weeks. An atmosphere of dread prevailed in Biharsharif, too, since many people from there were working in Calcutta, Ranchi and Jamshedpur. A funereal air wafted through their homes. Every day brought its own share of rumours to the town and its surrounding villages. The Muslim populace lost its faith in the news the Indian radio broadcasts and newspapers brought to them. They started listening to BBC and Pakistan radio. People escaped from curfews in riot-prone areas. And they carried with them their own versions of the carnage wherever they went. Fear and insecurity took hold of everyone. People kept the doors of their houses bolted round the clock. Akhtar Husain was about to leave for Ben to run an urgent errand. Some people asked him to postpone his journey, but he didn't see any reason to do it. Bibi Sahiba was very worried when she learnt about his travel plan. She was regularly briefed on the everyday happenings in the town and the adjacent villages by the woman, the fruit-and-vegetable vendor, who regularly visited Ben House to sell her stuff.

So, she called Akhtar Husain and asked him, 'I heard you're going to Ben? Is that so, my son?'

'Yes, Amma. There are lots of things to do there. I've given the patwari some tasks to accomplish. I must go and see.'

'There's so much of chaos going on all around. It's not safe for you to step out of the house.'

'But it's not happening anywhere here. It's occurring in Calcutta and Jamshedpur. Here, people are just getting panicky.'

'You can't trust anyone. No one knows what would flare up when and where. I've come to know that a lot of secret planning is going on here. Please, don't even get out of the house.'

Akhtar Husain laughed gently, 'Nothing bad is going to happen here, Amma. People are worrying in vain. And small incidents do happen every day, everywhere.'

'I don't understand why they are fighting when they have already carved Pakistan out of India.'

'Will they stop fighting when you and I migrate to Pakistan? Would you like to go there, Amma?'

'No, never! Why should I go there? I'm an Indian. This is my country, and not Pakistan!'

'Then stay here, with ease. Why live in fear?'

Bibi Sahiba failed to get his point, but spoke softly, 'Anyway, but please don't go out, my son. There's no male member in the house at the moment.'

'But if I confine myself here, people will think that I'm frightened.'

Bibi Sahiba remembered well her husband's difficult temperament. And now she had been noticing its reflection in Akhtar Husain. She said nothing in response to Akhtar Husain's intransigence. And taking advantage of her silence, Akhtar Husain left for Ben. On the way he realized that the atmosphere was not really relaxed. When he boarded the bus for the journey, he found no Muslim-looking person inside. A man clad in dhoti, with a gamcha (thin cotton towel) on his shoulder, appeared familiar to him. But the man gave him such an odd look that Akhtar Husain dared not speak to him. Sporting a grizzled beard, a sherwani, a churidar pyjama and a cloth cap, with a thin walking stick in hand, Akhtar Husain looked every inch a Muslim. It was possible that some passengers in the bus recognized him. They were staring at him, but no one tried to talk to him. He sat glued to his bus seat with evident indifference. At that moment, he realized that overcoming fear was not possible for everyone. There was an ominous silence in the bus, a moaning silence as it appeared to Akhtar Husain, a silence so unnerving that it threatened to burst the eardrums of a quiet person like him. He had taken two newspapers with him before boarding the bus. But the heavy atmosphere inside the bus made him so busy with thoughts that he could not read even a word. The newspaper lay open in front of him and his listless eyes kept running over them. It was an hour-long journey which seemed even longer and tedious to him. He had lost all sense of time when the bus eventually pulled over to the side of the road, from where a mud track forked off to Ben village. Along with Akhtar Husain, three more passengers got down from the bus and started walking on the mud road. Akhtar Husain always informed his staff at the village whenever he visited Ben, and they would arrange buggies for him that took him to his cottage there. But he had chosen not to do so this time, thinking that he would take a walk to his village home. The people walking with Akhtar Husain were watching him very carefully, which made him start the conversation with them.

'Where are you going? I'm going to Ben.'

His sudden query jolted them, but one of the fellows replied, 'We're going to Govindpur, Sir. Do you live in Ben?'

'Hmm . . . well, you can call it my home. In fact, Sheikh Altaf Husain was my father-in-law, and a maternal uncle.'

'Oh, so you are Sheikh sahib's son-in-law? Are you not the same person who was a deputy minister in the previous government? Sheikh sahib's name still commands respect in this area.'

'Yes. I'm the same person.'

One of them took Akhtar Husain's leather bag from his hand to carry it along out of respect for him, not listening to his refusals. Their journey on foot continued, and they began to talk to while away time.

Akhtar Husain asked them. 'Look, how tension is brewing in the entire region? So many years had passed since we achieved independence, but people still haven't become sensible. I don't know what ails us?'

'Sir, actually not everyone likes carnages and killings. But a handful of people for their own interests do stir unrests, and keep them alive,' one among them answered.

'It is, therefore, the duty of those who love peace, to come out and defeat those who are potential trouble creators. Otherwise, it is a contagious disease that if left unfought will hollow out the entire nation,' Akhtar Husain said.

'But, Sir, what happens is that such a situation is created in which no one is left free to distinguish the bad from the good. All people start thinking the same slanted way.'

'Just look at what happened in places like Calcutta, Ranchi and Jamshedpur. The whole atmosphere got tainted and grew extremely tense. Who is responsible for whipping up riots in these cities? Not in the least those Hindus and Muslims who reside there. Why then they suddenly become sworn enemies of one another?'

'But, Sir, the Muslims have an advantage that they can take off to Pakistan in the wake of any trouble here. But where should we escape in such a situation. We have to live and die here.'

'Those Muslims who have stayed back, too, have to die here. Some flee to Pakistan because that has become their escape destination. Had it not been there, where else would they escape?'

'Sir, that's why they have helped in its creation, to fly there when they can. These people dream of Pakistan while living in India, which is certainly going to create a tremendously disastrous impact on the others.'

'But Pakistan was neither created by Muslims nor by Hindus. It was born out of politics whose victims were both the Hindus and the Muslims.'

'Even then, the Muslims demanded and fought for its creation.'

'That's true. But some Muslims here committed a great mistake, and they were punished for it. In fact, a few people made that mistake, and the entire Muslim community has been penalized. You cannot constantly crack down on the entire community for so long. It can have dangerous consequences for a nation.'

Akhtar Husain's remarks calmed them for a while, and he continued, 'We need to think seriously who is affected by the riots. As long as the riots continue to occur, tensions will keep rising. And due to these tensions people will not work in factories and farms. They will remain closed in their homes. As a result, the country will stop making progress.'

'You are quite right, Sir. There's no village, no town and no neighbourhood, where there aren't Muslims. Conflicts and tensions affect both Hindus and Muslims alike. They become mutual enemies and try to vanquish each other. But what's to be done? Once something sticks in everybody's mind the most, it never goes out.'

'People like you and I have to offer our sacrifices for that. This is the call of our motherland, to which we all must respond readily.'

They reached a bend on the path where they saw a thatched hut that appeared to be a sort of resting-house or caravanserai. A few cots and benches were laid out in front of the hut. All of them sat on the cots. The hut owner was known to Akhtar Husain. He quickly brought a pillow for him. Akhtar Husain did not want to lie down, but at the insistence of his fellow travellers, he stretched himself out on the cot, and soon fell into deep sleep. He woke up with a start after a long sleep, and found everyone waiting for him. He felt quite ashamed.

'I'm sorry, friends. I slept rather long. That's why I didn't want to lie down. Age has its own demands.'

'Never mind, Sir. We, too, had the opportunity to take some rest.'

Tea was ready. Akhtar Husain looked at his watch and saw that it was time for the noon prayer. Finding him in some hesitation, one of the villagers asked him,

'What happened? Is there any trouble?'

'The noon prayer time is slipping away. I would have missed my noon prayer due to sleep.'

'Oh no, Sir. Please offer your prayer, first. We can wait.'

They asked the hut owner to bring a bucket of water, washed one of the benches, and dried it with a cloth. They then spread a clean white dhoti on the bench.

'Please, pray on it, Sir. It's a clean cloth.'

'Oh, thanks a lot! Sure, sure. It's a dry place. And dry places are clean.'

After Akhtar Husain offered his prayer, they took tea and left the hut to continue on their way. They had become very close to him in a short span of time. So, one of them shared their common concern with him, which revealed that they were, in fact, hereditary landowners and owned large tracts of farmlands.

'Sir, these days, we are confronted with very serious problems. We own large farms, and we have been always hiring tillers to cultivate our lands. We have never cultivated ourselves. These backward people, the Harijans, who have been pampered by our government, are now demanding very high wages for working in our fields. Tell me, from where can we pay such a high wage for farming? We've always given them some grains. All members of their families work either on the farms or in the houses. Their daughters and daughters-in-law, too, work. While it's quite the opposite with us. We'll be ruined if we go on wasting our money on those farmworkers.'

Akhtar listened patiently, and replied after the man stopped, 'Look, my friend, our country has now become independent. And our constitution has given equal rights to all the citizens of the country. It is necessary, therefore, to raise the living standards of the Harijans, and those belonging to other lower castes. If our government is trying to do that, we should try to help it.'

'Well, can these people ever come up? And God forbid, the day that happens, then neither you nor we can remain respectable anymore. After all, these people are working-class people. And if they don't work, how will they earn their living and work for our livelihood too? Are we going to bring our workers from Britain? They must work in our fields, and do nothing else.'

'My friends, we need to change that attitude. The zamindari is abolished so that the rich and the poor both enjoy the fruit of independence. The Constitution talks of equal rights to all. We have to respect that.'

'Then tell us, how do we grow grains in our fields? We are not going to work there ourselves.'

'The principle of farming that is accepted is that whoever ploughs the field, works hard on it, the field will be his, and he will have complete possession of its produce. Land to the tiller. You are disturbed just by the abolition of zamindari. Soon the government is going to introduce the land limitation act. What will you do then?'

'The government's only job appears to be simply making new laws every day. Who's going to see how much these laws are going to be implemented? If the landlords and jagirdars don't cooperate, these laws will always remain on paper. The true identity of India is from its villages where 90 per cent of its population lives. You put your laws into action on merely 10 per cent of the population and feel happy about it.'

'My dear friends, educated people must respect the law of the land, otherwise, it's quite true that laws will be just there on papers. If laws are not respected, then anarchy will spread in the country. The common man will never think of respecting the law. He will follow the words, acts and deeds of the sensible, educated people.'

'You talk of respect for the law. The ground reality is that the Harijans are thinking of capturing our lands. And the day is not far when they will raid our houses and make us homeless. You won't then be able to resist them, and surrender your prestige, your property, everything to them.'

Akhtar Husain pondered over what had been just said. The matter had been occupying his thoughts for quite some time now. He had foreseen that danger long time ago.

'The training of land grabbing has already been given to these people recurrently, so much so that now it has become their habit. Can you deny that the upper-caste people used them in confiscating houses and lands, and in inciting bloodshed and had given them their share in the riots? Those of the higher castes had benefited from all this in two ways. They took possession of the lands owned by the hapless deserters and bought their properties at a ridiculously low price. The lower-caste people have become used to those habits. They have tasted blood, and now you have to face the consequences.'

They said nothing in response to Akhtar Husain's observations, and walked in silence for a long time. Sounds of breathing and heavy footfall echoed through the landscape. Eventually, one from among them spoke to Akhtar Husain.

'Sir, those who were fleeing had to sell their properties. And somebody had to buy them. The truth is that every buyer tries to buy things at a cheaper price. And there was no one, except us, to buy them. Just imagine who would have bought their lands and homes, hadn't we been there?'

'So, you are inadvertently putting the blame on yourself. You are saying that had you not bought their lands they could not have escaped to Pakistan. This can be possible on a small scale, but you cannot say it was a general course of action. Those who were bent upon leaving India, had to go anyhow, leaving all their possessions behind. The main thing is that such a situation was deliberately created so that people had to either leave their property and go away, or sell it dirt cheap. The lower-caste people were used to grabbing whatever was left behind. They were given ownership papers, and later, these properties were bought from them. Tell me, if what I'm saying is wrong.'

'There's of course some truth in what you are saying. But there is more to it than meets the eye. Every community has its good and bad people.'

'Please don't talk about it. It's not only my belief, but my unwavering faith that every community has more good people in it than bad. But what actually happens is that a time comes when even the good walk on the path trodden by the bad. It happens especially when they stand to benefit from the deeds of the bad people.'

Everyone nodded in approval, but did not utter a word.

'So, I was saying that the people of the lower castes have now become inured to forcibly taking over lands and properties, and reap the crops. Had they not been employed to do that time and again, they probably wouldn't have dared to do it. They have gathered enough courage in the course of time. What is it that makes them so bold today?'

'I blame the government for the way things have come to shape today. By abolishing zamindari, the government has done us a grave injustice. It has also cossetted them to such an extent that now they have no respect for us.'

'But the government doesn't belong to a particular class or a sect of the society. It is everybody's government and so it thinks about the welfare of all of us. But what I want to say is that a government cannot build a society. It is you and I, all of us together, who shape and transform a society. The government works according to the principles we have created. And we reap what we sow. This is plain fact, and everything is happening according to that principle.'

'You know that land ceiling regulations are being enforced with full force in India these days. It will give rise to widespread unrest if it comes into force as a law.'

'There will be no uprising, I'm sure, if we follow the law of the land. We have to convince ourselves that the land should belong to the person who tills it. All unrests and agitations will come to an end the day everyone is treated equally under the law regardless of race or religion. Only he who knows farming can cultivate the land. You cannot ask farmers to go and work in factories where they need skilled workers. If the society grants equal rights to all its members, no problems will crop up.'

They had reached the path that turned off to Ben. Akhtar Husain's fellow travellers had to take the opposite path. He wanted to see them off from the bend, but they insisted on accompanying him to his haveli. The villagers at Ben were surprised to see the dhoti-clad people walking along with

Akhtar Husain. The atmosphere in the village had already become strained. Many Muslims from the village worked as urban labourers in Jamshedpur, Rourkela and Calcutta. Their village houses wore a look of mourning. The villagers started gossiping on seeing him with a few strangers.

'It is the old practice of these politicians that when something untoward happens, they come to teach the lesson of national solidarity.'

'He's a Congressman, after all—the friend of Hindus . . .'

'But now the hype created by Congress people is not going to last long. They had tried to do disservice to the Muslims by opposing the creation of Pakistan. Fortunately, the prayers of our saints have been answered and a country has come into being where one could take refuge in times of trouble.'

The villagers at Ben stared suspiciously at Akhtar Husain and his colleagues. Akhtar Husain had already noticed their glower when they did not greet him on entering the village. But he had dealt with circumstances worse than that, so he continued to walk towards his haveli with his fellow travellers, with feigned indifference. He found the gomashtha waiting for him at the gate of his haveli. The patwari had fallen ill and had gone back home. Akhtar Husain asked the gomashtha and a few of his staff to escort his fellow travellers to the main road outside the village. But before leaving, they extracted a promise from Akhtar Husain that he would visit their village sometime soon. A few hours of fellowship had erased years of distances.

Akhtar Husain found that the tense atmosphere in the village had once again reinforced in the Muslim youth the inclination of fleeing to Pakistan. Dozens of boys had left the village, and the rest were busy making financial arrangements to cover the cost of travel. It cost 2,000 rupees to cross over to Pakistan, and after that there was job and the sense of security.

The elders of the village came as usual to meet Akhtar Husain, and he asked them very concernedly, 'Please stop these boys from going away. In this way, an entire younger generation of Muslims will disappear from India. This is going to have a very bad effect.'

Ghassu Miyan, who was an old Congressman and had tolerated the abuses of the Muslim League, spoke out, 'Then tell us what to do, Babu. Life and property both are in danger here. To begin with, there's no job for them, and even if they find one, they are easy targets of rabble rousers. They are safe as long as they are in their localities and their village, but when they go out, they are at the mercy of others.'

'My dear, most of the Muslims were surrounded and killed in Ranchi. The doors of the houses were marked before they were attacked. Even senior Muslim officers were not spared their lives. People ten miles away from the carnage sites heard the victims screaming. Thousands were slaughtered. The Muslims lost their jobs, their businesses, their lands, their everything. When would they go to Pakistan, if not now? That is the only place left to save our lives,' said Mamu Dada who had retired from the police service twenty-four years ago, and was considered among the few educated and wise villagers in Ben.

Akhtar Husain asked him rightaway, 'Did they confront their attackers?'

'No, how could they? They had no weapons.'

'What if dacoits had attacked them instead of rioters?'

'Obviously, the dacoits would have killed all of them. Or they might have just ransacked their houses and left them alive.'

'Tell me, why do we possess all the luxuries of life but cannot keep anything for our safety? Remember, this country is as much yours as it is theirs. You have to live and die here. You do not have to leave the country at the behest of others. It is the destiny of the country that till now it has been running according to the will of a few bad people. How long should we allow these bad people to go on doing as they like?'

Nobody reacted to Akhtar Husain's discourse, and his words reverberated off the walls of silence.

'We have to challenge them, meet them head-on. We have to bring them to the right track, anyhow, in any way we can. And for that, we should not shy away from using weapons if it remains the only way out.'

'But, Sir, we are in minority. How long can we continue fighting against the majority?'

'Gentlemen, please let the concept of a minority and the majority stay on paper. It will be difficult to survive here if you constantly keep yourselves obsessed with these notions. You must know that the majority is not your enemy. It is another matter that sometimes those in the majority are led astray by certain wrong kinds of emotions. But still, you don't have to leave the right path. If someone hurts you physically, you must retaliate. You might be killed, but don't let this fear make you submissive. We have to die anyway, one day. But there is a difference between dying like a coward and dying fighting. Once you fight back and show your strength, your enemies will think twice before coming to you again. You need to have a lot of courage. Why at all should you leave the field and run away if someone attacked you? This is not the way to live.'

A complete silence followed Akhtar Husain's speech. Those who were listening to him were aware that there was a group of people from the other community whose members performed regular joint physical exercises and drills, received training in the use of weapons and were encouraged to keep weapons with them. Even though their community was not forbidden to do so, Akhtar Husain's visitors felt very nervous to think that they, too, could carry weapons. Akhtar Husain's words were not strange to them. Deep inside them, they too nurtured the same thoughts which never got any chance to be translated into words or actions. Akhtar Husain was speaking their mind.

31

A wild wave of anger had swept East Pakistan. Riots and killings had continued in Calcutta for weeks, and thousands of people crossed over the border and spread to many parts of East Pakistan. They had their own different stories to narrate. There were reports of organized killings from the steel factories of Jamshedpur and the mills in Hatia. At some distance from there, in Ranchi, people received reports of massacres of women and children, and when they gathered courage and reached there, they found nothing left there but blood and ashes. Many people had fled from those places and come to Ben where they were subsisting on leftovers. A new chapter in the partition of India had started. And this time the road to the east was the most heavily travelled. Relief camps were opened in Dhaka, Comilla, Rangpur, Syedpur, Khulna and Chittagong for which donations were being collected all over Pakistan.

Hamid had now taken up a key position in the Adamjee Jute Mills. He regularly wrote letters to his mother and grandmother at Biharsharif, to which both of them responded time and again. Akhtar Husain had never sent him a letter. But Hamid did not wait for any letter from back home, and sent them letters, gifts and money without fail through his acquaintances who often travelled to India. He desperately wanted to see his family but didn't have time for the visa formalities.

One day Chamo arrived in Dhaka. As Badrul Islam considered him the maternal uncle of Hamid, he spoke to him about his intention of marrying off his daughter Nazia to Hamid. Chamo talked to Hamid about it and suggested that he should not miss that opportunity. Badrul Islam was a very influential person, and Hamid had his blessings. The relationship would help him rise further in the future. He did not lack a good match for his daughter, but he liked Hamid as he was impressed by his nobility and goodness. Chamo's utterances made Hamid nervous. It was true that he had gone to Pakistan of his own accord, and had begun to nurture a liking for Nazia in his heart. But he was strongly tethered to his home and family and could never imagine marrying without their consent. In Dhaka, he was surprised to see, people who had married without informing their parents and living happily after having broken all relations with them. He came home and refused the offer, but Chamo extended his stay in Dhaka and continued talking to him about the offer every day.

Hamid quietly listened to him. He didn't understand what to say to Chamo. His refusal did not stop Chamo's gentle persuasion, and he had no one close enough to seek advice. He had Azimuddin there, but the man had severed his relations with Hamid. Shahnaz had run away with the Bengali soldier with whom she had an affair. The soldier was transferred to Rawalpindi, and now Shahnaz was with him there. On reaching Rawalpindi, she had sent her father a copy of their nikah nama (marriage certificate). It had the seal of a mosque in Dhaka and the signature of two witnesses. Azimuddin's house wore a look of mourning, as if grieving for someone dead. All his relatives and friends came to console the family, but Hamid could not muster enough strength to visit him. He appreciated Shahnaz's courage, though he did not dare to congratulate Azimuddin and did not know why he had broken relations with him.

Tired of Chamo's constant inducements, Hamid told him that he could not marry unless he got permission from his father. Chamo promised to get his permission but did not forget to remind Hamid that he had not felt the need to seek anyone's permission when he had fled to East Pakistan for the betterment of his future.

Some time later, Chamo showed Hamid a letter written by Akhtar Husain saying that he would not mind if Hamid took a decision about his future. All that he wanted was that Hamid should be happy and must learn how to live wherever went.

The letter opened the doors of happiness for Hamid. He loved Nazia and could not think of living away from her. And although far away from his home, he was still strongly attached to his parents, and sought their support every now and then. He read a hundred times the letter that his father had written to Chamo.

Badrul Islam had never intended to oblige Hamid morally to marry his daughter without his parents' consent. He wished that the marriage should be solemnized with everybody's agreement and in a happy atmosphere. He did not know what conspired between Chamo and Hamid, but was very glad to learn that Hamid's father had willingly approved the offer. Badrul Islam did not even see the need to read Akhtar Husain's letter. Obviously, he saw no reason to doubt Saminullah. So, on getting the green signal from Saminullah, he and his wife started preparing for their daughter's wedding. He believed that marriage ceremonies ought to be performed in a solemn way. Hamid also had just a few friends, and had none of his relatives there, so the wedding was a quiet affair.

Hamid was still staying in Badrul Islam's bungalow. After marriage he wished to move to his flat, and asked his father-in-law's permission, to which Badrul Islam said nothing. He knew that Hamid was well aware of the fact that the sole inheritor of all his property including the bungalow was none else than Nazia, his only child. Hamid took his silence as his assent and started arranging his move.

Just then, a new problem cropped up before him. The family whom Badrul Islam had allowed to live in the flat as long as it was not taken by Hamid, refused to budge from there. If anyone from that family had been employed in the jute mill, it would have provided them with a justification to stay there. It was not allowed to let out the flat to outsiders. It was allotted to Hamid and he had given its key to them on Badrul Islam's request. The family was allowed to stay there because the manager of the jute mill was Badrul Islam's friend. Hamid felt extremely worried when they outright refused to move. He informed Badrul Islam about the embarrassing situation. They fell into deep thought. Hamid was his son-in-law now, and Badrul Islam wanted him to stay in the bungalow. He had a right on that house. But he was silent because he could not say anything against Hamid's wishes who now desired to live independently.

After ruminating for a while, Badrul Islam told him that he could easily get the flat evacuated with the help of the officials of Adamjee Jute Mills, but he didn't consider it wise to uproot the miserable people. He assured Hamid that he would use his clout within the company to help a member of the family occupying the flat to get a job in the jute mills and have the flat officially allocated to them. He would also get Hamid shifted to a much better flat.

Hamid gazed admiringly at Badrul Islam. He had met a lot of people, befriended many, but he had not seen one like him. He was a sincere and generous person, with no trace of arrogance. He helped people in a way that it appeared as if that was the purpose of his life. He had helped hundreds of refugees. They were given jobs and housing. And he was still focused on helping them. It was a different matter that the refugees were never satisfied with their current situation. They felt that when they had left back their houses and properties and migrated to East Pakistan with empty hands, they had to be warmly welcomed. That was the reason why they did not even feel any sense of gratefulness to the Bengalis of East Pakistan. They also said that whatever they had attained in East Pakistan was solely by dint of their hard work. Hamid could not speak a word after his conversation with Badrul Islam.

A few days later, Badrul Islam informed Hamid that he was promoted to a higher position at the Jute Mills and had been allotted a wonderful flat. He could now move there if he wished. The Bihari migrants had also been assigned the flat they were occupying. When Hamid went to see his flat, he found it fully furnished with all the required items of a household. So, he and Nazia finally shifted to the apartment taking with them a few suitcases, Nazia's sitar and harmonium and a couple of pictures frames containing translations of the poems of Tagore and Nazrul Islam. He had also been assigned a domestic help for housekeeping. Hamid was a very happy man now. He had never imagined he would reach such heights of success. Nazia proved to be an excellent wife. Her attitude towards life was very poetic and artistic, while Hamid was a very straightforward character with very strong views.

A relief committee was established in East Pakistan to assist the victims of riots that broke out in Calcutta, Jamshedpur and Ranchi. Hamid was its active member. The committee collected lakhs of rupees in donations, bought blankets, medicines, clothes, shoes and other necessary articles from that money, and distributed them among the refugees. The biggest challenge was the reshaping of their lives. The country was heading towards a more temperate climate. And everyone was busy in their life. But for the new immigrants their basic struggle for survival had remained an uphill battle. Refugees, however, had been trickling into the country since its formation and settling into their new lives. But the mass exodus of recent riot victims to East Pakistan with their horrid tales of massacre, plunder and rape, made the hair stand on end.

Hamid made a round of the relief camp every day. Others, too, visited it. And he saw them listening to stories that he had already heard from the refugees. In one of his regular visits there, he chanced to meet among the migrants, one of his old friends from Biharsharif. The man had opened a small tea store in Biharsharif after finishing his Bachelor's. Hamid often met him at his shop. He was surprised but happy to see him there. The man told him that he had fled the country with a refugee group in the hope of a better future, because much bitterness and resentment had erupted between Hindus and Muslims in India, and it was no longer safe for Muslims to live there. When Hamid apprised him of the precarious job opportunities in East Pakistan, the man replied that he would at least live safely with his own people there.

Hamid was speechless. He had heard many weird tales from the refugees which he did not want to believe. But he promised his friend that he would present him as a riot-affected refugee from Ranchi. He should not worry about that.

32

Faiyyaz had come back after the completion of the psychiatric treatment he was undergoing in Patna. He kept silent most of the time, and when he opened his mouth, spoke quite sensibly. Akhtar Husain opened a small electrical store for him, and had appointed a trustworthy salesman for the shop who took care not only of the shop but of Faiyyaz as well. Faiyyaz stayed at the shop the entire day. His lunch was brought there. The shop had been making a small but steady profit. Akhtar Husain had granted permission to Hamid to marry Badrul Islam's daughter, but he had not discussed it with anyone at Ben House, not even his wife. In fact, he seldom talked about Hamid. Sajid sat for the competitive exams of the Indian Administrative Service, after his Bachelor's, and was declared successful. After his training programme he was posted in Champaran as a subdivisional officer. Akhtar Husain had married off his daughter Khalida to a medical doctor who was working in Saudi Arabia. Khalida joined her husband after the marriage. Akhtar Husain continued going to the lower court at Biharsharif, though with advancing age, his interest in law practice had waned, but he had no other vocation to spend his time on. He had taken retirement from active politics. Scores of people had now joined politics, and had become well-off. Politics had now become a milch cow that everybody wished to milk. Akhtar Husain was among those who believed in sacrificing their life to serve the cow. They were not acquainted with the craft of milking it for their advantage, so like residues, were left as undesired objects. People, however, had not thrown him away from politics. They often visited him for suggestions and guidance. He was still invited by the District Congress Committee when a national leader or a minister visited the town.

Nisar, the deaf–mute son of Asghar Husain, had acquired a remarkable skill in cloth cutting and sewing. The entire household got their clothes stitched by him. He had customers from outside, too. He had taken the outhouse room and arranged his sewing machine and other necessary articles there, and spent his days doing tailoring work. Bibi Sahiba had grown very old but was still fairly alert. After her Fajr prayer in the morning, she occupied her special low stool in the kitchen and guided the cook. Breakfasts particularly were prepared under her supervision, and she served it to each person in the house. When Waseem and Shamim visited Ben House with their families, everybody in the house sat together for their meals. But for Akhtar Husain—his meals were sent on a silver tray to his bungalow outside. His wife never interfered in the household affairs and helped her mother by working under her direction. Sarwar Husain's wife passed her days and nights alone, in her sequestered living quarters. Whenever she fell into fits, her screams, cries and curses were heard in every corner of Ben House. Everybody would then rush to her room, calm her down and give her what she needed. Sarwar Husain and Asghar Husain sent letters every now and then from Pakistan. Hamid's letters arrived every week. Asghar Husain's children had now grown up. One of his sons had joined a job in a Gulf country, the rest were studying in different colleges in Karachi. He had sent a family photograph, which was framed and hung in the living room. His children did not look like Indians.

After the 1965 Indo–Pak war, postal services between the two countries were suspended for months. The Indian Muslims were caught in a painful dilemma. Almost every Indian Muslim had a few relatives in Pakistan, and there was a regular flow of mails between them. This way they were related to Pakistan, though in an indirect way. But it was exactly for this reason that the Indian Muslims were looked at with suspicion by their Hindu countrymen.

Jawaharlal Nehru, who defended Indian Muslims time and again, had died many years ago. There was no one to counter the allegations that were now levelled against the Muslims. Calling the Indian Muslims 'Pakistanis' was considered the most offending slur cast on them. The Indian Muslims reacted so preposterously to that slur that people laughed at them and the abusers felt emboldened to continue their tirade. When Pakistani agents were arrested in the country and their names, which were not those of Muslims, appeared in the newspapers, the happiness on the face of the Indian Muslims was a spectacle to watch.

One day as Akhtar Husain was about to leave for the civil court, a police jeep, followed by a few more, entered the compound. People in the locality stood aghast when they saw so many cars entering Ben House. A crowd gathered outside the gate to watch what was going to happen. Akhtar Husain had not yet fully understood the situation when a deputy superintendent of police and a magistrate got out of their jeeps and walked towards him. They took him aside and told him that someone had reported to the CBI, the government investigative agency, that a wireless transmitter had been fitted somewhere in the house from where secret intelligence was sent to Pakistan. They were, therefore, sent by the government to investigate the matter, and had come with a search warrant. They asked Akhtar Husain to help them like a responsible citizen to carry a search of the house.

The news astounded Akhtar Husain. No one had till now dared to raise a finger on him or his family. He was incensed to think that the matter had aggravated to such an extreme that a search warrant was served on him. It was true that some members of his family had gone to Pakistan and they had not snapped their relationships with them because mere change of nationalities cannot break generations of relationships. But such a baseless, damaging allegation!

Akhtar Husain stopped going out of the house after that incident. He talked very little when his friends came to see him. Ajodhya Prasad was very angry and pained at the police search on Ben House. He went to Patna and met the chief minister, and complained to him about the high-handedness of the police. The chief minister showed his displeasure at the incident and said that he was helpless as it was not carried out by the state, but the central authority. He also wrote an apology letter to Akhtar Husain.

Akhtar Husain had always heard of frequent occurrences of police searches and house-search warrants. Urdu newspapers across the state were full of provoking and scandalous news and reports. But it was the first time in his life that he had personally experienced that happening to him. He had never realized that the first-hand experience would be so painful. When Sajid heard about the house-search incident, he took a few days leave and came to be with his father. He insisted that his father and others of the household go with him and spend a few days in Champaran. But Akhtar Husain refused. Perhaps he would have listened to him, had it been some other occasion. But Sajid had a government job, and he did not want to put his son in any embarrassing situation for his own sake.

33

Hamid had been watching with worry for a few months the strange restlessness that had spread over entire East Pakistan. The people of East Pakistan were a simple but politically conscious lot. Yet, they remained under-represented in mainstream governance. Although Pakistan had had a few Bengali prime ministers, but since the bureaucracy was dominated by those from the western part of Pakistan, these prime ministers could not effectively implement any policy independently. The country was mostly ruled by the army which had changed many colours up till now. There were very few Bengalis in the Pakistani military, and they were never close to the seat of power. West Pakistanis overshadowed them everywhere. The Bengalis complained that whatever they produced in East Pakistan was taken away by West Pakistan, as a result of which their part of the country always remained in need.

At the Jute Mills, many people took part in political discussions. Hamid never felt interested in those talks. But he fathomed the intent of their discussions. The quintessence of their conversations was that East Pakistan was one of the largest producers of jute and rice in the world, but West Pakistan took away all its earnings from those two products. The military government had put a restriction on the movements of people who openly talked about this inconsistency. But military governments in Pakistan changed hands frequently. Where the earlier military dictatorship had thought it necessary to continue and uphold its legacy, the subsequent leadership proved more sensible. Perhaps it understood the issue of legacy fairly better, and so, it tried to return the rights that belonged to the people. And in this attempt, the matter that had been pushed under the carpet for a long time, emerged suddenly and strongly, like a genie from a bottle. The national election was held which resulted in great polarization of perspectives and beliefs between the east and west of Pakistan. The elections favoured a national government led by East Pakistan. People in West Pakistan saw the daunting but clear prospect of the Bengalis assuming absolute power to form a national government. Politicians in West Pakistan impressed upon the military rulers to desist from making the mistake of handing power over to the Bengalis. They would breed and fuel widespread discontent in the entire country, and take revenge from each and everyone. They also drilled into the Muhajirs' minds that the Bengalis would throw them out of the country one by one, and so asked them to follow what the politicians in West Pakistan instructed them to do. The Muhajirs, therefore, readily agreed to their insinuations. They had been, from the very beginning, not very inclined towards the Bengalis. They had thought that they could get these Bengalis snubbed whenever they wanted. But now they were confronted with the danger of being ruled by them.

Suddenly, the military government of West Pakistan sent columns of military personnel to East Pakistan. Consequently, a most barbarous massacre ensued in the entire region. The Muhajirs in East Pakistan extended their immediate and considerable assistance to the army, and led them to the hideouts of the terrorized Bengalis. The difference and the distinction between the locals and the outsiders raised its vicious sceptre very prominently and bitterly, and thus became extremely obvious to everybody. Factories were closed in all of East Pakistan, and the farmlands wore a deserted look. Work in the government offices, too, would have come to a halt but for the fear of the military boots. The Adamjee Jute Mills remained locked. The number of refugees working there was very high. So, it was the first on the hit list of the locals.

But when the situation worsened intolerably, and dozens of Muhajirs were slaughtered within the compound of Adamjee Mills, Badrul Islam brought Nazia and Hamid, and their two small children, to his bungalow. The same evening, some people set fire to their flat. It was burnt to ashes.

The surrounding areas of the city were the worst affected, where systematic mass killings continued. High-ranking Bihari officials working in the railways, government offices and banks were singled out and slayed. At night, cars or vans would enter their houses and pick them up under the pretext of requiring them for some urgent government duty. They never returned to their homes after that. Occasionally, if some dead body was found, it was quietly buried. The sounds of gunshots and the roar of military vehicles were heard incessantly. Sleep was miles away from Hamid, Nazia and her mother's eyes. The main gate of Badrul Islam's house was kept locked. A security guard stood alert with his gun loaded.

Badrul Islam called Hamid in his study and said, 'Do you see Hamid what's happening here? I don't know what has suddenly gone wrong. How quiet this place used to be? Whose malignant eyes have darted fire on our nation?'

"Uncle, I'm sorry if I cause you any trouble. They know here that I am a Bihari.' Hamid's voice grew hoarse from a deepening sense of guilt.

'What are you talking, my son? You know, I've never discriminated between a Bihari and a Bengali. Though I know it very well that the Biharis have never considered me as one of their own, I have, nevertheless, always helped them, and they take me as their enemy.' There was pain in Badrul Islam's voice. Hamid had always noticed that agony ringing in his voice.

'You know, Hamid, I have been blacklisted by the army. One of my Punjabi friends, who is a high officer in the army, has told me that on the phone.'

'How can that be true, Uncle? You have done so much for the Muhajirs that their generations after generation should be grateful to you. Can I know what made them blacklist you?'

'Look, I have never been a member of the Awami League. But the truth is that I have always favoured what is right. And there is no doubt that I have voted for the Awami League in the elections. In fact, I have no grudge against any community, though I am against the policies of West Pakistan which has always exploited East Pakistan. I can only pray for those who are mistakenly holding me responsible for siding with the wrong and unjust people.'

Hamid heard him wordlessly. He had rarely seen Badrul Islam in such an intensely emotional state. But what he appreciated in him was that he had still not left his perfectly sensible way of thinking.

'Listen, my son! There's not much time left now. They may arrest me any time. So, I am going underground, and I am going to take my wife also with me, because they will not leave her in my absence. I'd like you to go under the protection of the army, for you are also not very safe here. And now, you have to think where to leave Nazia.'

Nazia, who had been listening to this from a corner, said she would dutifully follow Hamid wherever he would go.

'My dear daughter, this is exactly what I expected from you. Now both of you do as I tell you. Take your children with you and go to the barracks tonight. Nazia, you must forget that you are Bengali. We will depart to Comilla two hours from now. A car is coming to pick us.'

Badrul Islam's wife also joined them. There were tears in everyone's eyes. No one fathomed how and why they were to bid farewell to each other. The darkness of the night was lengthening every moment. And the frantic barking of dogs, the groaning of the bullets and the agonizing screams of the wounded had made the night into a symbol of evil and malevolence. Just then, they heard the sound of cars entering their compound.

'It's strange! They have come too early,' Badrul Islam said as he looked at his watch.

Within seconds, an army officer with a few soldiers entered the study. He had held a cocked pistol in his hand.

'Mr Badrul Islam, you are under arrest. Don't try to budge from your place.'

They were Pakistani soldiers. Everyone was struck dumb with horror. All their plans had fallen flat. The officer pressed the pistol to Badrul Islam's back and said, 'You are arrested for your involvement in anti-national activities.'

Hamid stood up and said, 'Captain, I am a Bihari, whom you consider as a patriot. Mr Badrul Islam has given me shelter. If you consider him anti-national, then we all are anti-nationals. None of us can escape this allegation.'

'Listen mister, we haven't come here to listen to your speech. We've been ordered to arrest him, and that's what we're doing.'

Badrul Islam's wife spoke out when she saw they were taking him away, 'Please take me, too, along with him. I've also participated with him if he was involved in anti-national activities.'

The officer thought for a while and asked both of them to sit in the vehicle. 'Officer, please take Hamid and his wife and children to the barracks. They are not safe here,' Badrul Islam pleaded.

'You don't have to worry about them. They are fine here. Nobody would dare to come here,' replied the officer sharply, and the cars sped out of the house.

Nazia started weeping inconsolably as soon as they left. Hamid stood aghast. The horror of the reality had silenced him. After some time, when his senses were restored, he realized that Badrul Islam had left him with a great responsibility. He had to protect Nazia at all cost. He comforted her, and planned to meet the army officer in the morning. There was no question of sleeping that night. At about three o'clock in the morning, an armoured vehicle entered the bungalow. Hamid and Nazia were standing in the hallway. Two young men got out of the car.

'Where is Mr Badrul Islam?'

'The soldiers took him and his wife away.'

One of the men talked to his partner in Bengali, 'This man appears to be a Bihari. He must have done some mischief. Why not take him with us? And this dame is a beautiful bird!'

Hamid understood Bangla well, but could not speak it fluently. So, he kept quiet. But Nazia confronted the two Bengalis and told them that Hamid was not a Bihari. He was her husband and a Bengali. She pleaded them not to paint the struggle as that between the Bengalis and Biharis. It was a battle based on oppression and it should be taken like that.

They started to make fun of her outburst, and told her, 'You also come with us. Mukti Bahini people need young girls like you. You'll be of much use to us.'

Hamid, Nazia and their children were asked to sit in the vehicle, taking nothing with them but the clothes that they were wearing. The car drove off, and rolled past countless lanes and streets until it stopped when the brightness of the day had spread its wings all around.

34

It was a huge enclosure, a low-roofed cowshed—like the one where zamindars and cultivators kept their cows, bulls and buffaloes. There were hundreds of them, not animals, but men, women and children. They were all tied up in the shed, like animals. The men were clad in filthy clothes, their beards had grown shaggy and their hair messy and matted. The women looked frail and withered, their clothes ripped and torn and their faces were filled with fear and horror. The young girls were tied up separately. Hamid at first thought it was a relief camp. But then immediately everything became clear to him. They were all Biharis there. Hamid's children were left with him, and Nazia was tied separately with the girls. Nazia cried and begged a thousand times, cried for mercy in the name of Bangladesh and Bengali. But their captors' hearts did not melt. All the prisoners were asked to shout 'Jai Bangladesh'.

The hapless hostages shouted with great enthusiasm, and kept chanting until their voices choked. The people who had brought them there laughed at their impuissance with great satisfaction.

They were kept hungry all day, and were given half-boiled rice and curd just before the evening fell. They were hungry since God knows when, so when they saw food before them, they devoured it like animals. And within minutes the meal was over. Hamid could not eat anything. However, he could not see his children starving, so he gave them a couple of tablespoons of rice in a pan. The delicate children, who had up until now all the blessings of the world, were so suddenly longing for a morsel of food. Their dogs ate better food than that they were being given now.

After midnight ten people entered the cowshed. They were dressed in lungis and vests, with gamchas tied to their waists and guns in their hands. They then made the prisoners shout 'Jai Bangla', and took away twenty or twenty-five of them. A few minutes later, the rest of the prisoners in the cowshed heard the trembling screams of 'Jai Bangla' coming from the other side of the wall, and just after that they heard as many gunshots as the prisoners that were taken away. An awful stillness swept over the place. The distraught captives were so shattered and fatigued that they began to doze off. The wives and kids of the men who were taken away cried their hearts out. Tears also came to Hamid's eyes, despite his efforts to control them. Suddenly, at that moment in time, Hamid's eyes fell on Azimuddin. He was in a very bad shape. As soon as he saw Hamid, he rushed to him, hugged him and started crying.

He burst out between sobs, 'Hamid Mian, everything is over. Nothing is left. They killed my son. My house and the press were ransacked and then set on fire. Your aunt died of deep anguish and trauma. I am as good as dead. I don't know how long I am going to live to suffer. I beg these people every day to shoot me, but these scoundrels don't listen to me.'

'Where do they take the prisoners?'

'This is the way they have been slaughtering the Biharis. They have kept them like animals. Every day, ten or fifteen of them enter this place, like butchers choose some people, carry them out and shoot them.'

'Oh, that's the story!'

Hamid thought that if he, too, lost his senses like everyone else on that day, every waking moment of his life would be a torture. Why should one die pleading and cursing if one were fated to die there? He strengthened himself and asked everyone to be calm. He explained to them that when they die, they should die like Muslims. Death was a reality, after all. They could not avoid it by crying and wailing, if they were destined to die there. His speech solaced the people in their misfortune. Hamid still remembered the lesson taught by Akhtar Husain that death should never be accepted with cowardice. One should fight it with courage and strength. Death was not stronger than life. And when death overpowered life, it was not actually a victory for death, it was merely the fulfilment of the duty which death had to perform.

The same scenario unfolded every night. Those clad in lungis and vests would pick and choose from among the captives in the cowshed, who were then were taken away, forced to chant the selfsame slogan and then shot. In the daytime, some people would come and take away some of the young women and girls. And in return, they would give the soldiers weapons, clothes and other supplies. Hamid could anyhow sneak a quick look every day to see the girls going, and thanked God for not finding Nazia among them. But he knew that his hopes were not going to last long.

It was a bizarre sight to see the executioners entering the cowshed every night, and selecting those that they decided to shoot. All the captives would be asked to stand in a queue. At that time, shades of death danced before everyone's eyes. They would select them after close scrutiny and then take them away. Perhaps they too didn't know why they did that. When their eyes fell on someone, the person would begin to count his last breaths then and there. But sometimes they would leave that man and pick out the other.

One night when the Bengali killers left after their night work, some people entered the cowshed. They had the same appearance—lungis, vests, gamchas and guns. They started to ask the names of the Bihari captives one by one, till they reached Hamid. They were startled when Hamid told them his name. They took him apart, and asked him to bring his children also there. The poor children could not even walk properly. Hamid realized that his last moments were approaching. He held his children's hands firmly. One of the incomers spoke to him, 'Go and get your wife out from the women's area.'

Hamid was taken into the women's enclosure. He was appalled to see the nightmarish scene there. Very few women were left there now. Most of the young women and girls had been taken away. The rest were waiting and were in an appalling condition. He recognized Nazia at a glance. Only Hamid's eyes could identify her, for Nazia had not remained the same. She was all skin and bones. Her clothes were soiled and tattered, her hair was dry and tangled and her eyes lifeless and sunken in dark sockets. Nazia was staring vacantly into the void. Hamid called out to her softly, but she did not respond. She did not even turn her head and kept her eyes fixed on one spot. Hamid realized that she might have lost her senses. But time was not permitting him to think long. He grabbed Nazia's hand and brought her out. He had at least one consolation in his heart that they had lived together, and were now all going to die together. When they started walking out of the cowshed, led by their new captors, everyone cried badly. Hamid also could not stop his tears. They came out in the open, weeping, leaving the others in the same state. The lungi-clad people walked ahead and Hamid and his family followed them on the sidewalks of a dark, seemingly unending street. One of the men was leading with a flashlight in his hand. Hamid had clasped Nazia's hand. And she walked with him like a lifeless doll. Their one son was holding Hamid's other hand, while the other held his brother's hand. The children's courage and calm were exemplary. Somewhere along the way they heard shouting of slogans and clamorous cries. Heavy vehicles roared past them and then silence overwhelmed the street.

They kept walking till they entered a large open maidan where a truck was parked at the corner with three armed men sitting in the front seats. They asked Hamid to climb into the back of the truck. Hamid helped Nazia get in first, then lifted his children into the truck, and finally clambered himself onto it. The lungi-clad men, too, jumped in. The truck began to move when everybody got in. As the truck gathered speed, Nazia, quite unexpectedly, broke into disjointed speech, and that too in Urdu. Everyone in the truck was talking in Bangla. Hamid made several attempts to silence Nazia, but did not succeed. Everyone was quietly listening to her. Nazia talked about politics, about the economy, about the subtleties of music, told stories of her childhood and continued her garbled discourse. The two children were asleep on the floor of the truck. Hamid was having a difficult time listening to Nazia's ill-timed outburst and wished she would speak in Bengali. He had always considered Bengali as a very sweet language, though he himself was not very fluent in it. When he used to be in a romantic mood, he would ask Nazia to sing Bangla songs. And as she sang, he lost his sense of time and place. He felt as if the earth, the sky, the entire universe was listening to her song in rapt ecstasy. Her voice was full of magic. Adorned in Bangla language, the profundity of her voice gave an ethereal experience. Nazia never refused Hamid's request for a song. Hamid recalled that and requested Nazia to sing. She quietly looked at him with blank eyes, and he continued with his request. Nazia broke down and wept copiously, inconsolably. Taking Hamid in her embrace, she was crying so hysterically that everybody in the truck fell into a hushed silence. And as she wept, she sang a mournful romantic song, punctuated by convulsive sobbing. She continued to sing, one song after another, for she remembered so many of them. The truck stopped with a lurch, but Nazia carried on, as if she was not aware of her surroundings, absorbed in her world of melody. The people sitting in the passenger seat ordered them to get down. Hamid helped his children alight from the truck, and then he and Nazia dismounted it. Nazia was still singing, which stopped when one of the lungi-clad men accompanying them yelled at her to shut up. She fell silent for a while and then started to cry so desperately that nobody dared to calm her down. The truck had halted very close to a jeep. They were directed to get into the jeep fast.

Fed up with the prolonged silence, Hamid could not hold himself anymore, and asked, 'Where are you taking us, gentlemen?'

'Keep moving with us, quietly. We can't tell you anything.'
He was answered tersely.

Hamid and Nazia boarded the jeep with their children.
Exhausted from crying, Nazia ultimately stopped, and fell
into a deep sleep. The vehicle kept running on desolate, unlit
streets and rough, uneven roads. It was stopped at many
places, and moved on after the Bengalis sitting inside it said
something in their language to the checkpoint officer. At a
few places, some Bengalis dressed in civilian clothes stopped
the jeep, flashed their torches and looked inside, and then
allowed them to proceed.

The driver willingly pulled over the jeep at an isolated
place and spoke to Hamid: 'Our next stop will be at a
Pakistani checkpoint. You have to talk to the officer in Urdu
and tell him that you are crossing the border at the order of
the governor of the province on a secret visit.'

When the other Bengali fellow noticed Hamid looking
quizzically at him, he advised him, 'You don't need to
think. Just do as you are told, otherwise you know what the
consequences are going to be.'

When they stopped at the final checkpoint, Hamid
stepped out and spoke to the officer telling him he was a
Pakistani government emissary. The officers signalled for the
vehicle to move on, clearing the way.

It was now daybreak, and the bright morning light
was spreading all over the place. The jeep travelled down
unknown paths for a few hours, and finally stopped in front
of a thatched hut. As the vehicle came to a halt, Chamo
emerged from the hut and ran towards it. Seeing Chamo,
Hamid jumped down, and breaking all barriers of patience
clung to him, weeping copiously. Nazia also got down from

the jeep with her sons, casting a vacant look around her, watching them crying. Chamo consoled Hamid, and walked towards her. He embraced her with affection while she said nothing and stood like a lifeless object. Chamo wept to see her so distraught, but her eyes were tearless and frozen. The people who had brought them there, stood a little away from their jeep, smoking bidis, waiting for Chamo to be free of the formalities. They came to him when he turned his attention towards them.

One of them said to Chamo, 'Look master, we have risked our lives to save them and bring them here. Please permit us to leave quickly now.'

'Yes, my brothers. I'm so thankful to you. Please keep this money with you. You will get the rest on reaching Dhaka. You don't need to come here for that now.'

Chamo pulled a bundle of banknotes from his pocket and handed it over to them. One of them tried to say something, but the other guy stopped him, and they hurriedly climbed into the jeep and sped away. Chamo brought Hamid, Nazia and the children into the hut. A basket filled with fruit was placed before them. Two large steel tiffin carriers were opened by unlocking a small catch on either side of the handles. Every box had food in them—parathas, chicken, fish, curry and sweets. Chamo sat down with them to a full meal. The children fell ravenously on the food. Hamid's eyes watered to see delicious cuisine after days of near starvation. Nazia stared blankly at the food in front of her for some time, and then the way she devoured whatever was served in her plate was a painful spectacle. Hamid could only take a few morsels and then pulled his hands back. A bed of straws was laid out on the floor of the hut, and it was covered with a large cotton carpet.

Nazia and the children soon fell fast asleep on it. Hamid was not feeling sleepy. He wanted to recount to Chamo all that had happened to them, but Chamo said that he would talk to him later about everything, and asked him to take some rest.

A few of Chamo's men stood at a respectful distance from them. The afternoon sun was sliding towards the western horizon. Chamo took his men with him and walked out of the hut. The inhabitants of the hut slept as long as they could and when they woke up it was morning again, and sunlight was filtering down through vents in the thatched roof. Hamid got up with a start. At that moment, Chamo entered the hut smiling.

'You know, how long you all have been sleeping?'

'Perhaps twenty hours, Chamo Mamu,' said Hamid smiling.

'Yes, my dear. I waited for you to get up for dinner, but you were sleeping so soundly that I didn't want to wake you up. Now, get ready. Quick. A car is going to arrive shortly, and then we will move from here.'

Hamid got Nazia and the children ready in no time. Nazia was still not in her normal state. No sooner had they primed themselves for the journey than one of Chamo's men brought choorha (flattened dry rice flakes), jaggery and tea for them. They partook of a typical Bengali breakfast. An armoured van arrived just then. Chamo asked all of them to get into it, after which the van's window blinds were lowered. Nazia said nothing along the journey. Hamid was very worried about Nazia's mental health. He felt there was no quick cure for her, especially because her loss was immense, and her wounds were fresh. She had seen the worst of life so recently, at such a young age. It was obvious to him that she needed time and he had to bear with her through patience and hope.

35

They heard the hustle and bustle of the day sitting inside the van. The children, once or twice, tried to peek out from the blinds, but Hamid had asked them strictly not to do so. After an almost entire day's journey when the van stopped, the evening was just around the corner.

Chamo got down first, and then asked them to come out.

'We have arrived home. Thanks to God. Get down, all of you.'

When Hamid and Nazia disembarked from the van with their children, they found themselves standing on the ground floor of Chamo's Calcutta apartment. Chamo's wife came running down the stairs on hearing the vehicle's sound. With shock and worry in her eyes, Nazia looked at her aunt and on recognizing her fell into her embrace, breaking down and sobbing like a child. When they all climbed up to the flat, Nazia seemed somewhat quietened. Hamid heaved a sigh of relief. He was feeling as if they had been given a new lease of life. Their book of life had almost closed, all roads of hope had reached the end, and just then the book again opened itself on a new chapter of life. But this tormenting gap between hopelessness and hope had left a disastrous impact on Nazia's mind. *She was cheered up somewhat, for the present, but what would happen after they left the place?*

'All of you are going to stay her for some time. The situation is very volatile. Calcutta is the only place in the entire country where refugees from East Pakistan can find some security. Travelling is not safe, however. We'll put Nazia under the care of a counselling psychologist. If she stays here for some days, she might return to her normal self.'

Chamo's advice was very appropriate. He took Nazia and Hamid to a psychiatrist who checked her thoroughly and said that severe emotional trauma and horrible incidents and scenes had affected her mind very badly. She utterly needed a peaceful, homely atmosphere, otherwise she was in danger of losing her sanity.

Hamid was disturbed when he heard that, but Chamo asked him not to worry and stay with him without any second thought. Hamid had no other option, though he did not want to give Chamo any further trouble. He was already indebted to him for so many things.

Hamid had spent a very comfortable life in Dhaka. But he had lost everything now. He wished to return to Biharsharif—to his parents' house, his own home, which was the only ray of hope for him. But then again, he had not lost sight of the fact that he was now a stranger in India. He had no future there. Like many others, he could not hide himself in the milling crowd for fear that someone or the other might recognize him and report to the authorities. And then all would end for him. He did not want to stay for a minute in Calcutta. Confusion, helplessness and fear overpowered his senses. He wanted to go to Biharsharif, but he had no money. After giving much thought to his dilemma, he decided to seek Chamo's advice.

After dinner, one night, he started a conversation with Chamo, 'Chamo Mamu, you have already helped me a lot. It's only because of you that we have bounced back to life. But I do not want to trouble you more. I want to go to Biharsharif. I'd like to meet my parents and see if I could scratch out a new future for us.'

Chamo heard him patiently, and said quietly, 'Hamid, I have done no favour to you. Who else could help you in need except your own near and dear ones? You call me Mamu, and so as your uncle I have my duties. And Nazia is like my own daughter. I won't stop you from going to Biharsharif. You must go there, but remember that the situation is very bad. The police have been carrying out raids on houses everywhere in the country, and arresting hidden Biharis.'

Hamid grew pallid on hearing this. Chamo continued, 'And you know, who were the informants who talked about their hideouts? They were their own relatives who informed the police about them. They feared that the refugee relatives of theirs would stay back and ask for their shares in the properties, houses and farms. I went to Bihar last month, and I saw the commotion and confusion that had broken out there. Oh, what a doomsday I saw with my own eyes! The Biharis are changing their sanctuaries by the hour. No one is helping them.'

Distressed by the revelations, Hamid shuddered and said, 'For what sins of theirs are they being punished like that, Mamu? God only knows that.'

'Now the only choice left for them is to go to Pakistan. They can't go to East Pakistan because it has become

Bangladesh now—a new independent country. They can't stay in India. But the route to Pakistan is closed. They can't go there from here. A major problem will arise if there is a war between India and Pakistan. And the danger is imminent. Tension between these two countries has been building up about the refugees from East Pakistan.'

Chamo was very much aware about the situations unfolding in the subcontinent. But his information had put a roadblock before Hamid. He bent his head and thought for a while.

'Mamu, what do you suggest? Should I go to Biharsharif alone, and take note of the situation there? Any decision can be taken after that.'

'I have, anyway, informed your father about your arrival. I won't stop you, if you want to go. I'll get your travel ticket reserved.'

There was hardly any arrangement that Hamid had to make for the travel. He was going to travel all by himself, and he had just some clothes to take with him. Chamo had bought him two pairs of shirts and pants from the shop which sold cheap European clothes. He had also purchased a few clothes for Nazia and the children. Nazia was recovering from her traumatized condition, and she had started taking part in conversations to some extent. Her aunt was always available for support and acted as good substitute for her father, since she was Badrul Islam's own sister. In two weeks, she had taken Nazia to almost all the tourist sites in Calcutta. But Nazia was still not completely normal. When Hamid informed her about his plan to travel to Biharsharif, she heard him but said nothing. After a few days, Chamo told him that the train reservation was confirmed. The day Hamid had to travel, he asked Nazia to take care of herself and the children. His train was to leave at nine o'clock that night. Chamo explained to him that the train would reach Bakhtiarpur the next morning, from where Hamid had to take a bus to Biharsharif. They reached the Calcutta railway station much before the departure of the train. Chamo handed the ticket over to Hamid, and pushed some money in his pocket. He advised him to take great care of himself, and keep very alert so as not to let anyone doubt him, and also asked him to return soon.

When the train started moving Hamid requested Chamo to take care of Nazia and the children, in response to which Chamo asked him not to worry about them at all.

As the train gathered speed, Hamid heard people talking about the current situation, and he realized that there was really much anger and resentment in people over the presence of refugees from East Pakistan. India's economy was badly affected by their mass arrival. The Indian government had introduced refugee taxes on many essential items. Though, in some quarters there was genuine sympathy for the Bengali refugees. But nobody had any place in their hearts for the Biharis who had returned from East Pakistan. They considered them as spies of the Pakistani government due to whose cruelty and barbarity about a crore people had to leave their country, depriving them of their homes and jobs.

The travellers spoke of great horrors terrifying Hamid. He bought a Hindi newspaper at the Burdwan railway station and sat down on his seat holding the newspaper over his face. The newspaper revealed to him that the war between India and Pakistan was about to happen. The blame game between the two countries had almost become endemic. India had loudly asked the whole world to help solve the problem of one crore refugees who had arrived on its land from Pakistan. In the border areas between India and East Pakistan, a government was declared with the name of Bangladesh. The names of its administrative officers and chargé d'affaires were displayed in the newspaper. As the night wore on, Hamid lay down on his berth but could not sleep. He was thinking about the perplexing situation in which he had found himself trapped. It all looked like a Greek drama to him. God first gave him everything one could wish for in life, and the drop scene was that the same God had taken away from him whatever he was blessed with, leaving him with nothing to survive on. He was, however, grateful to God that his life and the lives of his wife and children were saved, and if ever fate smiled on them, he could bring the life of his family back on track. He thanked God even more when he realized that so many people had lost their lives in East Pakistan that it was impossible to keep count. And many of those who were saved had gone from riches to rags in just a few years. Those who had been living safely inside the four walls of their comfortable houses till yesterday, were today thrown on the open roads, facing the vagaries of the cruel weather. Scores of young women and girls were kidnapped. There was no ledger, no record whatsoever of the terrible destruction that had befallen the land.

36

When the train arrived at the Bakhtiarpur junction, Hamid got off and boarded a waiting taxi whose driver was hollering at the top of his voice, 'Biharsharif, Biharsharif!'

When the taxi did not move for a few minutes, Hamid asked the driver to confirm, 'Arey, Bhai! Are you going to Biharsharif?'

'Yes, Sir, to Biharsharif.' The driver stared at him and again started hollering for passengers.

Hamid realized that it was a shared taxi, and sat relaxed in his seat.

In about half hour, the taxi was filled with passengers. As it pulled away, the passengers fell into conversation on the rising costs of potatoes and onions, and on the lack of cold storage facilities in the state. Hamid was relieved that they were not talking about regional politics as in the train journey. The taxi reached Biharsharif in half an hour. He took a rickshaw to Ben House from the taxi stand. Until now he had been travelling like a lifeless statue. But as soon as he sat on the rickshaw, it looked as if life had returned to him.

He felt a wave of apprehension and his heartbeat accelerated thinking about the fact that he would be meeting his relatives after a long absence. He had run away from there against their wishes, without informing anybody, and now he was returning in the same condition in which he had left, or even worse than before. Hamid was back after burying all those hopes and aspirations that he had carried away with himself. He had no future now. He was able to return with the financial help of a servant of Ben House, a person who was reared and brought up there.

Lost in reverie, Hamid could not fathom what routes the rickshaw plied through, what familiar paths welcomed him, till he reached Ben House. He had given the driver a very clear direction to his house. The rickshaw stopped in front of Akhtar Husain's bungalow. Hamid paid the fare, got down and climbing the steps that led up to the bungalow, entered his father's room. Akhtar Husain was lying sprawled in bed, reading a book. When he heard footsteps, he looked up to see Hamid. Father and son embraced each other, crying like children.

'My stupid son! Don't . . . don't cry like that. Chamo kept me informed about your well-being. Thank God, you are safe!'

Hamid's tears dried up after quite some time. Akhtar Husain took his son to the inner mansion, the women's quarter. Hamid's mother clutched him fondly and broke into heaving sobs. His sister was at her in-law's. Faiyyaz was at his tailoring shop, and Sajid was away on his posting. Bibi Sahiba had grown very old and mentally ill. She called Hamid near her when she saw him and said,

'Have you come from Pakistan?'

'Yes, Grandma . . . yes . . .'

'Haven't you brought your uncle with you?'

'Grandma, he is in West Pakistan, and I'm coming from East Pakistan.'

'How many Pakistans are there, my son?'

Everyone was silent. Hamid had no answer to her question. Bibi Sahiba too fell quiet and looked the other way. His mother told him later that Sarwar Husain had died in Karachi. The news of his death was kept secret from Bibi Sahiba, but one day when she cried frantically remembering him, everybody realized that she was somehow aware of the truth. The grief drove her insane. Sometimes, she would curse Pakistan, yet sometimes she prayed well for the country. It appeared as if the creation of Pakistan had completely broken her. She adored Sarwar Husain. Perhaps because he was her first child. Even during the days when she was displeased with him, she never allowed anyone to speak anything against him, and always gave him her blessings. After his death, the thought of Pakistan dominated her mind. The moment she swore vengeance on Pakistan, the thought of her son buried in its soil struck her mind, and then she began to pray for the country. Hatred and affection had become fairly ambivalent feelings in her mind. She tried to take part in the household chores as usual, but the moment she recalled Sarwar Husain's death, she would slump down in her chair, motionless. At times, it seemed as if she had not been able to accept that her son was dead. She would go on blessing him, and asked every visitor about his well-being. People at the house were very worried about her. Waseem and Shamim tried many times to take her with them, but she still had enough sense to tell them that she did not want to go anywhere because her husband had left her at Ben House, and what would she tell him if his soul came looking for her and did not find her there.

It was not the same house that Hamid had left. The vagaries of time had changed it drastically. Akhtar Husain had confined himself within the four walls of his house. He spent his time in prayers and reading books. Most of his friends had grown old, too, and had gone to live with their children. Those who were at Biharsharif could scarcely come out of their houses. Only Ajodhya Prasad and a few of his other friends came to him occasionally in the evening, and the customary evening meeting came to life. But even those meetings were now devoid of their earlier fire and fever. A heavy silence lingered in the air there. A day after Hamid's arrival, Ajodhya Prasad came to Ben House, and Akhtar Husain sent for Hamid to come and meet him. Ajodhya Prasad was like a father to Hamid. Even then he was hesitant to meet him, considering the circumstances under which he had come back to the town, but he could not disobey his father. Ajodhya Prasad hugged him, and asked him at length about the plight of the Biharis in East Pakistan. He then secretly queried,

'Hamid, I heard you've married a Bengali woman. Is that true?'

Hamid was surprised at this unexpected query. Nobody had yet asked him anything about his marriage. He stole a look at his father and answered softly, lowering his gaze, 'Yes, and I have two children from her.'

'Where are they now?'

'I have left them in Calcutta with one of their relatives.'

'I've also heard that the Bengali wives and Bengali husbands have left their Bihari spouses. Not only that, they have handed them over to the Mukti Bahini people. You must be aware of that.'

'No, I don't know much about that. But I know that my wife's parents were captured by the Pakistani forces only because they were Bengalis. My wife, nevertheless, has always been by my side in my good days and bad ones, and she is still very faithful to me.'

'That's strange! You are the first man from whom I'm hearing that. Otherwise, reports contrary to that have been reaching us here.'

'We have suffered whatever you have heard. But the bare truth is that my wife was there with me at the place where we were to be slaughtered, and she had lost her senses witnessing the cruelty and tyranny that was unleashed there.'

'My son, then you should have brought her here. We would like to see that great woman. The woman who left her parents, her family, her house, and her country for her husband cannot be an ordinary woman.'

Hamid gave no answer, and Akhtar Husain looked at his son but said nothing.

At night, Akhtar Husain called Hamid to him after dinner and said, 'I have no objection to your marrying a Bengali girl. That is your own problem. But the truth is that you all are foreigners here, not Indians. So, you can't stay here officially forever, as long as India does not accept it. And in the present circumstances, it is far from possible. At present, your situation is not very different from the one crore refugees who have taken asylum in India. The only difference is that the Indian government has extended a warm welcome to them, and is looking for fugitives like you in every nook and corner of the country.'

Akhtar Husain's speech was getting longer. Hamid failed to read his mind. He stared at him blankly when he stopped for breath.

'And my son, don't take it otherwise. Ajodhya Babu is an affectionate man. I respect his feelings and lovingness towards us, but never bring your wife and children here. The people here still remember what happened to Biharis in East Pakistan and will never accept your wife.'

Akhtar Husain gave him a detailed account of the police raid on Ben House, and said that he was so disgusted with that incident that he had stopped going out anywhere.

Hamid listened to him patiently. He had no knowledge about the police raid. He saw truth in his father's fears. He pondered for some time, and reached the conclusion that his long stay there might put them in danger. If, by any chance, the police and the state investigative agency came to learn about his presence, that would put the entire household in risk. He asked his father for advice.

Akhtar Husain told him, 'You are a Pakistani, and so you should go to Pakistan. That is the only country that can accept you now. Many Biharis came here and after taking note of the worsening situation returned to Pakistan. It was easy to cross over to Pakistan illegally, in the beginning. But that time has gone now. Biharis can come from East Pakistan but they can't go there. And on the borders between India and Pakistan the armies of both the countries are standing alert. So, the only hope for you is to fly to West Pakistan, which is now Pakistan, from Nepal.'

'But it needs a lot money, Father.'

Akhtar Husain thought for a while, and then said, 'Look, my son! I don't have any money with me, save some property. I can sell that. But if I do it now, people will become suspicious. They would infer that I am doing that to help someone near to me. And people close to me know you are here. I must tell you what has happened to the Biharis who had returned from Bangladesh in the hope of getting money from their properties. Their own relatives reported to the police against them and got them caught. Even now hundreds of them are in jail. No one knows what is going to happen to them.'

Akhtar Husain had validated whatever Chamo had told Hamid.

'What should I do, Father? I don't have a single penny with me now. I have lost whatever I earned there.'

'You have married the girl who is closely related to Chamo's wife, isn't that true? They are very rich and resourceful people. I've come to know that this fellow Chamo has also become a very rich man, now.'

He spoke in such a belittling tone about Chamo that it pained Hamid. He replied to his father, 'They were really very wealthy and influential people. Whatever I achieved in East Pakistan was completely because of their help and generosity. All is lost now. Nothing is left with me. The Pakistan Army took away my parents-in-law. And my wife was blacklisted as a Bihari in the eyes of the Bengalis only because she remained with me. It was Chamo Mamu who again helped me, which gave us a new lease of life. He paid a lot of money to the Bengalis to get us back, and he hasn't told me how much he has paid them. I can't now ask him to spend more on me.'

'But, Hamid, Azimuddin wrote to me that . . .'

Hamid cut his father short and said, 'Azimuddin Uncle lied to you. It was he who wanted a live-in son-in-law. He had amassed a large fortune and wanted me to marry his daughter against her wishes. When he became unsuccessful in that, he complained to you against me. After my marriage, I left my in-laws' luxurious bungalow to live in my flat, from where I moved only after the situation worsened there, and it was burned the same day.'

He could have talked more about Azimuddin's conduct, but he suddenly realized that he might have been killed by now. He had last seen him in the cowshed. So, he stopped there, and looked at his father.

'Alright, let's not talk about it anymore. At the moment, there are urgent matters to think about. Sajid is in Patna nowadays. He will definitely come here once he learns about you. Let's see if he can help you out.'

Hamid was quite disappointed with his father's uncooperative attitude.

Akhtar Husain had informed Sajid about Hamid's arrival. On the third day, Sajid came to meet him with tears in his eyes. Hamid had left him when he was still young, and now he had become a responsible government officer.

Sajid said to him, 'You must know, Bhaiya, if the government comes to know that I've met you, my job will be in danger. The cases belonging to the returning Biharis had been given to the central investigative agency to probe. The government keeps a vigilant watch on the Muslim officers. I am sorry that even against my best wishes, I cannot invite you to Patna. Where are Bhabhi and the children?'

'They are all in Calcutta right now. I came to see you all, and thank God I have met everybody here.'

'What's your plan now, Bhaiya?'

'What else could it be? I am a Pakistani citizen, and I have to go there.'

'But how can you go to Pakistan?'

'Perhaps, I have to go there through Nepal. Many people have taken that route to go to Pakistan.'

'But many people have been arrested, too, in trying to do that. After all, you will put yourself at risk when you travel to Nepal from here.'

Hamid had no answer. His hopes further dimmed after his conversation with his brother. He did not gather enough courage to ask Sajid for any financial help. Akhtar Husain, however, asked Sajid when they were alone to send Hamid some money. Sajid promised his father he would do that. Sajid left the next day, and on the third day of his departure sent a sealed envelope to Hamid through his stenographer. The envelope contained ten 100-rupee notes. Hamid thought for a while and put the envelope in his pocket. Undoubtedly this amount was not enough for him to even travel to Nepal.

37

The refugee crisis continued unabated. To cover refugee costs even poor Indians were taxed. Pressure was mounting on the Indian government from inside the country to recognize Bangladesh as a separate independent state, and send it military aid. Everyone knew that one day India had to recognize Bangladesh. But when?

Suddenly one day, unspecified Pakistani air force jets were reported to have launched aerial attacks on targets in Agra, Delhi and Jalandhar. In retaliation, the Indian government immediately recognized Bangladesh, and sent its troops to support it.

Lakhs of Biharis were still trapped in Bangladesh for whom the earth there was unwelcome and hard, and the sky too far away to listen to their lamentations. Among the Indian soldiers sent to Bangladesh, there were some Biharis whose one or two relatives or acquaintances had already migrated to that country. India had helped the Mukti Bahini forces a lot, and now its army had formally reached there to assist them. The independence of Bangladesh clearly implied that the Bihari population was certainly going to be exterminated.

The war started as Hamid planned to go to Calcutta. Akhtar Husain asked him to not leave Biharsharif at that moment. But he still wanted to plan his departure. The outbreak of war increased his restlessness. He spent sleepless nights. The Pakistani jets tried to drop bombs on Calcutta. A dusk-to-dawn blackout was ordered there. In the meantime, Hamid received a letter from Chamo asking him to postpone his journey to Calcutta for some days, and that his wife and children were doing fine. The letter relieved Hamid's worries.

It was winter in Biharsharif. Every evening Akhtar Husain would shut himself up in his room, oblivious of whatever transpired outside.

Despite Akhtar Husain's forbiddance, people in the house listened to Pakistan radio, and in this activity the friends of Faiyyaz and the neighbours took part with great excitement, enthusiasm and punctuality. At the appointed time all of them converged in Faiyyaz's room and locked the door from inside. The news was heard in low volume, so that the sound did not escape the room. Akhtar Husain never tried to peep into anyone's room, even when he suspected something inappropriate was going on inside them. Though Hamid did not participate in this clandestine activity, he listened to the sound of the news or reviews that somehow reached his ears, since his room was adjacent to that of Faiyyaz's. He was acquainted with most of the people who collected in Faiyyaz's room.

Hamid did not want to show up before the news-hungry visitors, although every one of them knew about his presence. He was quite apprehensive of their supposed queries that he had devised in his mind. Having lived out for long years, he could not recognize them by their voices, so he remained confined to his room, straining his ears to catch the news or conversation in the other room.

In the closed room, they listened to Akashwani first, because its broadcasting time was different from those of the other news programmes. And when Akashwani aired the news that the Mukti Bahini was achieving victory and marching ahead with the help of the Indian Army, Hamid could hear the comments made in the adjoining room.

'Never . . . it can never do that! What is this Mukti Bahini, after all? It is actually the victory of the Indian Army.'

'Akashwani never relays the correct news. Has it ever given the exact number of victims killed in the communal riots?'

'Bhai, why should Akashwani air the news of the defeat of the Bengalis? It would be India's defeat. And how could any warring nation just announce that it has been defeated?'

'The Akashwani news broadcasters think that they will help create the Bangladesh nation. This can never happen. The dreams of the Bengalis can never be fulfilled.'

'The grand idea of Sonar Bangla embedded in the minds of the Bengalis can be flushed out only with military might, and Pakistan is doing that excellently. India will regret its mistake in meddling with them, later on. Have these Bengalis been loyal to anyone, ever?'

'Just imagine, if Bangladesh becomes a reality, what will happen thereafter? What will happen to the Biharis who are stuck there in lakhs?'

'Why should we believe what is utterly wrong? After all, America's Seventh Fleet is not a toy that the Mukti Bahini people will drown in the sea. Let it reach their port.'

'China has also announced that it is not going to sit silently and watch.'

'When will the Seventh Fleet reach there? Just when . . . after all the Biharis are killed?'

'It takes time, Yaar! It's a very large ship, and not an aircraft which could reach in a few hours. It will take a few days.'

'Do you know how strong the fleet is? It is a huge ship with many fighter jets on its large deck, and it appears as big as a town. The jets fly from its deck, bomb their targets and then return to it. This fleet can save the entire Bihari population in East Pakistan.'

'It's time for Pakistan radio, now. Let's listen to it to learn how far the fleet has reached.'

Pakistan radio was broadcasting such confusing news that it was quite difficult to find out the truth. Nevertheless, it at least reported that heavy fighting was raging on the war front, and the defeat of the enemy was certain. It also played the comments of some political leaders who assured that the Seventh Fleet was soon going to enter the Bay of Bengal, and that Chinese help was within reach.

'Look at that! Didn't I tell you that the situation there is quite different? After all, America and China are not ordinary countries. Leave America for a while. It is a superpower. There's no doubt about it. China, too, is such a powerful country that even Russia fears it.'

'How powerful is India, to be frank? It's all Russia's power which is helping India to stand in the war. In fact, it's Russia which wants the Biharis to be massacred.'

'Biharis have done so much for Pakistan that it is definitely going to save and protect them, at any cost. It can't leave them like that. You'll see it.'

By the time their discussion had finished, the BBC news hour approached. The news relayed from BBC was so ambiguous and misleading that Faiyyaz's friends, poorly educated and unemployed people, who either owned small shops or subsisted on meagre zamindari compensation bonds, could hardly sieve out any meaning from the clever language typical of the BBC newsreaders and reviewers. On the other hand, Indian radio regularly transmitted news of the Mukti Bahini forces capturing many villages and towns of East Pakistan, which the disbelieving listeners never trusted. Actually, they were scared to rely on the Indian news, because that would mean believing in the decimation of Biharis. They still harboured a lingering hope that the Biharis were alive. The news-hungry listeners would leave quietly for their homes after the last news broadcast.

Hamid felt no upheaval inside him after listening to the news. His relationship with East Pakistan depended on Badrul Islam and his wife. And they had been taken away by the Pakistani Army. Though he could not yet completely believe Chamo who said that the army must not have left him alive, even then his contact with that part of Pakistan had broken off. To return to that place was nothing more than a utopian fantasy. He was surprised at those people who were so excited about the war between the two countries. Biharis were already butchered in East Pakistan, and those few who were still living there had no chance of survival. The refugees had to go to Pakistan at any cost, and for that Indian radio must necessarily speak the truth to impress upon them that they had no choice but to go there. When a drunken Yahya Khan boasted of victory in his slurred speech on the Pakistan radio and ended with Insha Allah (if God wills) those listening to it in the closed room of Faiyyaz chorused 'Amen'. Hamid knew that what Indian radio had reported was going to be true. Living in East Pakistan for some years, he had understood the Bengalis well, and knew that they would remain quiet and stupid as long as they could, but once they woke up to the reality, it would be hard to overpower them.

Akhtar Husain had strictly forbidden everybody in the house from listening to Pakistan radio. It would unnecessarily create suspicion without any benefit. He had a small transistor on which he listened to BBC, Voice of America and the Indian news broadcasts. Once Ajodhya Prasad had asked him to tune in to the Pakistani channel but he flatly refused.

'Oh, come on, Ajodhya Babu! When we did nothing wrong, the police came rushing here looking for a transmitter. Now if we listen to Pakistan radio, we will be sent to jail in handcuffs.'

Ajodhya Prasad was embarrassed, but immediately replied, 'Please don't talk about that anymore. Ours is a democratic country. We do what we like here. I, too, listen to Pakistan radio. You must listen to what the enemy is saying. And to tell you the truth, I listen to Pakistan radio to enjoy its Urdu which we don't find here nowadays. The language has no more remained chaste here in the hands of our newsreaders. They always substitute it with unsavoury Hindi words. I don't know what kind of Urdu they are introducing.'

'Listen to Pakistan radio at your home, for whatever reasons you like, but please don't ask me to do that.'

Their conversation ended, and Ajodhya Prasad left after some time.

Hamid had stopped going out of the house since the war started. He stayed in his room all day to avoid being seen by any visitor to the house.

Every day the newspapers carried reports of nationwide, house-to-house search to find hidden spies. Many people were arrested on suspicion. During those days, any Bihari runaway from East Pakistan could be charged as a Pakistani spy. Hamid was so scared to hear the disturbing newscasts that he felt completely disoriented.

He recalled his life in Biharsharif, his jobless days even after doing his Bachelor's, and his father refusing to help him get a job despite being a minister in the government. Even though he considered Akhtar Husain as a strong banyan tree that could not be uprooted, he was shocked to see him appearing like a weak plant which could be blown away by a slight puff of wind. The police search of Ben House had left him absolutely devastated. The incident had disparaged his roots. To Hamid, it appeared as if it was Chamo, alone, in the entire world, who was standing as a giant sturdy tree which no power could uproot. His feet remained steadfast, even in the worst of situations. *What would have happened to him, had Chamo not been there?*

In fact, the very existence of Chamo had created the passion for life inside Hamid. The moment his thoughts drifted away from Chamo, even for a while, he would become a model of mistrust and defeat. Two letters from Chamo came to him. In both, he forbade Hamid from coming to Calcutta until he gave him the green signal from there.

38

The atmosphere of Ben House had become quite gloomy. Bibi Sahiba suffered from periodic bouts of eccentricity when she spoke but remained quiet most of the time. She expressed her feelings of love and hate for Pakistan simultaneously, and then fell into periodic silence.

Sarwar Husain's wife showed no reaction to the news of her husband's death. She had broken all her bangles much earlier, and had already left wearing coloured clothes prior to the news. But when Hamid went to see her, she met him quite normally, and gave him a ten-rupee note when he took her permission to leave. Faiyyaz stayed all day in his shop. He did not talk much with people in the house when he returned home. Khaleda had come back from the Gulf and was living with her in-laws. She was in the family way, so she could not come to meet Hamid. Nisar was still unable to talk or hear, so Hamid communicated with him only through hand gestures and facial expressions. Hamid understood his gestures very well when he was living at Ben House, but having left the place many years back, he had now forgotten to figure out his sign language. And, therefore, not much communication transpired between them. Nisar had become an expert tailor and was earning good money. Cloth clippings and cuttings lay scattered on the floor of the room at Ben House where he did his tailoring work. Akhtar Husain lived in his own world. He was either busy in prayers or with his friends. He rarely went out of the house.

Hamid's mother was a very simple and virtuous woman. He could not talk to her on current affairs. On seeing Hamid back in Ben House, she started making arrangements for his wedding. She did not believe anybody when she was told that he was already a married man now. Hamid had to work very hard to discourage her from doing that, explaining to her that he had married, and had two children. But still, she did not believe him. Her justification was that Hamid could never think of marrying without the consent of his parents. Nobody has done that in the family. After failing in his efforts to convince her, Hamid finally told her that he was without any job, and so could not bear the financial burden of bringing a wife. He also asked her to get his elder brother Faiyyaz married, first. How could he marry when his elder brother was still unmarried? She then started finding a match for Faiyyaz. Akhtar Husain said that he wanted Faiyyaz to marry a woman belonging to a poor but gentlemanly family, who could comfortably adjust in the house.

The reports relayed by the Indian radio were turning out to be true, word by word. People's trust in news from Pakistan radio was waning. The quixotic news about the advent of the Seventh Fleet and the Chinese army was scarcely relayed now. But the scattered rays of hope were still flickering, though very faintly. Even then, a reasonable Muslim population in

India, whether refugees or citizens, waited day and night to hear about the movement of the American Seventh Fleet. But the Fleet refused to brighten their hopes. And the Chinese army could not cross over its long Chinese wall.

As people were lost in their hopes and dreams, suddenly, 16th December arrived. That day, from the morning, the excitement and fervour of the Indian news broadcasters were conveying a different story. A good part of East Pakistan was already taken by the Mukti Bahini forces and declared as Bangladesh. Rangpur, Khulna, Noakhali and Comilla were already captured by them. And Dhaka was going to fall any moment. The truth was that the Indian Army and the Mukti Bahini forces themselves could not conjecture that Bangladesh would become a reality within two weeks of the war, and East Pakistan would fade out of time and memory. Though some dreamers still visualized the Seventh Fleet laying siege to the strongholds of Mukti Bahini forces, ambushing the enemy at Dhaka. America was a superpower anyway, and Russia also feared it. The news about Kennedy's rebuff to Khrushchev which forced the Russian leader to leave Cuba, inspired these incurable romantics to rest their hopes on America. As they waited, Indian radio announced that Indira Gandhi would speak to the nation. Indira Gandhi spoke live on radio and declared that Dhaka had fallen to the Indian forces. Lt. Gen. A.A.K. Niazi, heading the Eastern Command of the Pakistan Army surrendered with 90,000 personnel to Lt Gen. Jagjit Singh Arora, who commanded the Eastern Command of the Indian Army.

The radio reported in detail the various stages of the surrender ceremony. The Pakistan radio suppressed that news and continued reportage of fierce war between the two forces. But now people had lost trust in Pakistan radio. Indira Gandhi's announcement between the various news relays had turned the tide.

The fall of East Pakistan was not a small incident. Millions of Biharis trapped there could now be saved only by the will of God. It was a defeat that subjected the Muslims of the subcontinent to utter humiliation. Time had played a cruel joke on them. They could neither laugh nor cry on it. The losers were Muslims, and the winners were also Muslims. An army of 90,000 soldiers of a Muslim country laid down their arms to Jagjit Singh Arora. And it was a calamity much bigger than the creation of Bangladesh. At no time in the 1400-year-long history of the Muslims, though punctuated by sporadic defeats, an army had surrendered with so many soldiers. It was a tragic chapter of their history. That night, a dark silence spread inside the houses of the Muslims all over India. Out of pain and shock, food was either not cooked or consumed in most of these homes. Sleep deserted their eyes. Widespread rumours concerning Lt Gen. Niazi swept through Indian towns and villages. Some showed him as a foreign agent who was heavily bribed to humiliate the Muslims; some claimed that he was a rakish, voluptuous man who remained drunk and had surrendered in that state. People were abusing Yahya Khan, blaming him for adding yet another chapter of disgrace to Muslims in their chequered history. The newspapers were full of exciting stories about the formation of the new nation of Bangladesh. The officials of the Bangladesh government who had hitherto been running the affairs of the country while in hiding, had now come out of their hideouts and reached Dhaka. They had taken control of the Bangladesh government completely. People were waiting to see when they were going to order the mass extermination of Biharis. The greatest grief was that those cornered there could not escape to India. They should be at least allowed to live.

All of this did not affect Hamid much; his only thoughts were of getting to Calcutta and, eventually, to Nepal.

39

Hamid was about to leave in a day or two when a great tragedy struck the house. His mother passed away. She took her lunch that fateful day, and after a few minutes fell unconscious. Doctors were immediately called. They came right away and declared her dead. She had a massive heart attack after which she could not survive. Needless to say, her death afflicted everybody in the house, and it was quite difficult for them to keep it a secret from Bibi Sahiba. She was an extremely sensitive woman. Sarwar Husain's death had devastated her. The news of her daughter's death would have brought unknown havoc on her diminishing frame. She was Bibi Sahiba's dearest daughter who had never left her mother alone. She was married within her own blood relations, so she did not have to leave her parental house. And Bibi Sahiba was spared the pain of sending her away. She looked after her mother very well, and obeyed all her instructions without any grumble. She never went against her mother's wishes. In her better days, Bibi Sahiba called her her right hand. The information of her darling daughter's death might kill her.

So, Akhtar Husain called everybody in his room, and said that they had to accept what had befallen them all, with patience and prayers. There was no need to cry aloud, and let Bibi Sahiba know about it. She should be left as she was, confined to her bed, and the matter should be kept a secret from her, in any case. He asked them to leave her in her room, and to make excuses if she inquired about anything. She was, anyway, not in her normal state of mind.

There were many rooms in the women's quarter, and a large hall was connected to all of them. Bibi Sahiba's bed and belongings occupied a corner of the hall. Two beds stood side by side. One on which she lay all day and night, and the other, a little lower, for her prayers. A prayer mat lay spread on it, and a book of prayers, and her prayer beads were placed near the pillow. Almost all the womenfolk in the house and the maid servants slept at different places in this sizeable hall. Faiyyaz and Nisar had their own separate rooms. The dead body of Hamid's mother was kept in a room which was on the other end of the hall. A wall separated the room from the hall. The body was placed there so that it should be quietly bathed and wrapped in a burial shroud, disallowing any sound to reach the hall. This room had only one door which opened on the opposite side of the hall. It was kept closed to avoid the full view of the room. Women were going in and out of the room, with slow, quiet steps.

Sticking to Akhtar Husain's instructions, people in the house, and those mourners who came to condole, were requested to remain peaceful. Bibi Sahiba spent most of her time in her bed. She did not go to the kitchen now. A maid was employed to take care of her. She used to help her take her meals also. When she finished her breakfast, Bibi Sahiba got out of her bed with the maid's help and walked feebly out of the hall, aided by her maid. When she saw the door of her dead daughter's room closed, she went near it and tried to give it a push. But it was locked from inside. She came back and tumbled into her bed. A feeling of vague unease grew inside her, and she asked anybody who happened to pass by the hall,

'Babu, why is that room closed?'

'It's nothing, Bibi Sahiba. Sacks of grain had arrived from Ben. They were kept in this room for the time being.' The person who was asked, answered in haste.

'But there is so much space left in the storehouse. Why not keep them there?'

Bibi Sahiba, even in that state of her health, remembered everything about the house, and kept herself aware of the happenings there. When she did not get any logical answer to her queries, her suspicion was confirmed that there was something amiss in the house. She lay in her bed for some time, and then started calling everybody in the house, by name, one by one to come to her. All responded to her call, but the one she was trying to see, the one she was waiting for, did not show up.

She asked them, at last, 'Where is Amna?'

Amna was the name of Hamid's mother. Akhtar Husain was called to answer her question. Very calm and collected, Akhtar Husain sat down beside her. Bibi Sahiba tried to get up, but he caressed her feet and request her to stay lying in her bed.

Bibi Sahiba thought for a while, and then asked him, 'Babu, where is Amna? I haven't seen her since morning.'

'Amma is busy doing something very important.'

'But where is she?'

'She's around. You were sleeping, perhaps.'

As Akhtar Husain got up to leave, she whispered in his ears, 'My son, has Pakistan taken her away?'

'Oh, no, Amma!' Akhtar Husain was caught off guard.

'I'm saying that because this Pakistan has been after my blood for quite some time now. Death to it! It has taken away all that I had. It might have come again, and taken Amna away. Go, go, and bring her.'

Akhtar Husain walked silently out of the hall. The dead body had been bathed and was being wrapped in the shroud.

Suddenly Bibi Sahiba got down from her bed and walked towards the closed room. She started thumping on the door, crying hysterically, 'O, Pakistan . . . O, doomed Pakistan. You've devoured my children . . . ruined my family . . . don't devour my daughter, now . . . for God's sake, go away from here . . . may you be cursed . . . I beg of you, Pakistan . . . leave me alone . . . I haven't harmed you ever . . . for what sin of mine are you punishing me . . . Pakistan . . . O, Pakistan . . .'

Akhtar Husain came running out of the room, and took her to her bed. She screamed wildly and fell unconscious. He orally administered to her a few drops of Coramine glucose in half a glass of water, and massaged her legs until she passed into a deep slumber. He hurried out of the room, and with the help of his friends and relatives took the dead body of his wife out in a coffin. A burial prayer for the dead was offered, and the body was buried in the nearby graveyard.

The sudden calamity had so jolted Hamid that he was stricken with grief. His mother' sudden and unexpected death without any illness was not a small matter for him. He felt her importance for him after her death and mourned her intensely. She had never asked for anything from her husband, brothers or children, and was content with whatever she had. Hamid's head drooped in regret every time he recalled her expressing her fondest wish to get him married.

Amna's death deeply affected Akhtar Husain and he mourned his partner-in-life. She often drew her sari pallu over her head when she saw him. In the presence of others, she did not talk to him directly, but through her daughter or son, whoever was there, and that too about matters of necessity. But after she passed away, he started feeling that she was so close to him that without her his life was meaningless. Hamid was distressed to see his father's pitiable condition. Bibi Sahiba had reached such an abysmal state of mental health that she would call out her dead daughter's name every now and then, and then start cursing Pakistan. That was her everyday routine. His mother's death had shackled Hamid to his house, although he had to travel soon. He had come to Biharsharif for only a week, and stayed there for about two months after his mother's death.

He had brought only one pair of extra clothes for himself, and the clothes he was wearing were soiled and torn. Akhtar Husain gave him two pairs of khadi pyjamas and kurtas. Chamo wrote to him regularly which served as a great relief for him. Hamid spent much of his time with his father, consoling and amusing him. Akhtar Husain's favourite subject for discussion was the Congress party, and Hamid kept him busy by asking him various questions about the party, to which his father replied in great detail and with great pleasure. Those were the moments when Hamid also felt quite helpless and forlorn. The occasional visits of Ajodhya Prasad and some of his friends were moments of panacea for Akhtar Husain. Suddenly, one day, Chamo's letter arrived, asking him to come back to Calcutta immediately. The letter disturbed Hamid. He knew that it was now dangerous for him to stay longer at Biharsharif. Chamo had his finger on the pulse of time. And Hamid knew that Chamo would never leave him to drown in the turbulent sea of time. He still had with him the money that Chamo had given him, which he could use to buy his ticket to Calcutta. He also had the money that Sajid had given him, and he had not yet decided what to do with it. Sajid had not talked or written to him since his departure to Patna, except when he came to hear of his mother's death. He had left only after a day's stay, because he had to go on a tour with the minister.

A day before leaving Biharsharif, Hamid left Sajid's money in a sealed envelope on Akhtar Husain's desk. He returned to his room and was lying on his bed with his eyes closed, lost in thoughts, when he heard some footsteps and opened his eyes. It was Nisar, standing very close to him. He gestured Hamid to follow him. Hamid could not fathom what Nisar wanted him to do. Before his flight to Dhaka, they were very close friends. He was considered an expert in the use of sign language, the language of Nisar. They often went out together to eat chaat from the roadside food carts and watch movies. Nisar had only those two hobbies, and needed someone to help him enjoy them. That was the reason why Hamid became his best friend. But now Hamid was a different man. He had forgotten the sign language that had once been his expertise. Though even now he communicated with Nisar in that language, but at that moment, he could not understand what he wanted to tell him.

So, Hamid went with Nisar to his room. Nisar entered his room and closed the door. He then opened the wardrobe, took out a small casket from it, turned its lock, and lifted the lid of the box. It was full of five-, ten-, and hundred-rupee notes and hundreds of small coins. Hamid was stunned to see that.

He asked Nisar in gestures, 'What's all that? Wherefrom?'

'I've saved all this money from my tailoring and cutting job,' replied Nisar in gestures.

'What will you do with all this money?'

'I will save a lot of money and then go to Karachi to live with my parents.'

Hamid looked at him dolefully.

'Take from this as much money as you need,' Nisar signalled to Hamid.

'But why, Nisar?'

'Am not I your brother, and a very close friend, too? I know you are in great need of money.'

As Nisar said that in his sign language, tears came to Hamid's eyes. Nisar quickly picked up his handkerchief and gestured for him not to weep.

'I don't need them, Nisar. Keep them with you,' Hamid told him.

'You don't consider me your own, then. Tell me, do you . . .?'

Hamid instinctively took him in his embrace, and said, 'Please don't misunderstand me, my dear brother. I love you so much! But you are saving this money for a purpose which is dear to you. I wish you success in it. I can do with the money that I have, and . . .?' All these he uttered verbally, and then again realized that the words were meant for Nisar who was deaf and mute. Hamid translated all that he had spoken into sign language and communicated them to Nisar.

Nisar gestured, 'I have a lot of money. This is just a part of what I have hidden at other places. You know it's not difficult for me to earn money now. I'll get a lot more from my cutting and sewing jobs if I need. Don't worry about it. But please take from this as much as you require.'

Hamid got into a fix. The matter was not just about taking the money or not taking it. It was Nisar's tender, sweet feelings that he did not want to hurt either way. He did not take time to decide, and counted out small notes worth 500 rupees.

Showing him the money and then putting them in his pocket, Hamid asked Nisar, 'Are you happy now?'

Nisar's eyes glittered with pleasure. He locked his box and put it back in the wardrobe. Hamid left the room, saying, 'Let me now go and pack my things. I'll see you tomorrow morning.'

Hamid came back to his room and tumbled into his bed. His experience had just now traversed centuries. Tears welled up in his eyes repeatedly as he dried them with his handkerchief. Hamid had never before imagined Nisar would reflect such a larger-than-life personality. Turning restlessly in his bed, he stayed awake for as long as possible, thinking about Nisar, and his incredible, selfless generosity against the cautious approach of his other relatives, and felt gratified that he had been gifted with the courage to bear the sobering experiences.

He had to leave the next morning and he had not yet had a heart-to-heart talk with his elder brother Faiyyaz. He came back exhausted from his shop every evening, and Hamid did not want to spoil his rest. He could have gone and talked to Faiyyaz at his shop, but Hamid had stopped going out of the house.

Hamid, therefore, got up early the next day, and scurried to his room. Faiyyaz had just woken up, but the red spots were still floating in his eyes.

'Bhaiya, I couldn't get time to talk to you at length. And I am going back now.'

Faiyyaz got up rubbing his eyes, threw a startled look at Hamid, and said, 'Why do you blame yourself. You're just on a visit. Even those who live in this house do not talk to me.'

'It's not that, Bhaiya. You keep yourself so busy, and there is hardly anybody here to talk to. Abba lives in his own world.'

'Hamid, it was only our grandmother who used to take care of everybody in the house. After her mental sickness, there is virtually no one to look after us. Our mother had always been a quiet and passive woman. As long as grandmother is alive, we will live easefully, but my heart pains to think what would happen after she dies, God forbid.'

'You are correct, Bhaiya. Our grandmother has always been a blessing for us. May she live long! But, even then, you needn't think so gloomily. You are now the oldest of us, and you have responsibilities on your shoulders.'

'It's only you who thinks like that, Hamid. Nobody tells me that. And your feelings don't matter since you don't stay here. You're going away and who knows when again we can see you.'

'These things are not to be told, but understood. Nobody tells this, Bhaiya. I talked to you about it just as a passing remark. Otherwise, I, too, wouldn't have uttered them.'

Faiyyaz did not answer him, but turned his face to the other side, and spoke in hushed tone, 'Isn't it time for me to get married? All my friends are married now.'

'Of course, you should have got married. It's getting late. Abba and Amma must have thought about it, but perhaps, they could not get a woman of your choice. Should I remind Abba?'

'No, no, you don't need to do that. I'll choose my own wife. Abba can't do that for me, even if he wants. He would need Amma, who is no more now.'

'It's true that only you are going to decide about your marriage. But it is better if you listen to Abba's wishes also. We haven't yet done anything worthwhile to please him.'

'Sajid is going to do all that we have failed to do, rest assured.'

'Even then, Bhaiya, I request you not to do anything that displeases Abba.'

'I am saving money, and I will marry when I'll have saved enough. There is no question of hurting Abba. I am not well educated, but I know this much that those who don't have money have no respect in this world. Nobody cares for them. I am, therefore, busy accumulating prestige.'

'As you wish! But please don't bring a bad name to the family.'

'I know, Hamid, that you too need money desperately. I am so sorry that I can't help you. In fact, I don't even take out money for my expenses from my savings.'

'Bhaiya, I've never asked you for money. You needn't feel sorry. How could you think I'd ask you for money?'

'I know you haven't said that, but I don't want you to harbour any doubts about me.'

'Please take that out of your mind. Your love and sympathy are enough for me. Why should I think about your money? I wish you buy your happiness with whatever money you earn.'

Faiyyaz heard his brother quietly, but he could not notice the storm brewing in Hamid's eyes whose rage he had smothered silently inside.

40

Hamid left Ben House before noon. Akhtar Husain wept as he bade him farewell. Hamid also met Bibi Sahiba before leaving the house, but he did not muster enough strength to inform her about his departure. He took leave of Nisar and Faiyyaz, and reached the station.

The atmosphere in the train to Calcutta was very different from his earlier train journey. Everybody was talking about the surrender of the 90,000 Pakistani soldiers, speculating about sending the refugees, who had been give the status of guests, back to their country. One of them believed that many of them would not leave, and remain in India lost in its surging population. Hamid did not take part in the discussion. He considered himself a foreigner who was escaping their gaze. The fact, however, was that he was still an Indian, and had no other citizenship.

When the train reached Howrah station, he found Chamo who met him warmly at the station, and said, 'I have made arrangements for all of you to go to Nepal, and you will soon get your flight tickets from there to Pakistan.'

It was a great news for Hamid. But Chamo's words left him emotionless and blank, and Hamid could not himself realize why. Chamo noticed a strange detachment in his manner. He was surprised, but did not say anything. Nazia's eyes lit up when she saw Hamid back, and her drawn face brightened. His two sons rushed into his embrace. Nazia was looking very controlled and the children neat, clean and healthier. He was much relieved to see them. Nazia had not met his parents, but she was sad to hear about the passing away of Hamid's mother.

Chamo informed Hamid that their journey to Pakistan was going to cost thousands of rupees, and he had made arrangements for the money. His agents had sold Badrul Islam's bungalow in Dhaka, as there was no hope for his or his wife's survival. Hamid looked shocked at the news.

Chamo explained to him, 'The situation there is that the moment the Bengalis see an uninhabited house or building, they storm into it and seize it. There is no one to ask them or to evacuate them from there. I have been trying a lot and finally got the bungalow sold for whatever money I could get. But that is enough for your journey.'

Hamid knew that Chamo had done the right thing. He had been honest enough to spend the money on them. And that was not a bad thing to do. Chamo also told him that his man would take him, Nazia and the children safely to Kathmandu, and return to Calcutta only after helping them board a flight to Pakistan. He also gave Hamid some money to buy necessary things. On the third day of his return to Calcutta, Hamid and his family boarded the train for their journey to Nepal. At the railway station, Chamo hugged Hamid and his children affectionately, weeping profusely. His wife was also tearful at sending her own niece away. She wanted to keep them all in

Calcutta, and help Nazia get a teaching job in a school there. But Chamo was against it. His argument was that someday someone or the other might somehow discover that they were Biharis who had fled Bangladesh. And then that would be really troublesome for all of them.

The man Chamo had sent with them to Nepal was a mysterious fellow. He did not sit with them but was in another compartment. He got down at every station that the train stopped and came to see them. He took great care of them throughout the journey. They reached Patna the next morning, refreshed themselves at the station and boarded the bus to Raxaul with Chamo's man. They arrived there at nine in the night, stayed in a hotel and the following morning hired rickshaws to take them to Biratnagar. It is the third largest city in Nepal, and is the country's hub for imported goods. From there they took a Nepal Roadways bus for Kathmandu. They got to Kathmandu in the evening and put up in an ordinary hotel, where many Biharis, like them, were staying. Hamid was amazed to find the Nepali Hindus' sympathy for the Biharis.

Thousands of Biharis had flown to Pakistan from Nepal, and thousands more were waiting to undertake the journey. The local people were helping them a great deal. Chamo's man asked them to call him Raju, and told them that they had to stay in the hotel for a few days. The flights that take people to Pakistan are small aircrafts which cannot take a lot of passengers. Many people were hanging around to fly. For Hamid the wait proved to be rather long. He wished to fly instantly to Pakistan. The longer the wait was, the greater grew his worry, as his entire life depended on that journey. Raju brought meals for them in their room every day. Hamid and Nazia stayed in their room, but Raju took the children around to show them the city. Nazia showed no enthusiasm, and remained quiet most of the time, but Hamid knew that this was not her normal self. He had noticed of late that she had developed two individual identities both distinct from each other, that routinely took control of her behaviour. He ascribed it to the severe emotional trauma that she had gone through. Outwardly it looked as if she was flowing with the waves of time. Hamid had decided that he would get her treated by a good physician on reaching Karachi.

Hamid was astonished to see how the other Biharis were behaving at Kathmandu. They remained outside the hotel all day, rambling around the town, seeing sights, watching movies, buying colourful clothes, watches and radios. And when they came back in the evening, they talked and laughed so loud and long till late night that other people staying there were unable to sleep. Their girls were busy buying cosmetics and applying and reapplying their makeup in front of the mirror. When five or six days passed liked that in Kathmandu, Hamid also tried to be as happy as those carefree Biharis and become completely unmindful of the past and the future. But despite all his efforts, he could not do so. Perhaps, these behavioural tendencies could not be acquired by efforts.

He asked Raju every day about their intended departure day for Karachi, and Raju comforted him by saying that he was trying his best to send them as soon as possible. Chamo had given four thousand dollars to Hamid, but never told him the price at which the bungalow was sold, and Hamid never asked. All expenses at Kathmandu including the flight tickets were borne by Raju. Chamo had already given him enough money, and Hamid did not have to worry about that. He was not asked to spend a penny on anything there. So, Hamid had kept the dollars very safely with him. He was intensely aware of the fact that he was going to a new country where he might come across unforeseen circumstances. He had lost the guts to face the might of time eye to eye, and was scared that his optimism and confidence might get punished by the changing moods of time. One night, Raju came late to the hotel. Nazia and the children were sleeping, and Hamid was trying hard to do that. His effort was thwarted by a loud knock at the door. He got out and saw Raju standing at the door.

'Bhaiya, your travel tickets are confirmed. Your flight is at seven o'clock in the morning tomorrow. I will come at five in the morning, and take you there in a taxi. Please be ready.'

His heart leapt when Hamid heard the news.

He didn't want to wake Nazia, so he crawled into his bed, and lay there with his eyes open and mind lost in thoughts. Asghar Husain was in Karachi. Hamid had his address, but he had not informed him about his intended visit. He had left India years ago, and Hamid had not seen him since then. He vaguely remembered his face and knew no one else in Karachi with whom he could go and stay. After long and careful deliberation, he decided to go to him directly on reaching Karachi, and seek suggestion from him about his future plan. He was not sure how Asghar Husain would treat him, but he had no other option. Fleeting thoughts kept running through his head until it was early morning. He woke Nazia up and asked her to get ready. They did not have much luggage. Raju came exactly at five o'clock and they departed for the airport. On reaching there, Raju handed him the travel papers, and stayed there until boarding was announced. Hamid thanked Raju a lot, hugged him and promised him that he would take Raju with him to Karachi on his next visit to Calcutta. From the small window of the plane Hamid could see Raju's white hanky fluttering at the top of others in the waiting lounge of the airport, until it became a dot.

41

Nazar Muhammad was a Pakistani Army officer. He was a Bengali and was posted in East Pakistan as a second lieutenant. Later, he was promoted, and before the formation of Bangladesh, was transferred to West Pakistan with a promotion. For Shahnaz it was like God's unexpected gift. She and Nazar Muhammad were in love. But he was a Bengali, and her family would never have accepted the match. Shahnaz was torn between her love for him, and her duty towards her family. Though Shahnaz, too, did not personally have a very good opinion about the Bengalis, as irony of fate would have it, Cupid drew her towards Nazar Muhammad, and she could not help it. He was the brother of a young lady who was Shahnaz's closest friend. Shahnaz met him through her friend and their love flowered in her friend and her brother's house. Her family and friends did not get the slightest hint about the affair. And before the news could explode and ruin their relationship, Nazar Muhammad was transferred to West Pakistan. He was asked to leave immediately, so they did not have any other choice but to do exactly that.

There was a small mosque at Dhaka where the imam
of the mosque kept a nikah register. He conducted the
nikah ceremony of willing couples at the mosque in the
presence of two witnesses arranged by the imam himself.
Nazar Muhammad and Shahnaz went to that mosque and
solemnized their marriage. They took the nikah document
and flew together to West Pakistan.

Shahnaz used to go to her friend's house regularly, and
would call home to inform her parents if she stayed there
for the night. When on the day of her nikah Shahnaz did
not reach home, her mother called her friend. The news that
was broken to her on phone devasted her so utterly that she
fainted with shock. Azimuddin was incidentally at home that
day. He seized the receiver from his wife's hand and held it
close to his ear; he could not for a long while believe what he
heard. Could his daughter do something so awful like that?

After that upsetting episode, Azimuddin confined
himself to his home. His wife and their other children also
remained virtually immobile for weeks. Their self-imposed
imprisonment did not last for long. Azimuddin had lost his
self-confidence and could not face the world. But when his
other children and their spouses came out of their house,
nobody asked them anything. Life outside went on at its
normal, usual pace, and the rivers flowed, and the wind blew
at their natural speed.

Within a few weeks of Nazar Muhammad's arrival in
West Pakistan, a general election was held in the country,
and the name of Bangladesh surfaced for the first time. The
government of West Pakistan had waged a full-scale, bloody
war against its own people, and after a few months the effect
of that war started unveiling itself. The balance tilted heavily

in favour of the people of the country. That was the time when the Bengalis working in the West Pakistan administration and armed forces became extremely worried. Despite the vigilance and surveillance of the West Pakistan government, many Bengali officers during the Indo–Pak war either took refuge in other countries or flew their fighter jets to ostensibly drop bombs on the enemy territories, and deserting their jets and all, took asylum there. Many war fronts were opened in the country, but the government was fighting on the front that it had opened itself. Nazar Muhammad was among those officers who considered loyalty towards his country as his ultimate faith, and he had proved himself in many difficult situations that the country faced. The government took full advantage of his faithfulness and fidelity. He was elevated to higher ranks very frequently. West Pakistan radio and television relayed his interviews, and awards and honours were bestowed on him. This exercise continued as long as his services were needed to fight the war. But as the war ended in Pakistan's defeat, the government stopped conferring laurels on him. He was removed from active field duties and assigned minor posts in the army office. He was later dismissed from the army on various unspecified allegations. However, as good luck would have it, with the rank of Colonel appended before his name, he was given a well-paid, decent job in an American firm in Saudi Arabia. All over the Gulf countries, almost inexplicably, the Pakistan armed forces were held in great repute and Nazar Muhammad was rewarded for exactly that reason.

As the indiscriminate slaughter of Biharis began in East Pakistan, Nazar Muhammad put all his efforts—even endangered his life—and saved Azimuddin's life anyhow.

Azimuddin had lost his mental balance after the emotional and physical strain that he had experienced as a captive of the Mukti Bahini. So, when he arrived at the Karachi airport onboard a military plane, he could not recognize Shahnaz. She got him the best medical treatment and care and made every effort to bring him back to normalcy, but just a few weeks after his arrival at Karachi, he died. Perhaps the soil of West Pakistan drew him there, otherwise he had already mentally died when he was in East Pakistan.

42

Karachi was a large city. But Hamid was coming from a sprawling city like Calcutta, so he was not overawed by the length and breadth of Karachi. What troubled him most there was his unfamiliarity with the place, and the more he tried to hide his worry from his wife and children, the more it was evident on his face. They got into a taxi at the airport and Hamid, with an apparent confidence, gave Asghar Husain's address to the taxi driver. The taxi traversed well-lit streets. His children gazed curiously out at the city through the car windows, and Hamid tried to read his future in its air. The taxi stopped outside a building. Asghar Husain's name was painted on a board fixed on its wall.

He asked a man standing nearby, 'Hello, gentleman! Does Mr Asghar Husain live here?'

'Yes, yes, press the bell marked number two, there!' He gestured towards the door.

Hamid saw many push switches on a board near the staircase. The switches were all numbered. Hamid pushed the switch numbered two with shaking hands. A very fair-complexioned boy looked down from the second storey of the building and shouted, 'Who's there? Whom do you want to see?'

'Is Mr Asghar Husain there?'

'Yes. Who are you?'

'Please tell him that Hamid from Biharsharif has come to meet him.'

The boy went in and after some time an aged man came down the stairs, and upon seeing Hamid, hugged him warmly, 'Arey, Hamid! How come, you're here, my son? You should have informed me. I'd have sent my car for you.'

Asghar Husain resembled Hamid's mother, otherwise it would have been difficult for Hamid to recognize him. It was not the same Asghar Husain he had seen in his childhood. He expressed his grief at the death of Hamid's mother and asked about others at Ben House. And then suddenly he remembered something.

'Oh, I've held you here for so long. Let's go up. Come, come! Shabnam, please come down. Take them with you.' He called out.

A very fashionable young girl, shaking her curly hair, came down and threw a glance at Nazia and the children. She said nothing to them but pretended as if she had recognized them all.

'This is your Hamid Bhaiya, son of your eldest aunt, and these are . . . umm . . . his wife and children.' He looked at Hamid.

'O yes, yes!' replied Hamid.

The girl held Nazia's hand, and all of them came to the second-floor flat of Asghar Husain. The drawing room looked very spacious, luxurious, well decorated and very flashy. Hamid recalled Badrul Islam's drawing room—a model of classical simplicity. It was decorated with books in such a way that it did not need any artificial decorations. Asghar Husain's wife had crossed the springtime of her age. She greeted them with warm affection, and asked them to refresh themselves and join them at the dinner table after that. Asghar Husain had nine children—four boys and five girls—from her. The eldest Nisar was in Biharsharif, two others were doctors in a Gulf country and the last son Shamsher was a businessman. His two daughters were married to Punjabis who were army officers. The third was married to a businessman, who was a Bihari migrant and lived with his wife in a different locality. He was also Asghar Husain's business manager. Asghar Husain's other two daughters Liza and Dolly were studying in a college. His cinema hall was doing a very profitable business.

The discussions at the dinner table revolved around Japanese cars, American televisions and clothes imported from Korea.

Liza remarked, 'The Indians are still obsessed with their Ambassador cars. They have no idea about the wonderful cars produced in America and Japan. Pooh! How ugly is your Ambassador car!'

'He is not an Indian. He's coming from Dhaka,' Asghar Husain reminded his daughter.

'Okay, it hardly matters! That is also a part of India. The only difference is that you can get Japanese cars there, but not in the rest of India.'

'Why do you pass judgments on others? What cars do you produce here in this country?' Asghar Husain censured her.

'We just don't need to do that, Daddy. Thank God, we get so many things imported into our country that we do not need to produce anything of our own.'

'Well, you are taking pride in your own weakness.'

Hamid quietly listened to the conversation between father and daughter.

'Brother, I had somebody bring me a khadi shalwar suit from India. Had I known you were coming I could have asked you to get me two pairs of khadi suits. They are the latest craze here,' said Dolly, Asghar Husain's youngest daughter, and brought her khadi suit to show them. It was a multicoloured suit with figures of peacocks embroidered on it. Nazia felt the clothes with her fingers.

'Where is your wife from? She doesn't say anything,' Hamid's aunt asked him.

'She . . . she's a Bengali.'

'What . . .?'

All of them chorused in surprise.

'So, your wife is a Bengali. How could you bring her here?' Asghar Husain asked him in a strange tone.

'She was not ready to stay back in Dhaka. She has decided to live with me through thick and thin.'

'She must then be a Bengali from Calcutta.'

'Yes, her ancestral house is in Calcutta.'

'That's what I meant to say. Otherwise, the Bengalis from Dhaka do not have to do anything with Pakistan. They are not Muslims, in fact.'

Hamid was speechless. Nobody said anything.

Asghar Husain spoke again, 'Even then, you shouldn't have brought her here. Does she speak Urdu?'

'Yes, she talks in chaste Urdu.'

'That's fine. Listen, then, nobody should know that she is a Bengali. Be careful about it you, too, Liza and Dolly.'

'Alright Daddy. But, Daddy, that means our Bhabhi knows how to sing and dance, isn't that so?'

'Shut up, Beti! Muslims don't do that. She has to forget singing and dancing, if she did that back home. This is the kingdom of God.'

Just then, Liza's small Pomeranian dog with its white fluffy fur jumped up on to her lap, and she started feeding it kheer with her spoon.

'Liza, so many times I have asked you not to feed Shushu with your spoon, but you don't listen to me. There are guests with me at the dining table, they must have objections.' Asghar Husain's wife scolded Liza mildly.

'You are talking about Hamid Bhai, Mummy? Why should he have objection with our Shushu, when he doesn't mind singing and dancing?'

'Mind you, Liza! You're again talking about singing and dancing.' Asghar Husain reprimanded Liza.

'Sorry, Daddy!'

Liza got up from her chair with Shushu in her arms and walked into her room, caressing her pet all the way. Dolly was going for shopping and she asked Nazia to come with her.

But before Nazia could say anything, Hamid said, 'I don't think she will be able to go out now, Dolly. She's very tired. We can do it some other time, as I have come to live in Pakistan now.'

When both the daughters left, Asghar Husain and his wife asked Hamid, 'Tell me now, Hamid! Is Nisar happy with his life there? How much money does he make?'

'He definitely earns so much that he has saved several thousand rupees.'

'That's very good! We are so sorry for him. He is a mute–deaf boy, so we can't bring him here. He cannot adjust to the life here. He would have become a burden on all of us.

Besides, his tailoring business will flop here, because we have Western-trained tailors and dressmakers.'

'Nisar is anxious to see you. He yearns for you.'

'We too want to see him. But I have taken a government contract for supplying military uniforms. So, I can't go to India because that will mean washing my hands off from lakhs of rupees that I am earning due to that, and putting myself under suspicion. I think he should get married now.'

'But, Uncle, who will marry him?'

'He can get a wife. But for that he should make some compromises. I mean stooping down to marry a girl of a lower status—a Bengali or an Oriya-speaking girl. The main thing is money which Nisar has in plenty, as you say. He would have been the owner of properties worth lakhs of rupees. That's why I left him there. But your father did not take any interest in it, and he did not handle well the court cases against them. Can't he bribe someone to present himself as Asghar Husain and get the property back? What can't money buy, after all? He was the elder of the house, our guardian there. But he was so busy pampering the Hindus that he had no time for the properties and other household affairs.'

Hamid could do little else than listen to him without uttering a word. That was not the proper time to indulge in any argument with Asghar Husain. After some moments of silence, Asghar Husain asked him, 'What were you doing there, I mean in Dhaka?'

'I was working as a sales manager in the Adamjee Jute Mills.'

'Oh . . . do you have any experience certificate or written proof you worked there?'

'No, I've lost everything there. But my name must be found there in the Mill's register.'

'How would you prove that's you, that you are that employee, I mean?'

'We can prove that with other records there.'

'Look, my son! I've told you that since I am a military contractor my hands are tied. But still, I'll try my best to get you a job. What's your qualification?'

'I am a BA from Nalanda University at Biharsharif.'

'What's a BA degree worth these days, my son? A technical degree would have meant a lot.'

'You are my only hope here, Uncle. I will do any job I get.'

'My son, the situation here has changed much. So many people have arrived here from East Pakistan that it is not possible to provide work for all of them. Many of them have gone to the villages to work as labourers there. What else could those poor people do? The Sindhis too are raising their heads, stoking the fear that the migrant population might exceed the local inhabitants. Nevertheless, I will do whatever I can for you. Can I offer you some advice?'

'Sure, Uncle. I'll do as you say.'

'You were at a very good post in East Pakistan, but put it out of your mind now. You can't get a job like that here. But please accept whatever job you get here as a blessing.'

'I've told you, Uncle, that I just need a job that would help me look after my wife and children.'

Asghar Husain ended the talk and fell into deep thought.

43

Hamid knew that his eldest uncle Sarwar Husain's family also lived in the same apartment building. But when for a long time he found nobody talking about them, he asked his aunt,

'Auntie, doesn't my badi (elder) auntie also live somewhere here?'

Instead of his wife, Asghar Husain answered him, 'Yes, she lives in a separate flat. My elder brother, your badey (elder) uncle had married a woman from another caste, and died leaving us to bear with your badi auntie. She doesn't keep any contact with us.'

'Why . . . what happened?'

'What else would happen? When brother Sarwar Husain came here, I extended all my help to him, gave him shelter here. And when his legal practice started shrinking, I helped him financially, and accommodated him anyhow. Now, after his death, his daughter, quite against our wishes, joined a teaching job at a school. I ask them to vacate my flat, and take any flat on rent outside. But they don't listen to me. I have been offered 1000 rupees every month and a good amount of consideration money for that flat.'

Hamid did not respond because he could hardly say anything that concerned the two brothers. He asked his uncle, 'If you allow, can I go and see them?'

His tone was such that if Asghar Husain forbade him, he wouldn't go there.

Asghar Husain replied, 'I don't have any objection. Try to impress upon them that they must leave my flat. Tell me yourself, Hamid, what a loss I'm suffering only because of them. It's my concern for them that I am doing nothing bad to them, otherwise I would have got their belongings thrown out of the flat in a matter of seconds.'

When Hamid walked up to Sarwar Husain's flat, he pushed the doorbell switch. Sarwar Husain's daughter Alia had come back from school and was taking tea with her mother. She opened the door and seeing a stranger standing in front, tried to move back.

'I am Hamid, your badi auntie's son. I've come from India,' Hamid said loudly. He could clearly see shades of Sarwar Husain in her face. He remembered his uncle's face very well. Sawar Husain regularly came to India. His aunt on hearing his voice came at the door, and both the mother and the daughter took him inside.

His aunt's face lit up on seeing him, and received him delightedly, 'Come, come, my son, do come in!'

Hamid entered the flat. It was arranged in a very simple manner, but had a decent appearance. They took him to their drawing room. Alia had done her MA, and after taking a teachers' training course, was teaching in a school. His badi auntie was very happy to see him. For the first time, a relative of her husband had come to meet her. She did not know about the death of Hamid's mother, and expressed her condolences when she heard it from him.

After finishing off with formalities, she spoke to Hamid, 'How should I tell you what I've suffered, my son? Asghar Husain had completely broken his relationship with us after his brother's death. After your badey uncle's demise we have been left helpless.'

Her eyes watered as she said that. Alia too placed the pallu (one end of a saree or stole) of her stole on her eyes.

'Auntie, why don't you move to a separate flat elsewhere? The conflict will automatically end, and you will be relieved. God may help you!'

'There's a problem in that, my son. Alia gets a salary of only 1000 rupees a month. And that is the only source of our subsistence. We have been trying to rent a flat for quite some time. I've asked Asghar Husain to search a flat for us, but for a rent that we can pay. And we will immediately get out of his house.'

'Badi auntie, we do not have many relatives, and a discord within the family has further reduced us. It gives me great pain to see that. The country has been divided into three parts, and our family, too, has split into many fragments.'

'Your badey uncle had risked his career for his brother and his children's love. He left his booming legal practice in Patna and migrated here thinking how his brother could live alone in a new country. But nobody cared for him once he came here. Asghar was definitely kind enough to ask his brother to live in this flat free of cost. But your badey uncle faced other financial hardships which compelled him to take home-tuition jobs. He never complained to his brother or asked him for money. It was God's mercy that we had a small family, and we lived on anyhow or else life would have been a hell.'

Hamid took leave of his badi auntie and came back to Asghar Husain's flat. Asghar Husain asked him, 'What did your badi auntie say? Is she moving out of the flat?'

'Yes, she said she will leave it the moment she finds a suitable place to live.'

'O, she has been saying that for years. In fact, she is saving her daughter's earnings for her marriage. Why would she spend money on a flat? She's here because she doesn't have to pay any rent.'

'Please don't say that. They are in discomfort, and they will surely leave your flat soon.'

'May your words come true! I hope it happens like that, but that's a distant possibility.'

Hamid and his family were given a room to live in Asghar Husain's spacious flat. Nazia stayed in the room all day. Dolly and Liza had declared her a bore. They were busy day and night in different activities. But all of them gathered during meals, and Asghar Husain also accompanied them, along with Hamid, Nazia and their children. He and Hamid talked on different topics, but Dolly and Liza always indulged in silly chit-chat, and Nazia and her children would gawk at them and say nothing. The two girls were an authority on the modern fashion craze. They had complete information about the fashion trends in every part of the world. They subscribed to many fashion magazines, and often talked about the latest articles published in them. Hamid was worried about his children. Their time was getting wasted, and he did not see any hope in the near future of putting them in a school. He often reminded Asghar Husain about his job, and every time he received the same reply,

'I am looking for that. It's not so easy. And why do you think so much. You are safe here in your own house. You will get a job if God wills.'

He had been there for quite some days when, one day, Asghar Husain told him that luckily a Bihari officer had been appointed at a very high post in Habib Bank, and they had to see him the following morning.

So, they went that day to the bank. Asghar Husain was immediately called in when he sent his visiting card. The bank officer was from Allahabad. Asghar Husain introduced Hamid as his distant relative, and said to him that Hamid was working in East Bengal, where all his relatives were massacred, and his house was ransacked. He had fled from there after much effort to India, but he was chased out from there too. He then escaped from India and had come to Karachi through Nepal. He had nothing to survive on. The story appeared quite pathetic. Hamid recalled his friend at Dhaka refugee camp who had asked him not to treat his falsehood as a lie. Hence, Hamid did not say a word.

The bank officer appeared quite affected by the tragic tale. He took out his hanky and wiped his eyes when Asghar Husain stopped. He ordered coffee for them, and talked to his subordinate officers on intercom. He then turned towards Asghar Husain, and said,

'Sheikh Sahib, there is a vacancy in our bank for a clerical cadre post. The salary is a little more than 1000 rupees a month. He can join it if he thinks fit. By the way, what did he do there?'

'Arey. Sahib, he had a very successful business there. I mean, he was earning lakhs of rupees there, but the Bengalis ransacked and ruined everything.'

'I'm really so sorry to hear that. It was all God's will. Yes, Mr Hamid, please join your job the day after tomorrow.'

'Thank you very much, Sir!'

Hamid's face brightened when they got out of the bank. Asghar Husain said, 'It was your good luck that you got a job so fast. And a good job, too. Things have really gone so bad here. The Sindhis want only Sindhis on jobs, and Punjabis only Punjabis. You've got the job so easily merely because the bank officer, incidentally, is a migrant from Allahabad and is known to me. It wouldn't have been so simple a story, otherwise.'

Hamid joined Habib Bank, and took Nazia to a good doctor on getting his first salary. The doctor checked Nazia and said that she was not suffering from any illness, and was normally healthy. Hamid narrated to the doctor that she was quite a cheerful woman, but the calamities that had struck Bangladesh had drained her pleasures. It seemed as if she had no feelings. She did not react to anything. The doctor was an experienced and elderly person. He told Hamid that he had seen many such cases, but he had no treatment for them. If she were to stay in a relaxed and pleasant atmosphere, she would most likely return to her earlier condition.

When situations got somewhat better for him, Hamid rented a flat in the suburbs of a newly built Bihari colony. Asghar Husain was very angry when he came to know he was leaving his flat. He asked him why he was going to a rented flat when he was free to live with his uncle. But Hamid anyhow made him agree to his decision. In fact, Nazia was living there like a second-class citizen, and she needed an independent, peaceful life to get herself back to normal.

The flat he had rented had three bedrooms, in addition to a drawing-cum-dining room. He went to his badi auntie and requested her to shift there with them. Two bedrooms were sufficient for him and Nazia, and he would leave the largest bedroom for her and Alia. All of them would live together in a relaxed atmosphere, and happiness would return to them. His badi auntie readily agreed, but Alia put one precondition— that she would move there only when Hamid agreed that she would pay half the rent. Hamid refused to accept that at first. But Alia stuck to her proposal. The rent of the flat was 400 rupees per month which Alia could easily afford to spend. At last Hamid had to concede, and all of them moved to the new flat. Asghar Husain came to see Hamid in the bank, one day, when he heard that Sarwar Husain's wife and daughter were living with him.

'I've come to know that Alia and Bhabhi are living with you. Is that true?'

'Yes, Uncle, and the good news is that now your flat is free.'

'That's all fine. But get it from me that we won't be able to come there to see you. You can, of course, visit us whenever you want.'

'Why, Uncle? Are you angry with me?'

'Yes, of course. Alia and her mother are not worth talking to. Bhaiya always lived in trouble after marrying Bhabhi. It is a woman's fate which brings either trouble or ease to a man. O, the woman has so terribly vexed us after Bhai Sahib's death. I had always helped Bhaiya when he was in a mess. But this woman flatly refuses to take my help. Her daughter has started earning and her pride has touched the skies, on her petty salary. I don't want to see their faces now.'

'Women sometimes act in a silly way, Uncle. We shouldn't, perhaps, put too much meaning into their ways and words. Please forgive them, Uncle. I am requesting to you, on her behalf, to forgive her.'

'Young man, who are you to ask me that for their sake? You needn't do any pleading for them. I haven't greyed my hair sitting under the sun. I have spent a long life experiencing such people.'

Hamid had to stay silent. Asghar Husain went away, and he really never came to his house. Hamid still failed to understand why he was so annoyed with them. He asked his badi aunty, 'Auntie, why is Uncle Asghar Husain so upset with you? What's the matter?'

'You could have asked him that, my son. We ourselves don't know why Bhaiya is so angry with me. All I know is that we have always respected him, and he has always looked down on our efforts to live with respect and freedom. Undoubtedly, he has helped his brother, gave him his flat to live. But your badey uncle had left his well-settled life to accompany his brother here. Yes, it's true that Asghar Husain had rallied round us. We are indebted to him for that. We really needed his help at that time, but when God has arranged our bread and butter for us, why should then we burden him with our troubles. Alia and I had managed all their household chores when matters hadn't turned that bad. Asghar Husain's wife never did the kitchen chores in those days.'

'But, Badi Auntie, Uncle Asghar Husain just wants you to ask him to forgive you.'

'But that's very strange. Why doesn't he tell us what mistakes have we committed? We don't know what our faults are. He wanted us to leave his flat. We have done that, too. Can he seek forgiveness from those who are younger in age?'

Alia did not open her mouth throughout their conversation. Hamid realized that the matter was not going to be solved so easily. It was an inconsequential matter, anyway.

Hamid was happy to find Nazia improving, returning slowly to her former self. To please her, he bought her a sitar. She spent her days quietly strumming the strings, filling the house with soothing, gentle tones.

They had no words in them. Perhaps words had melted down to become doleful tunes.

And the language of melody needs no words.

Everything else is dependent on one another.

And all are in need of one Godhead.

Those who could feel that need, are . . .

Time . . . flies, higher and still higher in its perpetual flight . . . touching the mountain peaks, their jagged, obstinate rocks, breaking them to pieces, scattering foam and dust all around.

O, Time, why don't you stop and stay, anywhere, any time!

PART THREE

44

15 August 1981. Letter from Akhtar Husain.

My dear Hamid

I have been receiving your letters quite regularly, becoming aware of the situations from time to time. It is most gratifying for me to know you are happy there. May God always keep you delighted! It was also heartening to hear that your sons Aftab and Waseem have passed their college exams with distinctions. I pray God grant them unparalleled success in this life and the hereafter. They are your worthy sons, and you should pay special attention to their education and nurturance. A person's life goes on, anyhow. But if children's lives are not well-run and streamlined, a rising regret keeps stabbing the heart all through life. Thankfully, both you and your wife are educated, sensible and wise parents, and I don't have to counsel you more about your duties towards your children. But as a father so far away from you, I could hardly do anything else than that.

The general situation here is just alright. It is quite natural for you to be concerned about what you hear or read about here. But you shouldn't worry too much. You have faced the worst. Every Muslim in the subcontinent has suffered physically, mentally and emotionally for years. Sometimes, I feel that all those years of woes and miseries were assigned by Providence as lessons or warnings, so that people must understand and implement whatever lessons they have learnt. If Muslims grasp this point, whether in India or Pakistan or in East Pakistan, now Bangladesh, they will survive whatever situations they have to face.

Mind you, my son, survival has always been a hands-on skill, an art, not everyone possesses. No greater art has yet been invented. The Biharis went to East Pakistan after the first partition of India. And that was just a coincidence. They could also have gone to West Pakistan. Many people went to West Pakistan, however. Those who fled their country, were not only displaced from their homes. They were also plundered and pillaged, many of them were killed. Those who headed to West Pakistan heard the Pakistani politician Ghulam Mustafa Jatoi saying that the refugees should be thrown into the Indus. Remember, my dear son, when one leaves his land, his homeland, forever, he has to forget about it and try to accept wholeheartedly, his adopted country. Unfortunately, the Muhajirs could not perform any of these moral imperatives, otherwise the pages of history might not have so nakedly and ferociously opened up to us the gruesome tales of horror. Now, I repent of talking about history. History is so indifferent to me, to you, to Bangladesh, to Pakistan, and to India, that it does not care about the wishes and suggestions of small people like us.

Though your worry is real, it should not destroy your peace of mind. The new migrants should be wary of people like Ghulam Mustafa Jatoi. He appears to me a very frank man. It's quite true that now the Muhajirs have nowhere to go except into the surging Arabian Sea. Where else can these poor people go? I am afraid of the day when I might have to see that unedifying spectacle in my life, of which, I'm sure, quite a little is left now. May God forbid!

I'm touched by your concern for me. I've been living like a recluse for a long time, after having spent a hectic life. Now, I see no more hope in life. I have nothing left to live for, but life doesn't leave me. There was time when I had taken great interest in politics. The punishment for which I have been suffering to this day. The Congress won the 1971–72 elections very easily. At that time, the party would still win even if it gave tickets to nonentities. I remember Muhammad Ali Jinnah very much on this occasion. His oft-quoted statement that if he raised a post with a Muslim League flag on it and asked people to vote for the post, they would readily do it, had become instantly famous. And it also proved true when Muslims really voted for the candidates who were good-for-nothing. Many dumb candidates fought the elections with the Congress flag, and were victorious. God alone knows the truth, but a Congress leader had been reported to comment that the party did not need any Muslim vote. The reason behind making such a statement was that there was a general impression that Muslims were very annoyed with the Congress because of the Bangladesh crisis. The Muslim discontent was a reality. Their wounds were still fresh. Thousands of Biharis were killed. And there had been a lot of talk going on about the gory carnage. They believed that the Congress government was backing the Bengalis in the massacre. Whether their accusations were right or wrong, was another matter. I just want to ask what could any other community have done if it had faced the same situations as the Muslims? It is a fact that if the relatives of the returning Biharis had helped them, these miserable people could have comfortably stayed back in India, lost in its milling crowd. They had no proof of their Pakistani citizenship. And their Indian citizenship was still intact. But their relatives in India feared that the returning Bihari refugees would assert their claims in the family properties. So, they forced them to leave India and go to Pakistan through Nepal, and believed that they had done a great job in helping them flee. However, I'd like to tell you that after the formation of Bangladesh, Indian Muslims have suddenly grown wiser. They have learnt to adjust themselves to changing situations. Communal riots do not frighten them now. They face them with courage. Perhaps, quite intuitively, they have prepared themselves to struggle, fight back and survive. I have been stressing upon this, time and again, but people never heeded me and fled from here. The reason was that they thought escape was the easiest alternative to take. It did not cost much to flee to East Pakistan. No visa, no passport, a little bribe and you cross over into that part of Pakistan. Once they reached there, the Biharis got jobs by recounting woefully their manufactured stories of sufferings and persecutions. Alas, little did they foresee that one day they might have to flee from there, too, for their lives. But whatever you and I have heard and seen has not shocked me, because I had already envisioned the entire bleak picture, but did not have the courage to express it. Time had stopped me from doing that, and had taken upon itself to reveal the horrible consequences in its own way at a more opportune moment so that they remain in our minds as a metaphor for human folly.

Coming back to the issue I was talking about, when the Indian Muslims found that all roads to their aid were closed, they came back to their senses. Prior to that, they had never felt they belonged to India, and were always looking for opportunities to run away to Pakistan. As a result, they had also closed their eyes to their legitimate demands. And if we tried to raise our voices for our community, we were decried for making a futile hullabaloo while our community remained silent. We then strove to awaken our community, but we found it sleeping like the dead. You don't get things without asking. The fact is that we have democracy in our country, where we have to raise our voices to get our needs fulfilled. In a military dictatorship, the ruler can pour rewards, on an individual level, on those he is gratified with. But in a democracy, you have to shape public opinion and give a collective call to get your demands fulfilled. The Muslims, here, have at last learnt to put forward their legitimate demands in a democratic way. They have realized what they really require, and they have recognized the importance of it for them. As a result, the government is also constrained to adopt a realistic approach. You would be surprised to know that most of the demands of Indian Muslims that had surfaced after the Bangladesh war were effectively fulfilled. In this way, it provided dignity to their lives, taught them the way to live, and in one go, placed them in the ranks of dignified peoples. The thing that Gandhi, Nehru and Azad could not accomplish, was attained after the Bangladesh crisis. You say that the war was a tragedy, but I believe that it was a blessing for Indian Muslims.

The blood of Biharis and Bengalis that was spilled in Bangladesh seeped into their memory, helping them to transform their thoughts and lives. We witness communal riots even today. Communal tensions have become a regular occurrence. But no one talks of leaving the country. Villages, towns and cities are not abandoned now. Animals are not tied up inside the mosques, and cow-dung cakes are not pasted on the walls of mosques to dry. Muslims now think of responding effectively and positively to the rioters, and efforts are initiated to ease the tensions between communities by taking far-reaching steps. Now when anyone asks the Muslims to leave India, they pounce on him and teach him such a lesson that he cuts a sorry figure in front of the world community. No one likes those stupid advisors today.

Whether or not Congress needed Muslim votes, the fact is that a large number of Muslims did not vote for Congress. I consider it a healthy trend. Though the Congress party had salvaged the fear-stricken Muslims and restored their confidence and self-esteem. But they had paid the party back long ago. It received hundreds of millions of voters for free. What did the Congress do for them after getting their votes? They already possessed the right to use their votes in favour of the candidate and party they wanted, and to refuse to vote for those they disliked. It is another matter that they came to know about their rights rather too late. The Congress party had often used them as a political pawn for their benefit. That game is over now. I say it loud and clear that the Congress party has an upper hand, as a ruling party, in the political game that is played during the riots. The rest of the players play according to the whims and fancies of the Congress party. Now, I am relieved that the Muslims will never again be wooed for their votes. Remember, Son, votes have their value and worth as long as the democratic system is well-established in the country. For this we should be grateful to Gandhi, Nehru and Azad. Pakistan is twenty-four hours older than India. That way, it is a little up the ladder. And it doesn't have the amount of problems that we have here. And yet, the masses are worth nothing there. They can be slighted and snubbed by any autocratic ruler. We have the power of the electoral votes which when loaded on a scale, tilt the balance in our favour. Otherwise, who cares for ordinary human beings like us in today's world?

Let me now tell you another political story. Indira Gandhi lost her election petition filed against her in the Allahabad High Court, although she got a breather from the Supreme Court a few days later. In the meantime, the other political parties took full advantage of this and launched a campaign against her. Jayaprakash Narayan, who had been watching quietly as a spectator for a long time, jumped into the political fray to become the people's messiah. You know, the Congress party, whose leader the inimitable Gandhi was not even its ordinary member, still commanded awe in the country. Indira Gandhi was so annoyed that she declared a political state of Emergency upon the country, arresting opposition leaders like Jayaprakash overnight. And thus, a new era of discipline started in the country.

Remember this, my son, that discipline without any fear becomes meaningless when people are not aware of their rights and duties. Indira Gandhi's police did not have to use much gun power to maintain peace. They just brandished their firearms which showed the protestors their limits. Nevertheless, it was really a good time, too. But sadly, what happened subsequently was exactly what is usual on such occasions. I'm not sure whether you really understand what the right or wrong use of power means. I am doubtful because young people like you are always attracted by the outward glow, and try to ignore the darkness of their homes. And in this way, they continue to fall victim to their feigned optimism.

Does it make you wonder how candidly a diehard Indian like me can speak to a Pakistani? My son, I must tell you that Pakistan cannot rival the amount of Indian blood that was shed in the creation of Pakistan. I had always been opposed to the formation of Pakistan, but I can never let my blood go to waste at any cost. And just see, how has Pakistan been responding to our sacrifices? The country has always been attempting to inveigle and mislead its people by indulging them with the free flow of imported goods. It is quite deplorable that even the most educated people there, proudly boast about possessing Japanese cars, American clothing and Swiss watches. Conversely, India produces goods in large quantities, and we export many of them to the outside world. We don't send them to your country because it is at war with us. Had you seen and used our products, you would have never dared to make fun of us.

Politics has little to do while defining the progress and backwardness of a country. But little do your countrymen know about politics. Look, how I've diverted from the topic I was talking about. Holding a pen between my fingers, I thought I was writing a speech. That's the problem I'm struggling with these days—a problem which can hardly be solved now at my age. I was talking to you about the Emergency rule imposed by Indira Gandhi, which worked well for a few months. But later it was used as a weapon to abuse power. The Prime

Minister, surrounded by her sycophants, was hardly aware what was going on in the outside world. They often told her things contrary to what she heard from other sources. And when confusions confounded her, she fretted and fumed, which gave the impression that she was drunk with power. Her weakness was that she never tried to assess and grasp the situation in the first instance. Therefore, the situation grew from bad to worse, and she remained oblivious of it. When she realized it, it was too late and had no option but to call an early general election. With her announcement, it appeared as if lava had spewed out of a volcanic mountain. Leaders like Jayaprakash Narayan still had the appeal to turn the masses in their favour. It looked starkly clear that Indira Gandhi was on board a sinking ship, and whoever boarded the ship would drown with her. Her people started deserting her in large numbers. Those who were seen folding their hands before her with respect in the morning, abused and abandoned her in the evening. But kudos to the woman that she is! Even in those trying circumstances, she showed she had lost none of her steely mettle. And she fought alone heroically with the adverse situations.

The Congress party had down the years become like an industry whose sharers were never in loss. The party had become the best means of gaining power and pelf. And these are the two ends modern man lives to achieve. As long as the Congress party could provide both to its adherents, they stayed glued to it. Those who were not attached to it, longed to join it. But the tide had turned now. The Congress party was no more a lucrative industry. So, people ran out of it towards there where they were hopeful of gaining both money and authority. Everyone was trying to leave Indira

Gandhi. The situation turned so bad that the party no longer had any proper candidate who agreed to fight election on its ticket. Just as undutiful children disregard their old parents in their youthful pretensions. But the love of children remains alive in the hearts of parents. The Congress party had indeed snubbed us, but how could we leave the party which we had nurtured with our blood? Indira Gandhi was the daughter of Nehru. The same Nehru about whom Sardar Patel had once said that there was only one Musalman in India and that was Jawaharlal Nehru. Indira Gandhi called me and Ajodhya Babu and asked us to take part in the parliamentary elections. We told her that we were ready. But the problem was that I wanted Ajodhya Babu to be the party's candidate and he was in my favour. You know that Ajodhya Babu did not care about power or personal gain; I wanted him to reach, at least at his ripe age, the country's highest legislature where the laws were made. I had already been there and had taken part in passing many laws, and in that regard, had to bear his jeers and jibes. I could have, perhaps, made him agree to my request, but before I could do that the name of the candidate was announced from Delhi. And I was nominated to fight the election from Biharsharif. I believe I was chosen because I was a known player in the field. And the place had become known as a Muslim-majority area. Ajodhya Babu was offered another constituency with which he was quite unfamiliar. He turned down the ridiculous offer. However, since the Congress party had now become an industry, the relationship between candidates and voters was of little consequence. The candidate was not important now. It was a vote for Indira Gandhi. So, the voters were no longer needed to know the candidate. They just had to cast their votes for the party or against it. What else could one do? Maybe, the stuff we are made of is no longer available. Ajodhya Babu was persuaded and urged in many ways to just stand in the elections, and the party would take care of all spending and arrangements. But the man did not budge from the stance he had taken.

Well then, after years of self-imposed retirement, I went back to the same place I had left with a broken heart. Even then, people kept coming to me from the towns and villages for advice, discussing their problems with me. And I did my utmost to help them. In this way, my relationship with the public remained as it had always been, but certainly it did not have the same warmth in it. But I never lost my trust in that relationship. I've lived with the common people my whole life. I had also had the opportunity to serve them from the seat of power, when I was a minister for some years. I was convinced that when I went in front of the public, my presence would dissipate any grudge they might have borne against me for whatever reasons. The atmosphere, though, had changed a lot. Congressmen were browbeaten everywhere. It was difficult for even Indira Gandhi to speak in public, had not her meetings been managed by the police and the administration. It was, however, difficult for other Congress leaders to face the masses.

Until now, Congressmen had won the elections with great ease and climbed the stairs of power with the help of Nehru and Indira Gandhi. They had never inculcated in themselves the habit of working hard and facing the masses. On the other hand, people from the opposition had been used to working tirelessly from the beginning. They reached the legislative assembly after a lot of toil and travail. The new situation was very favourable for them. Such an atmosphere was created where the distinction between truth and falsehood had collapsed. How true were Goebbels infamous words that if you repeat a lie often enough, it becomes the truth! I knew the situation was different. Yet, I was not afraid to confront the people.

After I filed my candidacy, I organized my workers. Just then, for the first time, it was revealed to me that there were no regular workers in the Congress. Nevertheless, the party could hire workers who were available in abundance, on daily wages. But even they were hiding away from the Congress party, at that time. Ajodhya Babu told me that most of these workers took money from the opposing parties and worked for them simultaneously, without letting anyone know about it. That was a very strange situation for me, and I could not compromise with it at any cost. I had told the president of the state Congress party that I would neither take nor spend any money, and had requested him to manage the expenses. He looked at me with confusion and disbelief. Perhaps, it was the first time that he had heard anything like that from an election candidate.

Interestingly enough, what happened was that when people heard that I had refused to take money, they felt so disappointed that they stopped seeing me. Fortunately, the representative of the party president came to my help and mustered a crowd around me. I, nonetheless, knew that elections couldn't be won by gimmicks alone. Therefore, I met my old friends, and wiped out the fog of dejection and dullness that had covered their minds and bodies. I also invited them to relive the past which they happily accepted and walked out of their houses to help me.

I have no qualms in accepting my folly that I was still not clearly aware how much the situations had changed. I realized that Gandhi, Nehru and Azad had lost their appeal, and people had become so frustrated with Indira Gandhi that they could not stand hearing or taking her name. Wherever I went for campaigning, people asked me questions that left me dumb and even tearful. I regretted my ignorance of the changed political scenario, to which I had no answers. People asked me on my face why, at my age, I was wasting my time in fighting elections. I was often advised to go back and lead a retired life and spend my time in prayers. Indira Gandhi's name would not enrich my life in the hereafter. Though I had answers to some of their questions, there was no gain in indulging in arguments. Congress had walked out of people's hearts and there was no wonder worker to lure them to the party. I deplored our long renunciation of active politics, which had left the party in such a dire state. In our days, there used to be a very organized democratic system within the party. It was not a matter of pride to be a part of the government, but was an honour to stay in the organization and work for it. The party and its organization were considered superior to the government, and it was believed that the government was born out of the organization. But the situation now was that the party organization had become a mere tool in the hands of the government. After all, it was the government that ruled, not the organization.

Remember well my words, because if by any chance your country becomes a democracy, you will come across similar situations. Even if it does not become a republic, my talks and experiences will deepen your knowledge and awareness and will never go wasted.

The results were announced after the polls. I lost the election. I even lost my security deposit. The man who defeated me was once my worker. Anyway, that was not something to be so sad or surprised about, because debacles do happen in politics. The strange thing was that those people who did not know him at all, voted for him—only out of their persistent opposition towards the Congress party. The Congress party was wiped out in entire north India. Indira Gandhi was also defeated. All those who were close to her were trounced, too. I was not personally affected by that loss. Victory and defeat are the normal and natural outcomes of an election.

I felt hurt that the party which was once the heartbeat of the masses, had suffered such a humiliating reversal. Congress was the other name of India. The tide had now turned and Janata Party formed the government. A case was filed against Indira Gandhi and she was sent to jail. The leaders in the new government were so intoxicated with power that they fought among themselves nastily and were not the least bit mindful of the consequences their squabbles would lead to. The Janata Party government lasted for less than three years. National elections were called again. Out of power for a couple of years, Indira Gandhi had weighed and understood the twists and turns the situations in the country had taken. The strategy that she adopted after her defeat was very unique and new. I am going to narrate to you an incident which would inform you about that typical political strategy.

There is a doctor here called Chandreshwar Prasad. He has a roaring medical practice and has toured many countries. He suddenly took interest in fighting elections, and so submitted his nomination as a Congress party candidate. A central observer of the Congress was sent to Patna to draw a list of candidates for the parliamentary elections. The doctor met him and they had a discussion, which transpired as follows.

'How much can you spend in the elections, Doctor Prasad?'

'About a lakh and a half.'

'And how much manpower do you have?'

'A hundred people or so.'

'How many firearms, I mean guns and other weaponries, do you possess?'

'One licensed gun and some spears.'

'Do you have the wherewithal to capture polling booths?'

'No, not at all.'

'You are a very decent person, Doctor Prasad. You are a very successful physician. Why do you want to put yourself in trouble? Leave it to others, please.'

'But I want to serve the people in a big way. And I think by joining the government I can work for them much more than the others.'

'Doctor Sahib, our only aim is to get a majority in the Lok Sabha, the House of the People. You cannot help people unless you are in power, and it is very important in the present circumstances that a candidate has at least 4,00,000 rupees in cash, a manpower of around 1,000 people so as to capture the booths, a cache of arms and other such things. Can you collect all that?'

The poor doctor returned hopeless, wearing a long face. Congress gave tickets to only those people who had fulfilled all the conditions specified by the Congress party central observer. And only people like them won the elections. One of your uncles was always taken as a Congress leader, though he had never been directly affiliated with the organization.

The reason was that he always lived and behaved like a leader. Members of the legislative assembly and ministers visited him and he shuttled between Patna and Delhi every so often. I wished to ask him where he got all that money from to maintain his considerable expenses. But I stopped short of doing that because it might have put a dent in our relationship. Whenever any political leader needed a lot of people for his political rallies, he would contact that uncle of yours, who would bring to the meeting ground a huge crowd from God knows where, to make it successful. In the recent elections, Congress nominated him to fight elections from the Koderma constituency which was not only too far from his hometown but was quite unknown to him. But, in spite of that, he succeeded in the elections with the help of money, weapons, manpower and other resources that were supplied to him from places and persons shrouded in secrecy.

We were not consulted in the recent elections. During the entire election period, all of us, the Congress old guards, closed ourselves in our houses, learning about the outside world through newspapers in the absence of any other alternative. And when we went out to caste our votes, we were informed that our votes had already been registered by someone in our absence. Who did that, when and how, were questions that went unanswered, so we plodded dejectedly homeward.

Truly, it's now time for us to live a retired life. We have been left with little time to prepare for the hereafter. If we do not heed this fact, we would get neither this world nor the other that awaits us.

I feel like talking to you about the Muslims. Up till now whenever a problem raised its head, the Muslims were the first to leave the field and run away, because there was nothing easier than that to do. Obviously, their disappearance from the scene of trouble led to the unilateral solution of the manufactured problem. But with the partition of the country and the sealing of borders, all escape routes have been closed. They have to face the problems hands on now. With the creation of Pakistan, many people had left their villages and towns, abandoning the mosques and graveyards that lay on large Waqf lands that were mortmain property. They lay deserted for some time, and then people started tying animals in the mosques, and using graveyards as grazing land. Times changed and the land prices started touching the skies. The luck of these hopeless lands also turned for the better. People looked at them and vied to possess them. Canny, underhand schemes were devised to capture these lands. And a practical, wily way was invented to initiate the scheme. Even needy Muslims were caught carrying out that scheme. They created fake court documents to establish their rights over a Waqf property, and sold them for a pittance. There is great power in money, my son. Its need makes man do the meanest and vilest of deeds. The sellers and buyers both are happy in this kind of deal. And this way the matter comes to an end. But actually, it doesn't stop at that. The oil boom in the Gulf and the exodus of the Indian Muslims to that region led to a drastic change in their financial status. For a certain period, their sudden affluence inebriated them with money. But when their senses returned, they thought about preserving their mosques and cemeteries back home. They had to die one day and face God. To their dismay, they found that those places were now occupied by others, not the Muslims. The new owners had registered legal documents with them. They were not at all going to vacate what they had legally bought.

Attempts to evacuate them from there had led to communal flare-ups. The Hindus suspected that Muslims were bringing in truckloads of money from the Arab world and they would buy the whole of India and oust them from the country. The Muslims, on the other hand, say that they had suffered incredible cruelty when they were poor, and now when they had acquired wealth, they were not going to bear any more.

Land prices have shot up so exorbitantly that the time is not far away when people will be deprived of buying even two yards of land for the burial of the dead. Now land has become costlier than precious gemstones. Social prestige is decided solely on the basis of a person's landholding status. The problem has reached the dimensions of a social and economic catastrophe. Villagers and townspeople often come to me with their complaints. But I can do precious little for them. When they go to their own leaders, they don't meet them. And even when the leaders do, they enthrall them with such beautiful promises that they become conscious of the realities after years. I had repeatedly asked responsible people from the highest to the lowest echelons of the government, to identify the official papers in which the lands for mosques and cemeteries are earmarked as Waqf properties and take them into government management. But their responses were lukewarm and often discouraging.

Some months back a savage communal violence erupted in Biharsharif. The reason was a piece of land disputed for years by the two communities who were also engaged in a lawsuit over it. The tension had been simmering like an internal fever for many months. A few heavily-drunk Hindus and Muslims got into a squabble over drinking tadi (palm wine) in a tavern. And in a flash, the entire town was engulfed in flames. The authorities could not find a way out, so they imposed a curfew in the town. And the peace-loving people locked themselves in their homes. They didn't know what was going on outside. An eerie silence had spread over the place. But quite clandestinely, the fire had reached the villages. The roads outside the town limits were like open fields for the bloodthirsty rioters, and they had a field day there. In the villages, only those were saved who had either already got the wind of the worsening situation and escaped, or those whom their neighbours hid in their homes, risking their own lives.

The characteristic feature of this carnage was that the upper-caste Hindus did not take part in it, and they went beyond their limits and saved the lives of the Muslims. While the people of the lower castes participated in it wholeheartedly. The fact was that in the year 1942, people of the same castes were used in slaughtering the Muslims. Although they did not directly benefit much from the killings, they had nevertheless tasted blood. In free India, these are the people who now receive all rewards and benefits from the ruling government. The higher-caste people are no longer taken into consideration. In the villages it has become difficult for them to live with their honour. People from the backward castes enter their houses and dishonour and abuse their women. These people have been given their quotas of reservations in jobs, too. The era of the upper-caste people is now over. A yawning gulf of hatred and mistrust has opened up between the two castes, which can hardly be bridged. Since the upper-caste people still have their safe cottages and walled bungalows, and guns to pursue their hunting hobbies, many poor Muslims could survive. The rioters lay in ambush on the bypass roads outside the town precincts, and searched every passing bus and car for their victims. Whoever was found wearing a beard or holding an Urdu newspaper in his hands was recognized as a Muslim, and killed. Colonel Gupta's only son was mistaken for a Muslim for his beard and murdered brutally. Do you remember Colonel Gupta from Patna? The day curfew was lifted, the bloodbath also stopped. Lots of hustle and bustle ensued. The ministers toured the affected areas, the chief minister came thereafter, and the prime minister also paid a visit. Tears of the miserable survivors were wiped. Promises were made. Aids and donations started pouring in. Everything that needed to be done on such an occasion was put into action. But I noted one strange and interesting phenomenon. The Muslims were not shocked and terrorized by this atrocious episode. They, of course, regretted that they were caught unawares. They were deluded and fell in false hope because they had confined themselves to their houses in obeyance of the curfew order.

It appears now that the year 1952 has once again livened up. Earlier, people used to flee to Pakistan, but now they take flight from their villages and settle in towns and cities. The dangerous thing is that those migrating from the villages to the towns have started settling there according to their sectarian and religious considerations. Hindus do not want to visit the Muslim-populated areas, and the Muslims do not choose to live in Hindu-dominated localities. Each of them is running away to their safe zones. Consider it yourself, since you, too, had been an Indian: if this stressful situation continues to persist, just how many parts will the country split into? We are still suffering the aftershock of the first partition, and people are sowing seeds of several divisions. What pleasant dreams had we cherished in the past, and what grim realities we have woken up to! We are just wringing our hands, wondering helplessly.

Perhaps, my letter is getting longer. My mind keeps wandering, and I realize that I have much left to tell you still.

Your grandmother Bibi Sahiba has passed away. Her entire life embraces a complete chapter of Indian history, which contains her sheer love for her country that would bring to naught all those fat patriotic books. Her husband was a great nationalist. I regret that he did not live long enough, otherwise he, too, would have been among them who had written down the destiny of this country. Bibi Sahiba was a very simple, family woman. Her husband never tried to teach her politics. But she knew very clearly that to love one's country is a necessary part of religious faith. And fuming at its enemy is like worshipping.

The formation of Pakistan was going to put in the eye of scorn all, by their own countrymen, the value and worth of those Indian Muslims who wanted to live in India anyway. Everyone who worked with your grandfather Sheikh Altaf knew that very well. Your grandmother, too, had realized that. But when her sons left her, she found herself lost in a desert where she burnt herself between love and hate. Pakistan would not allow her sons to return permanently to India, so she started hating Pakistan. But when your eldest uncle died there and was buried in its soil, Pakistan stood to merit her love. She wanted to hate Pakistan, and whenever her abhorrence for it escalated, quite unconsciously, a feeling of love rose from inside her, and she at once stopped hurling abuses on that country. And she withdrew to her world. She was imprisoned in a no man's land whose back door was locked and the front door unsafe and shaky. She remained inside it all her life. We tried to keep it a secret from her when your mother died. But she had been so alert and active in her better days that it was not easy to hide things from her eyes. Even in her state of mental derangement, she felt that Pakistan must have played a cruel trick on her. She both cursed and blessed Pakistan, alternately. God must have wondered what to accept her curse or her blessings. She uttered the name of Pakistan on her deathbed. God knows what was on her mind during her last breaths.

After her demise, the house has changed a lot. It's not quite encouraging to talk about your aunt—I mean, Sarwar Husain's first wife and my sister. She has never considered herself alive. Faiyyaz has once again returned to his earlier stages of insanity. He either stays silent or behaves quite like a lunatic. He has almost shut down his shop. His servants ran away tired of getting beaten every day. He has not yet married. Who will marry a mad man? Nisar is making a lot of money from his tailoring profession, and is saving it all for a future about which only he can predict.

Your uncle Asghar Husain is a strange man. He has not come to India even once after his flight to Pakistan. The love of a mother and a son could not compel him to visit them. God knows what will happen to this house! There is no active, alert person to look after Ben House. My days are numbered now. I have lived my life, and am now not able to do anything worthwhile. But as long as I am alive, I will not let the walls of this house fall.

I must tell you about Sajid. He has married a Hindu girl and no longer comes home. They performed a court marriage as per Indian law. He had called me before his marriage, not to invite me but to inform me. I had no answer for him, so I said nothing.

Who knows, how far away, the two-yard land, our last abode is from me. But before I am interred in it, I wish to travel thousands of miles away to perform Hajj. I don't know whether the land would listen to me before calling me to its dark wall.

I bid you farewell, my son. Be happy with your wife and children! I could not give you anything as a father. I have only my prayers and my duas, for all of you. But give to your children all that you can, and I pray you live long to do that.

With love and blessings
Yours
Akhtar Husain

PART FOUR

45

16 December 1981. Letter to Father

My dear father!

May God keep you all well!

I have not received your letter for quite a few months, though I keep myself anyhow informed about your well-being. My letters must be reaching to you regularly, if the postman has been not unkind. I am fine here. Thank God.

I have told you in my earlier letter how with Asghar Husain Mamujan's kindness, I was able to get a job here. The monthly salary was a little more than 1000 rupees. I lived with him for some months, but in order not to trouble him more, I shifted to an independent flat. My badi auntie and her daughter Alia also moved to the flat with me. Alia and I shared the rent. There were problems quite naturally, as we lived frugally, but still we lived on. Those who arrived in Pakistan immediately after the partition of India were undoubtedly at an advantage. Jobs were aplenty, and the abandoned houses were waiting for them. But those who migrated here after the Bangladesh catastrophe were looked at as snatching the morsels out of the mouths of the local populace here. The situation grew even worse every passing day. The local inhabitants, therefore, hated us, and it assumed an enormity that might have burst into disaster any time in future.

Alia got married within a year after she came to my flat. She left her job and went to America with her husband. After a few months, Badi Auntie also went there. I had, therefore, to bear alone the burden of paying the full rent. Life became difficult. There were days when we had nothing to eat. Nazia wanted to work and help me, but hatred against the Bengalis had not lessened in those days. Mamujan, too, had asked me not to let anybody know that she was a Bengali. All her certificates and degrees are from the University of Dhaka. Without them, she was as good as an uneducated woman. She again started losing her mental alertness, imprisoned day and night within the four walls of the flat. Our days passed in hardships and despondency. I took up home tuitions in the evenings, and earned some more money. Fortunately for us, we were living in a locality which was away from the real population of Karachi where there was very stiff competition, a rat race to earn more money in order to live better. We could hardly survive in that crazy competitive world.

The situation took such a turn that it became hard for Biharis to survive here. The army had gone back to their barracks. Bhutto had become the prime minister. He talked a lot about democracy. He had emerged as the only leader of import in the whole of West Pakistan, with the return of democracy. The greatest favour he did to Pakistan was that he successfully made it possible to let India release 90,000

Pakistani soldiers. He had certainly breathed hope and respect into a humiliated and shattered nation. Otherwise, it was quite impossible for a nation caught in a disgraceful situation to survive with respect. Not only a big part of the country had separated from it, but as many as 90,000 soldiers had also surrendered in a very disgraceful manner. No other example of a tragedy of such immense proportion has been found in Islamic history. Victory and defeat are two different realities, but both are transitory. It doesn't take time to turn victory into defeat or vice versa.

For a long time after that, the people here tried to forget their acute embarrassments by keeping themselves busy with different kinds of amusements. A centuries-old book written by Shah Nimatullah, the Sufi master, was discovered after some research. This book became very popular all over the country. In this book, the Shah had talked about an eastern part of the world which, he had predicted with his divine inspiration, would be soon conquered by a western part of the world. The reality was that the tragedy Pakistan faced was so enormous that had its people not overlooked it by feeding themselves with fervent hopes, the nation would have suffered untold miseries. Most people in the country did not have a clear idea of what had happened to Pakistan. They only knew that a great calamity had befallen India, and as in the past, a good number of Muslims had migrated from there to Pakistan. Bhutto cashed in on their ignorance. First, he welcomed the Biharis wholeheartedly, but later the Sindhi in him got better of him. In the suburbs of Karachi, the Sindhis stared so hard at the Biharis that the poor Muhajirs would cringe with fear, as a mouse on seeing a cat. Every Bihari had been waiting for quite some years for a major incident to strike the nation. Only a spark was needed to be thrown into the lava that was bubbling inside. Believe me, Abbajan, if any day the Biharis and Sindhis crossed swords that would not be an ordinary event, but a ghastly episode in the annals of history. Luckily, Shah Nimatullah's predictions do not say anything categorically, or else, we would not have lived so long here.

Mr Bhutto also conducted a national election. A power hungry and flamboyant politician, Bhutto led the country as a dictator and was convicted of corruption and murder. The nation which had slept for years must have had some hangover for sometime after its waking. And there must be some people who would take advantage of its inebriated state. Democracy has matured in India. How transparent are elections there? In fact, Pakistan should have tolerated Bhutto's election. It could have opened a lot of ways for the nation's progress. It would not have been so difficult to establish a good democracy in a small country like Pakistan. The problem is that the politicians here have been trying for the past thirty or forty years to reach the seats of power. The goddess of power afforded them only a fleeting glimpse of her, and then disappeared in the dark, leaving them repenting in despair. For many years, the military government kept on lengthening its rule in different garbs and uniforms. When elections were held at last, the country was split into two. Bhutto came to power to stay for five years. But how long could the hopeless politicians wait? They misled and tempted the army and got him toppled. The army unseated Bhutto and captured power. The crafty politicians implicated him in court cases and had him hanged. But the army was also not going to be fooled! It had tasted power for the past many years, and was bored of lying idly in the barracks. Why would it transfer the power that it had snatched by its prowess to others? It did not, and would never hand it over to anybody. The army again enforced its old policy by encouraging and pampering the Muhajirs. A strong democracy might pose trouble for the Muhajirs. Two distinct groups of native Pakistanis and Muhajirs emerged on the national political stage. The native Pakistanis were fed up with the military government, and the Muhajirs lavished praises on it. The military establishment had established itself on the seat of power for some years to come. Pakistanis had to wait with their fingers crossed.

One day, I suddenly met Shahnaz in a market. I must have told you that she is Azimuddin Uncle's daughter. The same Azimuddin Uncle who had escaped to East Pakistan and had built up a vast fortune there. Shahnaz had married a Bengali military officer against her parents' wishes, who was later transferred to West Pakistan. The Bangladesh episode happened in his absence from Dhaka. Azimuddin Uncle was there with me in the Mukti Bahini slaughterhouse which was readied for the Biharis. I was convinced he would not survive long when I was taken out of that killing ground to safety. But as is commonly said, the grave calls its occupant; until then he cannot die. So, it did not call him and he was saved. He reached Pakistan anyhow, and within weeks of arriving here died, only to be buried in the two-yard land waiting to devour him.

Shahnaz came very close to me in Dhaka, like my own blood sister. Her husband left the military service after the creation of Bangladesh, and is now working as an executive in a major American firm in Saudi Arabia. Shahnaz lives with him there, but has left her two children in Karachi for their studies. The children live in their magnificent bungalow. Shahnaz and her husband visit Karachi every three months or so to see their children. Shahnaz always meets me with the same warmth of feeling. There is no arrogance in her despite being a very wealthy woman. I never told her about my financial hardships. She came to my house once, and everything was exposed to her. The wretchedness of the house, every brick of it complained to her about its sorry state. She asked me to accompany her to Saudi Arabia. I could not understand what to say to her, and asked her to give me some time to think. After a fortnight, Nazar Muhammad, Shahnaz's husband, came to Karachi. He compelled me to travel with him to Saudi Arabia. He got my papers ready, and I, too, decided to accept their offer. So, finally I went to Saudi Arabia with him. He had got me a job in his firm on a salary of 4,000 riyals. I was also allotted a flat by the company. After a few days, I called Nazia and the children to Saudi Arabia to live with me. The biggest problem here is our children's education. I had to send both our sons to Karachi after a few years. I have bought a flat in Karachi. Both our sons live there. We go there twice every year to see how they are doing. Nazia has returned to her full mental and physical health very satisfactorily.

Abbajan, I have met countless people from Pakistan and India who are working here in different cities. Most of them are those who have left good jobs in their own countries and have come here for a few thousand bucks more. There are also a number of those who have arrived here on the promise of a good salary, but are working on much less than they were promised. There is no dearth of money, food and all possible comforts of life here.

There is no respect here; the respect we fought and longed for in Pakistan. Here everything that money can buy is available. I wish to live here for three or four years more. I cannot afford to stay more. Whatever I will earn in these four years, would be enough for me to spend the rest of my life.

Nazia and I have performed Hajj. I have also done proxy Hajj for my grandmother and mother. Please come here, Abbajan, and do your Hajj. Just take a flight and come here. I will arrange for your visit. What more should I write to you. Please try, Abbajan! Come here and perform this greatest obligation.

Your son